nuggets

A TALE OF THE CARIBOO GOLD RUSH

Susan K. Kehoe

◆ FriesenPress

Suite 300 - 990 Fort St
Victoria, BC, V8V 3K2
Canada

www.friesenpress.com

Copyright © 2019 by Susan K. Kehoe
First Edition — 2019

Cover: Gold nuggets in the pan of an old-fashioned balance scale.

All rights reserved.

This is a work of historical fiction. All the main characters are purely figments of my imagination. Some of the historical people and places were indeed real to give flavour to the structure and background of my story. SKK

No part of this publication may be reproduced in any form, or by any means, electronic or mechanical, including photocopying, recording, or any information browsing, storage, or retrieval system, without permission in writing from FriesenPress.

ISBN
978-1-5255-4937-3 (Hardcover)
978-1-5255-4938-0 (Paperback)
978-1-5255-4939-7 (eBook)

1. FICTION

Distributed to the trade by The Ingram Book Company

Other books by author:

Ireland: Snapshots in Time

Acknowledgments

A sincere thanks to Mel for initial proofreading and suggestions, always constructive.

VANCOUVER ISLAND AND NEW CALEDONIA CIRCA 1860

1. Fort Victoria
2. Fort Langley
3. Chilliwack
4. Fort Hope
5. Fort Yale
6. Spuzzum
7. Boston Bar & Hell's Gate
8. Lytton
9. Cache Creek
10. Kamloops
11. Clinton
12. 70 Mile House
13. 100 Mile House
14. 150 Mile House
15. Williams Lake
16. Quesnel
17. Barkerville
19. Horsefly

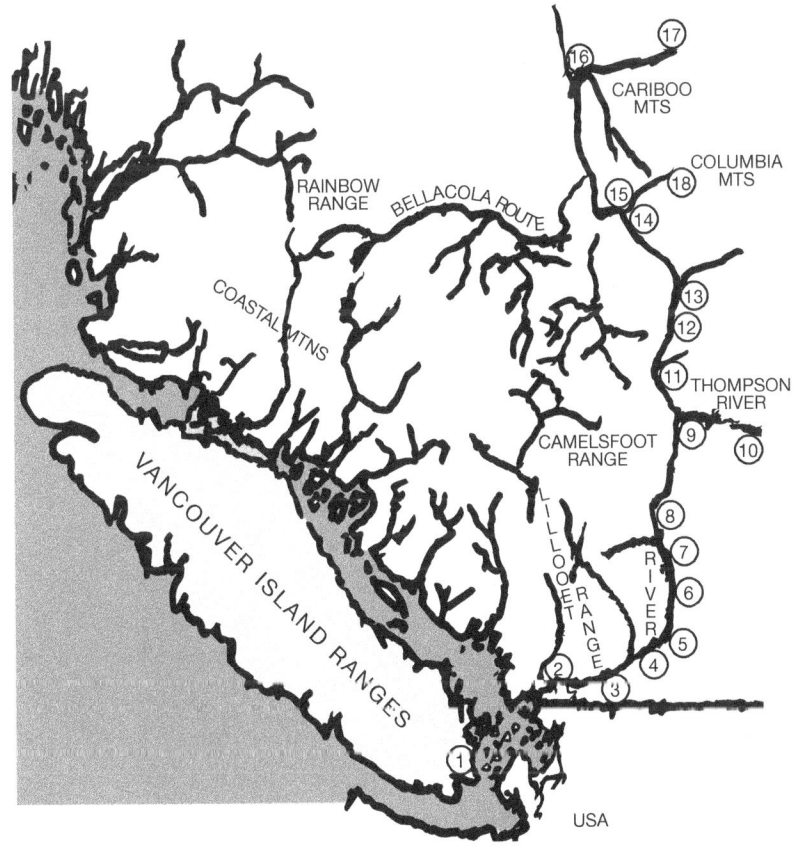

Map of British Columbia showing Victoria and the water route to the interior via the Fraser River, including the towns of Hope, Yale, Creek, Lytton, Williams Lake, Horsefly, Soda Creek, Quesnel and Barkerville.

Chapter 1

VICTORIA, VANCOUVER ISLAND, APRIL 1860.

As Robb climbed into the heavily laden Hudson Bay cargo canoe, he quickly scanned Victoria's main street, hoping to catch a glimpse of Emma Freeland, the elegant daughter of a local surveyor. There was no sign of her trademark blue silk bonnet. He hadn't seen her for several days and resented missing any opportunity to talk to her. His brother Matt was eager to push the canoe away from the dock, completely oblivious to his younger brother's reluctance to leave. With a sigh, Robb thrust his paddle forward and they headed into open water, en route to their rendezvous with the local Songhees.

A pale sun peeped through, showing hazy coves of wave-rounded pebbles. Robb eyed the shoreline where dark-green spiky tips of the shore pines punctured the low mist. Some trees were stunted and twisted into fantastical shapes from the prevailing winds. Screeching gulls scavenged and squabbled for stranded clams in the tidal pools. Through gaps in the cloud cover, an eagle on outstretched wings cruised the morning air currents, receding to a tiny dot high above.

An hour's paddling brought them out of Victoria Harbour, leaving the small town besieged by slumbering, booze-laden gold-seekers camped in acres of tents. Robb was thankful the miners were finally quiet. Nightfall was usually an orgy of alcohol, card playing and general roughhousing that sometimes became violent.

Their regular meeting place with their Native trading partners, the Songhees, was at Finlayson Point. The fog was starting to lift, revealing a hazy seascape of blue offshore islands shapeshifting in the changing light. Robb was watching for the Songhees on the headland. "I'm glad we meet them here now and not in town. I don't think they like the miners much," he casually remarked to his older brother.

"Hold it, Robb!" whispered Matt. Both their paddles paused in mid-air, dripping diamond droplets of seawater. "Something's not right. The beach is empty – no canoes, and there's no smoke from the big house. Where are they?" said Matt frowning.

Both men loaded their muskets, watching the undergrowth for any signs of activity. They quietly beached the canoe and cautiously approached the big gray cedar-planked house, the home of the Songhee chief, Whalecatcher. The totems of beaver, raven and whale stared down at them with blank eyes.

Robb cautiously pushed the plank door open with the toe of his boot and peered inside. The big house was bare, no fires, no baskets, no looms, no clothing, just abandoned space. Empty, the room seemed even larger; the impressive hand-hewn, seventy-foot-long Douglas fir trunks stretched the entire length of the ceiling. They walked around the encampment looking for signs of disturbance. The firepit was intact, and when Robb touched the ashes, they were cold. The drying racks were bare – all the filleted fish were gone. Robb just stood looking puzzled.

"I don't understand. They don't usually leave the winter house for another month. They asked for the axes and blankets we've brought. Last week there were at least fifty families here. I don't see any sign of violence. Surely Whalecatcher or Long Feather, would have said something if they were planning to go. Something's happened."

"Maybe it's the miners. All of us have had confrontations with the drunks wandering around Victoria. I'm always telling Edna to make sure the door is locked when I'm gone," said Matt, his forehead wrinkled in concentration. "I haven't heard of anything in particular, although I did hear a rumour that a miner went missing a few days ago. I don't know if he ever showed up."

"They could have gone east or west along the coast. It's all their territory. You'd think we'd have seen them though, wouldn't you?" said Robb.

"You know them better than most. Where do you think they've gone?"

Robb thought for a few moments. "I don't see much advantage to them moving further east to Duncan. I'm sure all the boat traffic here to the mainland is interfering with their fishing. My guess would be they've headed west, deeper into the bay closer to View Royal."

"Let's go back and pick up your canoe. No point taking a loaded one until we know where they are. We'll have to tell Father and Sir James about this."

As they paddled back to Victoria Harbour, the fog was clearing and Robb kept an eye out for smoke on the numerous small islands. "Matt, I don't see any canoes in their camp across the bay either." Most of the Natives who worked as casual labourers in town lived over there. Entering the harbour proper, he could see a three-master unloading supplies at the dock.

"Father will be happy to see that delivery. He's been having a hell of a time keeping the Bay's shelves stocked."

Matt said, "At the prices HBC's charging, they can't complain about the profits. Mind you, the town merchants are starting to give them stiff competition." He flipped open his pocket watch. "Another hour and the *Commodore* from Port Angeles will be in with two hundred more miners," he said, tucking the watch back into his vest pocket.

Robb grinned thinking about his hard-headed Scottish father bargaining down to the last penny. His mind took him back a couple of years to when he'd helped stock the shelves after school. He'd watched his father barter and bargain with the Indians for pelts, furs, dried fish and canoes and with the gold-crazy miners for everything else. "He's ranted about not wanting settlers coming in and ruining the fur trade, but the miners have done that on sheer numbers alone." There'd been so many Americans coming through that it was now common practice to use dollars instead of British currency in the stores.

As they pulled in beside the dock, they could see another group, which included the local constable, all clustered around a fishing boat. "I wonder what's going on there," said Robb, walking over to join the curious. "What's the problem?" he asked a bystander.

"They found a body out in the bay."

Robb wormed his way through the crowd to look down at the pallid corpse lying on the dock.

From his clothes and scraggly beard, the dead man was obviously a miner. The constable was checking the pockets for identification and removed a soggy miner's licence and a wad of US bills, so robbery hadn't been the motive. There was a slit on the left side of the man's shirt. "He's been stabbed," said Constable Hastings. "Do any of you know this man?" he asked the crowd, eliciting a murmur of denials.

Robb moved closer, peering at the wound. His heart skipped a beat, as he'd seen that mark many times before on seal carcasses – the double-sided, two-inch slit. It shook him to realize that the man hadn't been stabbed but speared with a fishing spear, and he contemplated the possibility this was the cause of the

Songhees' sudden departure. "Constable Hastings, do you want me to take the licence and money up to Sir James? Matt and I are heading up there now."

"Certainly, Robb. We'll take the body to the fort for the surgeon to look at."

Already there was a long lineup of miners at the Hudson Bay store, men with hard faces, ragged clothes and long beards, toting heavy back packs. "Most of them sound American, but I can hear Chinese, Italian and some British accents too. I wonder how long their nice clean suits are going to last," said Matt, looking at four young men in suits and dress boots.

"With that lineup, we'll never get in there; we may as well go up to Sir James' office," replied Robb as they walked inside the gated palisade and trudged across the parade ground past the schoolhouse to the single-storey log building that served as the administration office. "It won't be long before they'll dismantle the palisade and make room for real buildings. They'll have to compete with the new store being built by that San Francisco outfit. Did you hear they paid a thousand dollars for the building lot? Somebody made a killing on that; I'd bet it was either Sir James or maybe Pemberton, the surveyor. Both of them bought up plenty of property around here ten years ago."

The clerk was shuffling a mountain of paperwork and stared at them over his spectacles. "Good morning, Robb, Matt. Shouldn't you be out at Finlayson Point?"

"That's why we're here, George," replied Matt. "When we got there, the village was completely empty."

"Empty?!" said George in astonishment, putting down his quill pen.

"The Songhees have left; no one's there or in the camp across the bay, either, by the look of it. We've come back to report to Sir James and get further instructions. The other thing is that you've got a dead miner on the dock. Constable Hastings is dealing with it. Robb's got his money and miner's licence," said Matt as Robb placed the soggy papers on the blotter.

"Good heavens, that's odd. The Esquimalt and Songhees have been quite reliable since they signed the Te'mexw Treaty with us. Let me speak with him," George replied, knocking on the door of the inner sanctum and disappearing inside when the deep hidden voice commanded him to enter.

Matt and Robb looked at each other, well used to the formality typical of Victoria's British upper class. Sitting there waiting, Robb could hear the low murmur of voices in the office, so he looked at the log walls covered with maps, a portrait of the queen, the British flag and several Paul Kane sketches of the Songhee encampment, including a portrait of Whalecatcher that depicted the essence of the intelligent face. George opened the door, ushering them in.

Sir James Douglas, Governor of the British colony on Vancouver Island, sat there in his tailored, formal black suit, the coat tails split on either side of the chair, his stark, white-starched collar and black tie framing his cafe-au-lait skin and white, bushy side whiskers. Robb looked at the broad face, with its high forehead and the dark eyes that seemed to take in everything. Robb could feel the power of the man behind the mask of deep reserve and dignity. The desk was covered with maps and correspondence. Behind him the wall clock ticked the seconds with precision as the pendulum swung back and forth. *He's the most powerful man here, governing Vancouver Island and the New Caledonia mainland to protect British interests.*

"George tells me the Songhees have gone and their camp is empty. Is this true?" he said.

"Yes, sir, it is," replied Matt, standing respectfully with his hat in his hands. "There was no sign of violence or disturbance, but all their belongings are gone."

"Robb, what do you make of this? Over the past two years, you've been our unofficial liaison and have probably got to know them better than most of us."

"Sir, it's too early for them to move to their summer grounds. I can only assume that there's been some kind of crisis and they've left. I'd hazard a guess they may have gone deeper into the bay closer to View Royal or Esquimalt. I didn't see any smoke from the islands on the way back. Do you want me to look for them?"

Sir James pondered that question for a few moments. "Let me think on that. Do either of you know about the missing miner?"

"Only what Constable Hastings told us. The body was found out in the bay this morning. He was stabbed in the chest," said Matt.

I'm not going to say a word about the wound until I speak to Whalecatcher. It would be very easy and convenient to pin a murder on the Natives rather than a white man, Robb thought.

"George, bring that licence in here. If the salt water hasn't ruined the ink, we may find out who he is. The Americans reported the missing man as David Sutton."

George returned with the folded piece of paper. Sir James gently laid it out on his blotter and unfolded it with care. "Ah, it's very faint, but David Sutton it is. His friends have already left but we'll try to contact them by letter. It might catch up with them at Fort Yale. I doubt if this is related to the Songhees. Could have been anybody with the carousing that goes on. In the meantime, we'll bury him. At least we can put his name on the marker. George, get hold of Reverend Cridge. He can take care of the burial. Robb, take a run up the channel and see if the Songhees have gone to View Royal. If you don't find them, you can help James at the licence office. There were hundreds of miners, five-deep, waiting for licences yesterday. They were lined up all the way down Wharf Street. Good thing the patrols kept them orderly. Matt, you can help your father at the store." Formally dismissed, they nodded, walked out and went to unload the big canoe.

"If we don't unload all the supplies, they'll disappear by morning. Far too tempting for that lot," said Matt, glancing at the miners. It didn't take the pair of them long to move the stores into the shed.

"I'll take a blanket and an axe with me in case I meet the Songhees. See you later," said Robb.

Matt headed for the back entrance of the store while Robb went further down the waterfront, hefting his musket and the trading goods. Once again, he scanned Wharf Street hoping he'd catch a glimpse of Emma. He'd really been hoping he would see her working at the church food booth, but since she wasn't in sight, he knew for sure she'd be at the social Saturday night and church on Sunday. She'd never miss an opportunity to show off her latest gown.

There were very few women on the street, none of them the dainty, exquisite blonde who made his heart race. The thought of looking at those blue eyes and the pouty little mouth was more than he could bear, and the tantalizing glimpse of her bosom behind the lace trim of her gown set his blood on fire. In his imagination, he felt his hands touching her hair and the soft white skin of her neck and shoulders. He felt the rising anticipation in his body and, heaving a big sigh, came back to reality and the long lineup of miners at the licencing office. He didn't look forward to the prospect of being stuck inside all week filling out paperwork.

At the boathouse he lifted his canoe from the wall and chatted briefly with Bill Balding, the proprietor, while he stocked his backpack with one of the roast beef sandwiches Bill's wife always had available. "I'm off to View Royal to see if I can find the Songhees. I should be back by dark," he said as he pushed off from the dock. The wooden posts were encrusted with barnacles and pink starfish below the tideline. He kept a watchful eye for the incoming ferry and outbound small boats loaded with miners heading for the Fraser.

He scanned the sky, noting a relatively calm sea, sunshine and little wind. He knew he'd make good time under those conditions and put more muscle into his paddle. Soon his canoe was moving steadily into the bay, the bow cutting a froth of white bubbles through the small waves. The noise of tent town and the harbour faded as he continued along the channel with green, rounded steep hills plunging in from both banks. The waterway was dotted with small islands, too small for habitation but full of cormorants sunning themselves with their black wings outstretched. There were a few scattered log cabins with small docks on the eastern shore. If the families were out working their gardens, Robb would wave at them. He could hear the thud of the axes across the water.

He caught sight of three tall black fins cutting the waves. He had no desire to test his luck against three orcas. They were twice as long as his canoe. He knew the Esquimalt and Songhees occasionally harpooned them from their dugouts. Whalecatcher had a reputation for killing them. Robb considered the man much braver than himself. He directed the canoe closer to shore. The whales passed him at a distance, but he was awed by the sleek black-and-white curves of the majestic beasts and their effortless speed.

He remembered watching the Songhees hunt porpoise, with Whalecatcher in the bow, harpoon poised, and a dozen half-naked men behind him, paddling like fiends. His harpoon was right on target and they hauled the dying porpoise alongside the huge wooden canoe. There was enough meat on that carcass to feed the whole village. Robb had always been impressed with Whalecatcher's hunting prowess.

He paddled for two hours then paused, placing the paddle beside him. Taking the sandwich from his backpack, he happily chomped through the thick, crusty homemade bread and the generous slab of beef. He caught the sound of warblers high in the forest canopy and continued monitoring the treetops for smoke.

He hadn't seen any sign of the Songhees yet. He figured he'd be in View Royal within thirty minutes. His thoughts turned to his father, who was inclined to think Robb should take over running the HBC post there in the future, but Robb knew he didn't want to spend all his days inside. He also knew that Emma Freeland wouldn't want to live out here in the wilderness. Victoria would be far more her style. His whole family, with the exception of his eldest brother, Henry, lived there too.

Cleaning up the last crumb, he started paddling again and noticed more canoes, manned by Natives, coming down the creeks feeding into the narrowing channel. They were all heading in the direction of the store. Robb pulled his canoe onto the pebbly beach and took a good stretch. He noticed a few more log houses had been built since the last time he was there. *More newcomers.* The Esquimalt were unloading big bundles of furs. Robb knew those would be the last pelts for the season, as the muskrat, beaver and fox were shedding out. Robb walked into the store and waited for Jim and Harold Anderson to serve their customers.

"What do you think of these, Robb?" said Harold, passing a bundle over to him. Robb went through each pelt looking at the condition of the fur and the quality of the hide. He rippled his fingers through the soft, dense sea otter fur.

"These are good," he replied, handing them back.

"What are you doing up in this neck of the woods?" asked Jim. "We haven't seen you for a while."

"The Songhees have moved from Finlayson Point, and I'm trying to find them for Sir James. Have you seen them?"

"They went up the channel a couple of days ago but didn't stop in here. Unusually early for them, I thought," Harold replied.

"I found that curious too. Maybe these Esquimalt know something," he said, approaching one of the Native men and launching into Salish trading jargon, a mix of English, native Lekwungan and hand signals. Robb spoke basic Salish, but had to supplement his words with his hands. He knew enough to trade but not enough to be fluent.

The man he spoke to shook his head but walked out and beckoned Robb to follow. He pointed to the creek branching off on the eastern side of the bay. Robb thanked him. "Well, Harold, if I want to get back home by dark, I'd better get going," he said as he waved goodbye and got back into his canoe. He paddled across the river towards the creek.

Chapter 2

The church women had set up a booth with stew and sandwiches to feed the miners. The whole congregation took turns either serving the meals or preparing the food every day except Sunday. The four women were busy handing out heaped tin plates to the miners, who were enjoying the home cooking.

"It just amazes me that no matter how many sandwiches we make, we never have enough," said Mary McDonald, Robb's mother, as she carved slices of beef from the roasted haunch hanging on a hook. "Millie's got another pot of stew on," she said, adding another log to the fire. "Ann and Edith are baking dozens of loaves every day. We'll need to slaughter another steer this week to keep up our supply. We never have enough pies, either."

Mary waved at her two daughters, Jane and Emily, as they entered the booth, both girls carrying bags of freshly baked bread.

"Here, Mum," said Jane, tossing the bags on the table. "These are still warm."

"Very good. You two start making sandwiches and that will free me up to serve the customers," said Mary, looking at her daughters with pride. The fourteen-and sixteen-year-old girls were pretty and clear skinned, attractive in their long, plain dresses with their dark-brown hair pulled back in simple, shiny braids. She also noticed the miners paying attention and fussed like an old mother hen.

"This was a great idea as a fundraiser," said Ivy Hamilton. "At fifty cents a meal, we're making a tidy profit. Getting a bowl of stew, a roast beef sandwich and a wedge of pie for that price is a good deal. I wonder how long it will be before we get the new church built. I hear Sir James is going to donate the land for it. I never expected this gold rush to last so long."

"At least the miners are polite to us. I just wish they'd stay sober in the evening and have a bath," said Mary. "Most of them smell dreadful. They wear the same clothes day in and day out. Most of them have rotten teeth. It's a pleasure to see my clean-shaven menfolk when I get home."

"I saw Robb heading west in his canoe after he left the fort. Where's he going?" asked Ivy, who kept track of everyone, including seventeen-year-old Robb.

"I've no idea. Sir James must have sent him out. I'm actually glad to see him out of Victoria for a while. He's following Emma Freeland around like a lovesick puppy. Mind you, she encourages him, cuddling up to him and fluttering her eyelashes, all coy and winsome. But she does that with all the men, and poor Robb takes it seriously. He's fallen hard."

"Mary, I've heard she's got a suitor and her father approves."

The two girls were listening intently to the conversation behind them and looked at each other.

"Jane, I don't think Robb knows that," Emily whispered to her older sister. "Do you think we should warn him? I think he's totally smitten with her. It wouldn't surprise me if he proposed."

"I'll talk to him as soon as I see him," Jane whispered back, not wanting to miss a word of the ongoing conversation between her mother and the neighbourhood gossip.

"How did you find out? Who's the lucky man?" asked Mary.

"I was talking to Reverend Cridge's wife after church on Sunday. She says his name is Jackson and he's a commissioned officer with the Royal Engineers, much above Robb's station, and he's well off," said Ivy in a conspiratorial tone.

Mary took the comment for what it was worth, knowing no one in the whole community was more sensitive to people's social status than Ivy, and she'd be the first one to be critical.

"I just don't want to see my boy get hurt when Emma takes up with some rich man's son. I'd rather see him with a nice, sensible girl who can cook, clean and be a good wife rather than that fashion plate who expects to be waited on and looks down her nose at the rest of us," said Mary with conviction.

"He's not like your other boys, is he?" said Ivy, handing a steaming plate of stew, a wedge of pie and a sandwich to the waiting miner then dropping the coins into the cashbox.

"No, he's different, I'll grant you that. All our other boys, including Henry in Alberta, like to dress well and do civilized things. Ever since this gold rush started, William has been too busy to spend as much time with Robb as he did with the others. Robb loves to be outdoors hunting, canoeing or fishing. He's not that comfortable in a suit and rarely dances. I don't think Emma would be a good match at all; she's too uppity. I just want to see him with a good, sensible girl. He also tends to be a bit tactless, just like his father, and that can ruffle a few feathers," she said, thinking of her older husband's sometimes caustic comments.

Chapter 3

Robb could smell the wood smoke, but the forest was so dense he couldn't pinpoint the direction. He scanned both banks of the creek looking for the landing site, and around the next curve saw the high-prowed dugout canoes tethered to tree roots and a faint trail winding from the creek up into the towering forest and moss-covered boulders.

As he pulled his canoe on shore, he heard faint noises behind him, and turning, saw three bronzed, half-naked men standing there, their spears pointing directly at him and their faces expressionless. The stance was definitely hostile. He'd known these men for four years and couldn't understand their reaction. He gave his usual greeting and quietly resumed removing the goods from the canoe. He tucked his musket under his arm in a relaxed manner, keeping the barrel pointed down, hoping he wouldn't provoke them.

"I'm looking for Whalecatcher or Long Feather. Are they in the village?" he asked. One of the men pointed to the path. The trio remained silent, so he headed onto the pathway that meandered between the buttressed roots of giant firs, hemlock, spruce and cedars, the cathedral-like green gloom broken by stray filtered rays of sunlight. Moisture dripped from the ferns and the moss-laden branches. The forest was unusually quiet except for the chirps of unseen chickadees and the faint whisper of footfalls behind him. He was acutely aware of the spears aimed at his back.

He had no idea what was wrong but noted that even the women and children huddled around the cooking fire were avoiding him. There was no friendly greeting and there was a tension in the air he couldn't explain. The little ones usually came over to him, but not today. Robb sat down on a log and waited, his guardians still within spearing distance. He could hear people coughing, and several of the children were scratching red rashes clearly visible all over their bodies. He heard a baby crying somewhere and the low murmur of its mother. The rashes reminded him of the measles he'd had as a boy. He couldn't see any pustules, so didn't think it was smallpox, but knew that either one of the white man's diseases could wipe out the whole tribe. He noticed small carved wooden boxes under the trees and realized with a sinking feeling that they were child-sized coffins, confirming his suspicions.

Above the coughing, Robb heard the keening, shrill wail of a woman. It was an eerie, primitive sound soon joined by other voices that echoed into the trees, raising the hair on the back of his neck. Long Feather emerged from the tent with the shaman behind him. Robb stood up, feeling his skin prickle, and guessed that someone important had died.

The shaman made an announcement to the clan that Robb couldn't understand, and a loud wail passed through the crowd. The nobles of the tribe were making a big fuss around Long Feather and Robb realized that Whalecatcher's cape was being placed around his son's shoulders and his fishing spear officially presented. *Whalecatcher must have died and Long Feather's now being made chief,* he thought. One thing he had learned was that succession for the Songhees' leadership was a hereditary one. He also knew that he must not say Whalecatcher's name out loud, as it was taboo to mention the name of the dead. He couldn't even begin to think that measles had taken out a man like Whalecatcher. *That old man was in far too good shape for that.*

Robb quietly waited as the villagers openly grieved for their chief. The shaman was performing a ceremony, smudging Long Feather from an abalone shell of smoldering herbs. He was ignored until finally Long Feather walked towards him and paused an arm's length away. His expression was inscrutable, and the dark eyes bore into him.

Robb couldn't see any friendliness there. What he could see was anger, but he didn't know why.

The villagers formed a semi-circle around Robb. He drew himself up straight and looked directly into Long Feather's eyes. He knew all too well that any sign of fear could provoke an attack. "I came here to find you after you left the village so unexpectedly. I am deeply saddened that your father has died. He was a good man and a great chief. He taught me many things. I admired him for his wisdom, his courage and his strength. I wish to see him one last time to honour him before I leave. I've brought an axe and a blanket as my final gift to him," he said, handing them to Long Feather. Robb knew the axe would be highly valued. *I'll have to repay the Bay for those items.*

There was a long pause then Long Feather accepted them, still appraising Robb. "Come," was all he said, turning toward the tent. The crowd opened, allowing Robb to follow. He silently exhaled, his heart thumping.

As Robb entered, the women kneeling around Whalecatcher's body stopped singing. He slowly knelt beside the body. There was a round, blackened hole in his abdomen – a bullet hole. Shocked, Robb turned and looked up at Long Feather. "He's been shot. What happened? Who did this to him?"

Long Feather pointed to his younger sister, who was now standing with their mother and many other family members around the corpse. Robb could see her arms and face were badly bruised and swollen, distorting her features. There were also dark stains that could have been blood on her torn cedar-strip skirt. She had obviously been assaulted. She averted her gaze when he looked at her. Long Feather went into a tirade.

Robb didn't understand a lot of the words, but the fierce, crude gestures and rage made the scenario explicit. She had been working the oyster beds with her mother and sister when the miner came on the scene. He was drunk and he had grabbed her, raping her right there on the beach. Whalecatcher heard the commotion and speared him in the chest but the dying miner shot him. They dumped the miner's body in the bay and fled here to their refuge, knowing full well the consequences of killing a white man.

Robb stood there for a long time. "If it had been my sister, I would have shot him too," he said with conviction. He'd seen this girl grow from a child to a slim, proud young woman in the time he had known the family. As a chief's daughter, she was a noblewoman. *She'd not be out whoring like some I've seen in town.* She was avoiding his gaze. "She didn't deserve to be treated like that by any man. I'm going back to Victoria. When you are ready to trade again, come and find me. I don't know if our paths will cross again, Long Feather, but I wish you well."

Long Feather nodded but said nothing. Robb turned, picked up his musket and walked out of the camp past the crying, spotty babies and the coughing, sickly parents. He noted the slaves were already making a raised scaffold where Whalecatcher's body would be placed, open to the elements and the spirits of the forest. Locals had reported the practice of sacrificing slaves when a chief died but Robb didn't know if the Songhees still did that. *With the sickness present, it isn't likely they'll have a potlatch for the new chief just yet.*

He walked to his canoe. No one stopped him or followed him out. He realized that at this moment he was just another white man, and if it hadn't been for his good working relationship with Whalecatcher, they might have killed him. That thought made him shiver.

A light rain started to fall, dimpling the water. It was later than he expected and too late to paddle back to Victoria. He opted to spend the night at the trading post, feeling sure Jim and Harold would have somewhere for him to bunk down.

"I wasn't expecting to see you back here," said Harold when Robb went into the store.

"Can I stay over? Business took longer than I thought; it's too late to paddle home."

"Surely, come up to the house. Martha's always got enough to feed an extra mouth, and you can bunk in with the boys. What's going on with the Songhees, anyway? Did you find out?"

"That's the other reason I came back. I've got a lot to tell you after you close up" said Robb, not wanting to have that conversation in front of customers.

Harold was quick to take the hint and spent the next twenty minutes completing the sales of flour, beans and tinned goods to the remaining settlers. After Harold locked up the store, they walked across the road to one of the small log houses. Inside was warm and dry, with heat radiating from the cook stove and coal oil lamps lighting up the room. Martha, Harold's wife, was stirring the pot on the stove and a delicious, yeasty aroma of baking came from the oven.

"Martha, I found a stray and he's hungry," joked Harold.

"Hello, Robb. Come on in and make yourself at home," she said, wiping the perspiration from her forehead with the corner of her apron as she stirred the pot, her cheeks flushed from the heat. The two girls were setting the table and automatically set a place for Robb.

He hadn't seen them for two or three months. He noticed the boys were growing up. Harley was rapidly closing in on Robb's five-foot-ten, and the others not far behind that. Soon Robb was in deep discussion with them on their latest escapades. It was a welcome change from the rain and damp outside, and it felt good to be with a family after such a turbulent day.

The eight of them sat down for the meal. After Harold said the prayer, Martha served up the venison stew filled with potatoes, onions and a thick, rich gravy. There were mounds of warm rolls and rich, yellow butter.

"I see you've still got the cow," Robb said, as the butter instantly melted on the steaming roll.

"Yes, she's doing well. The boys have cleared the trees on about four acres and fenced it. The grass is coming in quickly, so she's got enough for grazing now and the heifer calf is doing well," said Harold.

"Martha, this meal is delicious. Where'd you get the venison?" asked Robb. "The coastal deer are scarce around Victoria."

"I shot it up by the creek," Harley bragged, puffing up with thirteen-year-old pride. "We don't see them around here too often either. It was a nice mature buck. I was lucky to get it."

After the meal, Robb and Harold sat by the fire. "Well, Robb, what happened over there today? You've avoided saying anything about it."

Robb spoke in low tones. "They have sickness over there. I think it's measles – red rash, coughing. I didn't see blisters, so I'm hoping it isn't smallpox. The children are dying, and the adults don't look well either. Your community here would be vulnerable too, but it seems to affect them worse than us. Whalecatcher has died."

"Died? I'm surprised. He had the constitution of an ox. You had to admire him, even if he was an Indian. I've seen him take out porpoise and whales and last all day paddling that big canoe. He had to be close to fifty years old. What happened?"

Robb framed his reply carefully as he wasn't sure just how much he should be telling him. "I'm not entirely sure. I can't understand all their language, but the gist of it is he had a confrontation with one of the miners. He'd just passed away when I got there. Long Feather is chief now. I'm telling you, at the moment they are hostile to white men, so be cautious if you're dealing with them. I don't think they will raid you or anything like that. Right now they just want to be left alone, and white men are not welcome. They let me leave."

"Thanks for the heads up. I'll pass the word to everyone in the morning; the last thing we need is an epidemic or an Indian war," said Harold, sucking on his pipe and staring into the fire. "On the whole, we've had very little problems with them compared to the other posts when I worked in Alberta. Some of them help us out with tree cutting or working the vegetable gardens. We've had a good relationship with them. Guess we'll have to see how it goes."

* * *

Later than night, Robb was lying on the lower bunk vacated by the youngest boy who was now sharing the upper one with his brother. He lay there realizing he had really expected to die at the camp. His mind was overflowing with memories of his time with the Songhees. He remembered the one occasion he'd met them when they were spearfishing from the rocks for salmon. They had made it look so easy. It had been all he could do not to fall in, let alone catch something. At the time it made him feel pretty stupid, but in the end, he'd laughed at himself. The water seemed to distort his aim. Even the younger boys were good at it. The women filleted the fish and hung them on drying racks. If they smoked them, the flesh lasted right through the winter.

As hard as he tried, sleep would not come that night. He'd doze for a while and wake up again, thinking of other things, of Long Feather walking through the woods and meadows, showing him which plants were edible and which ones weren't. Mushrooms, flower roots, he knew them all. Robb had a gut feeling he might never see him again. He decided to head back to Victoria at first light, as he had so much to tell Sir James.

Chapter 4

Sir James Douglas watched and listened as Robb McDonald told his story. He sat there getting the details in order; so David Sutton raped Whalecatcher's daughter, Whalecatcher speared him and Sutton shot him before he died.

He looked at Robb and was impressed. He had sent him on a mission, and the boy had been resourceful to get the job done. They could have killed him. It had taken guts to walk into that camp alone. As administrator of the mainland, he needed a trustworthy courier to take confidential messages to the forts along the Fraser. He thought that sort of job would suit Robb, since he couldn't see him working in the store like his father and brothers; the lad liked to be on the move. His first priority was to finish preparing for the American delegation who would be arriving over the weekend. After that, he'd offer Robb the job.

"Robb, I'm going to ask you to keep this information confidential. I don't want the rape and the shooting to become public knowledge, so don't tell anyone, not even your family, about that part. Had Whalecatcher lived, I would have had to charge him with murder even though there was extreme provocation. It would only cause more problems between the whites and the Natives. If anyone asks, we'll keep to the original story – David Sutton was stabbed by persons unknown."

"I understand," replied Robb, relieved.

"Good. In the meantime, you'd best go and work with James in the licence office. He's swamped down there," he said and dismissed him.

Sir James watched Robb leave and then he called George in. "Robb brought me some interesting news. The Songhees are at View Royal but have a measles outbreak. It appears there have been a lot of deaths in the children. Whalecatcher's dead, and his son, Long Feather has taken over. Council's already banned the Natives from coming into town because of the drinking and whoring. The good thing is that the ban will stop the spread of disease here. At least the trapping season is over. We weren't doing much business with them anyway. Hardly any game around anymore with all the miners. We make far more profit on miners' supplies than on pelts."

George returned to his duties in the outer office while Sir James sat and pondered the situation. He contemplated the issues of a public trial. A trial between Natives and whites was always problematic and could alienate either side or both. There were enough tensions with the Americans as it was. The murder of an American miner by a Native would just add fuel to the fire. They were having their own problems with the

Indians in Washington state with the miners heading north to the Fraser River through their territory. *No, I'll leave Sutton's death as an unknown – that's the best course of action.*

The measles epidemic was another matter. The less public exposure to the disease, the better. Measles or smallpox could spread like wildfire in places like tent city or the steamships. That would be bad for everyone, and trading as well. *Time will tell. By winter, I'll know if the Songhees are coming back. Whalecatcher was a canny bargainer when it came to trading. It will be interesting to see how Long Feather deals with it.*

Chapter 5

Robb spent the rest of the day beside James at the counter in the licencing office, processing the certificates. He would take the five-dollar fee, fill in the name in the register and issue the licence. He was at the point he could probably do it in his sleep. He wasn't even paying much attention to the miners, as their faces had become a blur. Some came in bunches, all clamouring to be served, and a few were alone, like the one in front of him. He didn't see too many of them coming back rich. Robb eyed the man who was about six feet tall and relatively clean, with a trimmed beard and clear blue eyes in a sun-bronzed face. He was wearing the traditional trousers, jacket, heavy boots, brimmed hat and backpack, which showed heavy wear.

"49'er?" asked Robb.

"Yep, how can you tell?" the man queried.

"American accent. You seem to know exactly what you're doing, like you've done this before," said Robb. He entered the information on the certificate and signed it, handing it over to him. "Well, Henry Farnsworth, good luck to you," he said, and the man quickly slipped out the door to be instantly replaced by another applicant.

James and Robb both heaved a sigh of relief when five o'clock came and they locked the door.

James opened the vault in the back room and deposited the day's cash. "Do you realize we processed three hundred and twenty-four permits today?" said James. "It was good to have you helping me. By myself I can't do more than one hundred and fifty, less if I get a bunch who don't speak English."

"That's over sixteen hundred dollars in fees in just one day! Sir James will soon have enough money to start building that road up the Fraser valley he's been talking about," said Robb as they walked down the main street.

"I've heard the surveyors from the Royal Engineers have started surveying the farmland and the canyon itself," James replied. "There's just a mule track up the Fraser right now. One step off the path and you're in the river. No one, man or beast, survives a fall into that gorge."

"You wonder if it's worth it." Robb thought gold fever was like a disease. "Some of the miners aren't going to live to reach the goldfields, and there's no guarantee they'll find gold if and when they get there. I haven't seen too many come back with much to show for it. They slave away and find some then squander it on booze and saloon girls, if you can believe the tales they tell."

"We need to build a stamp mill on the mainland. The last few who did strike it rich had to take the steamer to San Francisco to have it processed, and I read about that one fellow who got conned out of his gold by someone claiming to have a bank-style storage vault. They stored it, alright, right in their back pockets. A lot of people got caught in that scam. You'd need to have an armed escort just to get it back here. Gold dust is awkward to deal with too. It's bulky and heavy to carry. If you use it as currency, a pinch of it's worth a dollar. It sounds to me like the trail's a death trap, an open invitation to other men's greed," said James as they parted to their respective homes.

* * *

Robb's family was keen to hear about his trip up the bay. They sat for supper with William presiding at the head of the table. "Well, Robb, we were concerned when you didn't come home last night. What's happening at View Royal? Is everything alright at the store?"

"As you probably know, when Matt and I went out to Finlayson Point the other day, the village was empty, so Sir James sent me to look for Whalecatcher further up the channel. The post there is doing well, with some new families from Upper Canada settling further along the creek. Their cabins are up and roofed already. Harold's boys have cleared another four acres of land to make grazing room for the cow," he said, savouring his mother's roast chicken.

"Did you find the Songhees?"

"I did and that's a sad tale. Whalecatcher died just after I arrived in the village. Long Feather is the new chief."

"Was that anything to do with that dead miner?"

"Not likely," said Robb casually. "Worse news, the Songhees have a measles outbreak."

"Measles! Good Lord, I'm grateful they moved. That's the last thing we need here," said William. "Business hasn't slowed down at the post. We'll be down to bare shelves in a couple of days again. The supply ships can't get here fast enough."

"By the way, I owe you for one blanket and one axe. I gave them to Long Feather to honour his father. Do you think the new stores will have an impact on the Bay's business?" Robb asked to distract his father from the topic of Whalecatcher.

"We'll have to wait and see on that one, but business is good right now. Once we have supper over and done, we'll get ready for the social. Sir James has a meeting with some senators from Washington state. They are still negotiating the boundaries for the Oregon territory, and the Americans are still having Indian problems along the Columbia River. The miners keep traipsing through Indian land looking for gold."

Jane and Emily attempted to speak to Robb as they cleared the supper table but were interrupted by a knock at the door as Matt and his wife, Edna arrived. Robb quickly shaved, combed his hair and put on his good suit.

His mother paused and straightened his tie. "There, that's better," she said with pride, looking at her dapper youngest son with his wavy black hair and deep-brown eyes. "Now you're looking quite civilized, but you could do with a haircut; it's over your collar." They all hurried out of the house, with William locking up, and briskly walked over to the fort. Music and laughter were coming from the hall, competing with raucous noises from tent town.

"Robb, will you please slow down?" said Jane

"I'm in a hurry; I want to see Emma," he replied, irritated with the delay.

"Robb, listen to us. We've got something you need to know," she said stepping in front of him. "Just stop. I've been trying to talk to you all evening, but we kept being interrupted."

"What is so important that you're getting in my way?" he demanded, frowning at his sibling, who was blocking his path.

"Emma's father has approved a suitor for her," she blurted out.

"What? How could he? She's not sixteen yet. How did you find that out?" he said brusquely, looking at her in disbelief.

"Ivy Hamilton heard it from Mrs. Cridge and told Mum a couple of days ago when we were serving up meals in the food booth."

"Do we know the man?" he said, wondering if it was someone local.

"All we know is that he's an officer in the Royal Engineers, his name is Jackson and he's rich."

They walked slower now as Robb contemplated the enormity of that development.

"Thanks for telling me. Obviously, Mum wasn't going to say anything. I'm not happy with the news but you just stopped me from making a complete fool of myself. Go on ahead and catch up with Mum and Father; I've got to think on this for a bit," he said.

He wondered what he was going to do.

He knew the courtship ritual well from what his brothers had gone through. It was a societal expectation that a young man had to get permission from the girl's father before he was allowed to visit the girl, always with the goal of marriage in mind. Often, the girl had to be chaperoned by a relative so the two were never alone. It was permissible for the two young people to meet at socials to mingle and enjoy each others company.

The formal expectations were that the young man had to have finished his schooling and have a job. The woman was expected to be skilled in household chores such as cooking, cleaning and other skills, making her a good wife.

The hall was brightly lit, with the doors wide open and the sound of violins. He paused at the door, observing all the well-dressed townsfolk. There was laughter and chatter. It looked like most residents of Victoria were in attendance. His family dispersed, his father to the bar, his mother to a group of church women and Emma and Jane to the Robertsons over in the corner.

Young Billy Robertson was immediately by Jane's side as he had been of late. Their attraction appeared to be mutual.

Robb cast his eyes around the room looking for Emma. He saw her beside her mother, her father Henry Freeland, and a tall, square-shouldered young man in the red-jacketed, gold-trimmed uniform of the Royal Engineers. He watched as Emma slipped over and gazed up adoringly at the man, her face alight.

He immediately felt sick and turned away to speak with Bill Balding and his wife, giving himself time to get his equilibrium back. He could see Sir James with several dignified senior statesmen talking in the corner and Amelia Douglas, his wife welcoming the local women. The men were strangers, and Robb took them to be the visiting Americans. Slowly he circulated through the room trying to keep up the pretense that he was having a good time. He nodded to Emma when their eyes met, and she smiled sweetly but didn't come his way. He eventually met Mr. Freeland at the bar.

"Good evening, Mr. Freeland," he said.

"Good evening, Robb. I hear you just got back from View Royal. Things don't sound very good there with the epidemic."

"No, sir. I have something I need to discuss with you. Could you spare me a few minutes?" Robb said.

"Certainly," he said as they walked outside.

"Mr. Freeland, I have a very high regard for Emma, and I came here tonight to ask your permission to court her." Robb said, keeping his eyes firmly on Freeland's face.

There was a long pause as Mr. Freeland looked at him. "Robb, I'm aware of your interest in Emma. There is no nice way for me to say this to you, son. I want my daughter to marry a man who has a position in society and income enough to support her. You, your father and brothers are clerks for the Bay. You earn a dollar a day, and other than the family home, you have no prospects of owning property or any means of getting it.

"Captain Jackson earns over seven hundred a year and his father, a surveyor on the Fraser River road, has property both on the island here and the mainland. I'm sorry, young man, but I cannot jeopardize my daughter's future. I cannot give you permission to court her," he said and with a nod, quietly turned and walked back into the hall.

Robb stood there feeling completely deflated. *Damn him. I'm just not good enough and not rich enough.* He knew he couldn't go back in there and watch her dancing and laughing with Jackson. He had no idea what he was going to do to get her away from the man. He turned on his heel and walked back home. He sat on the porch mulling over his options, the raucous cacophony of the miners echoing from tent town.

Thoughts ran unbidden through his mind. Somehow he needed to earn more than a dollar a day, but didn't see how he could do it. He thought about joining a bunch of miners and heading off to the goldfields. The more he thought about it, the better he liked the idea. *If I can find enough gold and not squander it away like those fools, just maybe I can be rich enough to buy a good piece of property and be worthy of Emma in Mr. Freeland's eyes.* He was so mad he felt like hitting something.

His thoughts were interrupted as he saw his family coming back from the hall. He could hear the high-pitched giggles of his sisters and his mother laughing as they separated from the Robertsons and came up the front walkway.

His father looked at him. "So, this is where you disappeared to. Didn't see you all night. What's going on?"

"I didn't care much for the company Emma was keeping, so I came home," Robb replied.

"I see," his father said with one eyebrow raised, unlocking the door. His mother herded the girls inside and Robb reluctantly followed.

* * *

Robb slept poorly. He kept seeing Emma's face in his dreams. The more he thought about Mr. Freeland's rejection, the angrier he got. Sunday morning brought no relief. He knew he would see her again in church, and he couldn't think up any good excuse not to go; at least not one that would satisfy his father.

Just before they left the house, his mother gave him a hug, knowing the source of his discomfort. "Robb, don't take it so hard. You're a good-looking man and you're a hard worker. There will be lots of other girls," she said.

"It's not other girls I'm wanting, Mum," he said quietly as they walked sedately up the church walkway along with the other parishioners decked out in their Sunday best. Billy Robertson was firmly planted between Jane and Emily. The men removed their hats and led the way to their respective pews. Reverend Cridge hadn't come in yet and Robb looked at the empty pew belonging to the Freelands, dreading what was coming. He sat quietly, his teeth clenched, as he heard the rustle of skirts and Mr. Freeland's voice followed by a brief comment from Jackson as they moved into their pew. Robb refused to look over at them even when he heard Emma's voice replying to her father; he kept his face forward. He could feel his father's eyes on him at times, watching.

Cridge's sermon seemed to drag on and on. Robb went through the motions and somehow got through it. He prayed not to make a fool of himself, for his parent's sake. *They have to live here with these people. If I do something stupid, it will discredit them. This town is small enough that nothing is private.*

With the final Amen, the crowd rose to their feet and slowly began to exit the church. Robb could hear Emma's voice through the chatter and saw her walking ahead of him. She looked radiant in a pale-blue dress and bonnet and was walking beside her mother, ahead of her father and Jackson. The sight of Jackson's broad, upright back in its bright-red jacket had Robb biting his lip to the point where he tasted blood, so he kept well back. A firm arm around his shoulder brought him up short and he stared into his father's stern face, seeing a look of deep concern under the shaggy gray eyebrows.

"Take the girls home, Robb. I'll talk to you later," said his father, ushering him out of the church, away from the Freelands. Robb took a deep breath and nodded.

Robb's last glimpse of Emma was her coyly smiling at him. Jackson was eyeing him too, with a slight frown. Jackson said something because Emma turned and fluttered around the uniformed man like a mesmerized moth.

He quickly walked over to his sisters and moved them in the direction of home, leaving his parents to mingle with the after-service throng. Jane and Emily flanked him on both sides and kept up with him as they briskly walked home in silence. He moved with purpose now. He decided right there and then that it was time for him to go. *My future is with the miners.*

Chapter 6

On Monday, Robb worked at the licencing office with James, processing another three hundred applicants, quite a few of them from China. He found it tricky to get their registrations done as their last name went first and the spelling was peculiar, with lots of a's, o's and ng's. Carefully, he managed to make out a licence in his own name and enter it in the register, the name somewhat scrawled but unnoticeable amid the many others. He added five dollars to the cashbox, folded the certificate casually and put it in his jacket pocket when James had his back turned.

The *Eliza Anderson* was scheduled to leave port in the morning to do the Fort Langley run. She usually left at seven, so he had to be on the dock at midnight just to make sure he had a chance of getting on board. She only carried one hundred and sixty passengers and there were probably two hundred miners waiting for a ride. He'd managed to get his backpack ready with his clothes, compass, an axe and a knife. He'd hidden it in the woodshed for now, planning to buy tools and food later as they were too heavy to take all at once.

He remembered he had to take a large piece of canvas and some rope. He'd withdrawn most of his savings; it wasn't much, but it would have to do.

The rest of the day was uneventful. When Robb got home, he kept himself busy chopping wood and trying to be as nonchalant as possible. He saw the girls occasionally look at him in speculation, as if they sensed something was going to happen. *They'll find out soon enough.*

Over supper, he listened to his mother prattle on about some local gossip; she said new people had moved into the former Smith house two streets over, someone's daughter was pregnant, and mentioned the price Ivy Marshall had paid for the new hat she'd worn to church. It all went in one ear and out the other, but it passed the time. Robb savoured every morsel of his supper, knowing he wasn't going to be getting another home-cooked meal for a very long time. What he was really going to miss was her apple pie. He licked the last pastry crumb from his fork. "That was excellent, Mum," he said, and she just beamed at him.

After the meal, he sat by the fire across from his father, who was wreathed in clouds of aromatic pipe smoke, reading the newspaper that the steamer had brought in from Olympia, Washington, on her regular weekly run.

"Anything interesting?" Robb asked.

"Looks like there's a civil war brewing south of the border, a lot of it to do with slavery. There have been skirmishes with the Indians on the Colorado River again. More gold is coming down both the Fraser and the Colorado; more miners coming in all the time, crossing Indian lands. I wonder how Sir James made out with his negotiations with the Americans over the weekend. It's official now – Britain's formalized the mainland as New Caledonia. Sir James has given up his Bay post because of the conflict of interest situation. Can't be administrator of New Caledonia and chief of the Hudson Bay. There's serious talk of Britain creating one country from the west coast through the Rockies to the east coast, joined by a railway. At least for now, we have claimed the coast up to Prince Rupert."

"Do you think the Americans will be buying Alaska from the Russians?" Robb asked.

"That wouldn't surprise me in the least."

Robb was glad he had avoided any mention of Emma and diverted his father into power and politics. The clock finally struck ten. Robb headed up to bed, lying on his cot in his travelling clothes, waiting for the others to settle for the night and listening to the steady beat of the rain on the cedar-shingle roof. When gentle snores emanated from his sleeping family, he quietly wrote a brief letter to his father.

He placed the letter on the dining room table then went into the pantry, taking a two-day supply of flour and beans from the china jars and filling his small cloth bags. He took the last loaf of bread from the shelf. He stood for a moment looking around the house he'd known for the past ten years. He hoped he was making the right decision but couldn't think of any other way to get Emma. He hoped they wouldn't hate him for it. His father was going to be disappointed in him and Mum would probably have a "spell." Silently, he unlatched the door and slipped out of the house. The miners were still carousing, so he hoped any noise he made would go unnoticed. In the woodshed he picked up his backpack, rechecked every item, rolled up his bedroll in the piece of canvas and tied it in place with two lengths of rope. Swinging the pack onto his back, he decided the weight wasn't too bad and adjusted the shoulder straps. He had some coin in his jacket pocket for his fare but had put the rest in his pack. *I can't trust anyone from here on.*

He threaded his way down the darkened street, past the tents where the miners were still drinking and playing cards. Around a dilapidated shed, he tripped over a drunk sleeping against the wall, the whiskey bottle clutched in his hand, oblivious to the world. Robb kept his eyes open for the midnight patrol, wanting to avoid recognition from the locals.

The *Eliza Anderson* sat in darkness at the dock with only her stern lanterns lit. Her engine was quiet, no smoke from her funnel, and the side paddle wheel was stationary. Already there was a lineup, dark shadows of anonymous men in rain gear sitting on their backpacks waiting. Robb counted the men ahead of him. There were at least fifty, so it had been a smart move to come down early. He guessed that by morning there would be hundreds more. He pulled the brim of his hat down and slung the tarp around his shoulders, covering himself and his pack as the rain started to steadily pour down, puddling around his boots. He dozed periodically but was too excited to sleep much.

By four o'clock, many more miners stumbled down to the docks and Robb found himself crushed in the lineup. He kept a firm grip on his backpack and his hand on his pocket. He was elbowed and pummelled as several fights broke out when some tried to cut in. The losers limped to the back of the line. The mob had its own rules. Lights came on all over the ship and the engine started, sending clouds of smoke and steam up the funnel. Robb's heart was thumping with excitement. It wasn't until five o'clock that a seaman lowered the gangplank and the miners surged forward.

Captain Hustler stood at the top of the gangplank with a rifle in his hands. There was instant silence. "There'll be no fighting on my ship. Single file up the gangplank, gentlemen," he said brusquely, handing the rifle to his second-in-command and starting to collect the two-dollar fare from each man. The line seemed to move slowly but once Robb had his feet on the gangplank, he knew there was no turning back. He handed over his money, got his ticket and found a position against the wall under the shelter of the upper deck. He glanced over the heads of the men around him. There was no sign of his father on the pier and he was grateful for that. He knew he needed to find a group to join. Being alone was a death sentence on the trail. Men simply disappeared, with their corpses left to rot in the woods. He had no intention of letting that happen. *Who can I trust?*

Merchants showed up with loads of cargo, which were winched on board. At 6:25, Captain Hustler sold the last ticket, much to the disappointment of a hundred miners still on the dock. The gangplank was hauled in, the hawsers released, and the anchor raised. Promptly at seven o'clock, the *Eliza Anderson* blew her whistle and pulled away from the dock, the paddle wheel churning steadily.

Robb could feel the throbbing of the engine through the deck planking. He watched as the gap between the ship and Victoria Harbour widened. Looking at the bay he'd paddled for the last few years, he realized he might never see it again. He had no intention of coming back to Victoria unless he was a wealthy man.

Chapter 7

William McDonald came out of his bedroom prepared to have a quick breakfast then go to the store. He could hear the rustling of the rest of the family as they were getting up. The first thing that caught his eye was the envelope on the table. With a sense of unease, he picked it up and saw "Father" in Robb's scrawled handwriting. Taking a deep breath, he tore the envelope open and unfolded the single sheet of paper.

> Dear Father,
>
> I know you will not be happy with my decision, but I am heading up the Fraser to the goldfields. Mr. Freeland told me I am not worthy of his daughter since I am only a clerk working for the Bay I'm not earning sufficient to support her and have no prospects of owning my own home. I love her and intend to prove him wrong. I will write when I can. Robb

William put the letter down on the table, looking at it a second time. "The stupid young fool! He knows damn well the odds of striking gold are close to nil. Damn him! Damn Emma Freeland and damn her father!" he ranted out loud.

Mary flew out of the bedroom still in her nightdress, her dark hair hanging loose over her shoulders. "William, what's the matter?"

He handed her the letter, which she read with trembling hands, and tears started to well up in her eyes. "I don't believe it. He's gone. All over that useless girl."

Jane and Emily ran down the stairs in their nightclothes and gazed at their parents in amazement. William was pacing, still swearing, and Mary was in tears.

"Robb's left. He's gone with the miners," Mary said holding her arms open to her daughters, who came and hugged her.

William opened the front door and looked at the harbour, empty except for a few British naval ships from Esquimalt. The *Eliza Anderson* was out of sight. He slowly closed the door, realizing there was nothing he could do. "I should have known he was up to something when he was so quiet last night. Freeland is doing all of us a favour. Emma's the last person I would want for a daughter-in-law. Robb's worth ten of her," he muttered.

Mary quickly made breakfast, noticing that some of her supplies were missing. "I've run out of bread," she said to William. "I'll have to bake some more this morning. Sorry, love."

William was too distracted to notice. When he was ready to leave, he looked at her. "I may be late coming home. I'll have to see Sir James and let him know, as well as the boys."

When the door closed, Mary sat down, Jane and Emily beside her. "I'm not looking forward to what Ivy Marshall's going to say about this."

"Mum, I'll make another batch of bread. We need some for the miners, anyway," said Jane.

"I feel it's partly my fault. I told him about Captain Jackson before we went into the hall."

"Jane, he would have found out anyway. He saw them as soon as he went in, so don't be blaming yourself. Your brother's a strong, stubborn man, a lot like your father. He'll do what he feels he must. We just have to pray it works out well," she said, her eyes welling up with tears again.

* * *

William slumped into the chair, the first time he'd sat down all day, and started talking to George while he waited for Sir James. "Aye, it's been another busy day. I can't keep up with the supplies, even with Matt helping me. The ship should be in tomorrow, with any luck. I'm out of axes, picks and pans, and there's not much flour left."

Sir James opened the door to the office and called him. "George tells me you have an urgent personal matter to discuss. Come in," he said, ushering him into the room and indicating he take a seat.

"Yes, sir. Robb left on the *Anderson* this morning for the goldfields, all because of that Freeland girl getting engaged to Captain Jackson. I had no idea he was going. Came as a real shock."

"I see," said Sir James. "That really is unfortunate. I was going to ask him to be my personal courier now that I'm administrator. I'll be moving over to the mainland shortly. The mail is so slow here and with the ongoing negotiations with the Americans on the boundary, I need someone I can trust. The timing for this is lousy. It would have been a good posting for him and a steady government job. Pay's better than he would have made in the store."

"When are you finished with the Bay?" William asked.

"My replacement should arrive in a couple of weeks. In the meantime, let me know if you hear from Robb. I might be able to talk some sense into him. This is an opportunity that he's going to regret missing."

William trudged home. Both Matt and James were waiting for him, alerted by the family grapevine.

"Father, I checked the licence register. He made one out for himself yesterday and he did pay for it, so he's legal," said James. "It never crossed my mind he'd do that. It was just yesterday that we talked about the stupidity of these miners going to the goldfields. So few of them strike it rich, and the conditions are dreadful. I can't believe he's done it. Can you talk to Sir Douglas for me? With Robb gone, I'm going to need someone else to help me in the licence office."

"Aye, I will. All we can do is wait," replied William, shaking his head and feeling a deep despair at the colossal challenge his youngest son had taken on. "Well, in his favour, he's a good hunter and woodsman, and he's used to dealing with the Indians. He's in good physical condition and he's not afraid to work hard. He's used to dealing with the miners in the store too, so I hope that will stand him in good stead. It bothers me that he didn't take his musket. Most of the American miners are armed, even if Sir James has forbidden it. A lot them carry pocket derringers; they're lighter to carry, I suppose."

Matt was shaking his head. "Robb's usually cool-headed and sensible. I didn't realize the depth of his feelings for Emma. I thought they were just flirting. They've been doing that since they went to Craigflower primary school. I can remember him when she first started there, all those blonde ringlets and silk ribbons. There's no way he can compete with Captain Jackson socially."

"I'll have to write to Henry to let him know about this calamity. It'll probably take a couple of weeks to reach him in Alberta," said William. "Robb's missed a great opportunity for a job with Sir James."

Chapter 8

The *Eliza Anderson* chugged slowly into Oak Bay, then along the channel into the strait, the paddle wheel leaving a churning wake. Although he'd moved from the mainland to Victoria as a child, Robb had no recollection of it. It all seemed new.

The rain was easing off and he found an opening on the rail and leaned over to look at the islands, his pack firmly wedged in front of him. There were many small boats following in *Eliza's* wake. He watched the crowded boats sail by, sometimes faster than the *Eliza* with her single engine, and marvelled at the lively trade ferrying miners to Fort Langley. He looked over the men crammed together on the hundred and forty feet of deck and listened to conversations. There was excitement but also a grim determination or even desperation to succeed. He wondered if he would become like them. Would he strike it rich and fritter it all away? *Not if I can help it!*

He looked to the southeast at San Juan Island. Both the British and the Americans had troops there until the boundary dispute was formally settled. Sir James had a pig farm over there but lately there had been articles in the paper about problems.

The islands were blue in the early light, and the colour changed to greens as rays of sunshine pierced the clouds. Robb realized he was hungry and thirsty. He lined up for a ladle of water from the communal water barrel then found a space to sit down on the deck and have a bite to eat. Some of the passengers were buying their breakfast from the ship's galley, but Robb decided to save his money and rummaged around in his pack for the bread and beef. He quartered the loaf and cut a slice of beef with his knife, returning the remainder to his pack. Bread instantly reminded him of his mother. She'd be out in the booth now, making meals for the miners and probably getting an earful from Ivy. Thinking about Emma didn't help. He kept seeing her and Jackson together. She should have been with him.

He started looking at the groups of men on the deck. He needed to team with someone in order to survive the trail. He looked at the four young Brits in the suits and ruled them out. *They won't last long in the wilderness.* There was a group of six young Americans playing cards and drinking, but Robb didn't like the look of them. They seemed a rough and shifty bunch. He saw the Chinese group he had processed licences for, but while they were experienced, they likely wouldn't take a white man with them, especially since he didn't speak their language. He passed the time between looking at the changing scenery, open water now with the mainland hills coming closer, and assessing the other men on board, recognizing the faces of many he'd completed licences for in the past week.

He'd have to change ships at Fort Langley. From there, the *Enterprise* did the Langley to Yale run, if the conditions were right. She had a shallower draft and more engine power than the *Eliza*. The river was shallow in places, but the water of the Fraser moved faster where it narrowed, and with spring melts he'd heard it could be treacherous. From Yale he'd be on foot.

He watched for the mouth of the Fraser River as the *Eliza* negotiated the many islands and sand bars of the South Fraser Arm. He chatted casually with the men beside him. Most of them were American; some were 49'ers, some were San Francisco city men looking to get rich quickly, and others were men who had left their wives and children behind to seek the elusive nuggets of gold. They all had stories. Some had been doing this for years and still hadn't found enough gold. He knew he had to keep his head and not succumb to booze and women. He absolutely had to save all his money so he could buy a house and a business to support Emma.

The land was relatively flat, forested with evergreens and extensive swampy, low-lying areas, but in the far distance were higher hills, their peaks tipped in snow. Small homesteads dotted the riverbanks where the land flattened into lush pasture with grazing cattle. The river was busy with canoes and small boats heading upstream with miners and supplies, and downstream with lumber, cedar shingles and barrels of salted fish.

The *Eliza* passed Annacis Island, and beyond the next curve in the river the Fraser forked.

"What river's that?" Robb asked as one of the deckhands manoeuvered through the crowd.

"That's the Pitt River. We'll be keeping south of Douglas Island over there and staying on the main channel," the man replied.

Robb sat on his backpack and mentally made a list of the supplies he needed. He was accustomed now to the noise and vibration of the engine and the paddle wheel. He'd need a pick, a shovel, a gold pan and ten pounds each of flour and beans. He really would have liked to get another musket but was concerned about the weight. There would be at least sixty pounds in his pack. He decided to try his luck at the fort. Langley had been a Bay post since '41. His father had worked there for a while and Robb had been born somewhere close by.

Another miner sat down beside him. He was in his early thirties, tanned and bearded, looking lean and hard, his pack well used.

"Hello," said Robb, looking at the man carefully. "I'm Robb McDonald."

"I'm Bill Hartford," he said, giving Robb the once over. "Is this your first time out?"

"Yeah, thought I'd give it a try. I could use the money. You look like you've done it before. Where are you from?" said Robb.

"California. The gold fields are played out down there and I've been working my way north for the last couple of years. From what I hear the Fraser is just beginning," said Bill, finishing a plate of beans. Bill wiped his mouth and beard with his red bandana. "Where are you from?"

"I'm from Victoria, but I've never been up the Fraser," Robb replied, thinking this man could be a possibility. They spent the afternoon together, sitting on their backpacks, watching other groups play cards and casually chatting.

"I've never played cards. How does it work?" asked Robb.

Bill obliged by pulling a deck of cards from his pack and going through the basics. "I'm surprised you don't play cards. I thought everyone did."

"Not in my parents' house. My father's an old-fashioned Scot. He might sit down for a drink or two, but he doesn't think much of card players. Waste of time to him, and too much chance of losing money. He'd never spend an extra penny unless he had to," Robb replied, thinking fondly of his surly father. "He works at the Bay post in Victoria, in the store selling supplies and trading for furs. That's what my brothers and I do too. Father makes sure he keeps us busy and out of trouble." He could clearly visualize his father's face.

* * *

It was early in the evening when Robb felt the *Eliza's* engines start to slow. They were entering a narrow channel on the south side of an island and he could see buildings on the southern shore. *That has to be Fort Langley.* The *Eliza* pulled alongside the dock and was soon secured. Quickly, the gangplank was lowered, and the miners streamed off. The crew were soon unloading supplies and mail for the fort, and there was a steady stream of horse-drawn carts bringing freight bound for *Eliza's* return trip via Olympia, Washington.

Robb saw there were already two hundred miners waiting on the dock for the *Enterprise*. "I don't think we're going to be able to get on this sailing by the look of it."

Bill motioned him over. "We'll probably have to wait for the next run in two days' time. Why don't you come with me, Robb? My tent's big enough for two." Robb agreed and they managed to secure their place in the lineup for the *Enterprise* despite the shoving and pushing.

Chapter 9

The distant whistle of the *Enterprise* brought every waiting miner to his feet. They watched as her engines slowed and she came slowly into her docking place. It seemed forever before the gangplank was lowered and the miners were allowed to disembark. Robb watched the newcomers closely. Out of sixty men, only one man looked happy. Robb surmised he must have found gold. The rest looked dejected, worn out or ill.

"Bill, I've got to pick up some tools. Maybe someone will sell theirs," said Robb, heading off and leaving his pack sitting beside Bill's.

Robb approached several of the disembarking passengers to inquire if their equipment was for sale. They shook their heads. There was one particularly tired, disheveled individual who looked much older than the others. The old man was almost skeletal, his thin wrists protruding from his loose shirt. When Robb asked if he would sell the pick, pan and spade, he handed them over for Robb to examine. Although well used, the tools were still serviceable and in good condition. They dickered for a few minutes then there was a look of resignation on the wizened, wrinkled face as the man nodded and handed everything over. Robb paid him. Transaction completed, the old man shuffled off towards the local tavern.

Robb headed back with a grin on his face, carrying his prizes.

"How much did that cost you?" asked Bill.

"I got them for five dollars; would have cost me twenty-five if I'd bought them at home," said Robb. "Geez, these guys stink. They haven't had a bath or changed clothes for weeks."

"Wait 'til you've been stuck in a cabin all winter with five or six guys," Bill replied with a grin.

He laughed at the grimace on Robb's face and realized he liked the kid.

They quickly gathered small sticks for a fire and got the tarps put up as a light rain started to fall. They had just enough room for their bedrolls. Then they sat around as beans slowly simmered in Bill's gold pan. "It saves carrying an extra pot," he said.

Robb had made himself another beef sandwich while Bill hauled some jerky from his backpack. Bill listened to the voices outside. "When you're in tent town or on the trail, listen to what's going on around you – usually there are a lot of fights. You get to know who are buddies and who aren't. Most of the guys are alright, but some are just plain dangerous; they're predators just waiting for the newcomers. They're totally unpredictable if they're drunk. You walked off and left your pack with me. Not a good thing to do with a stranger."

"Well, you didn't touch it, did you?" said Robb. He'd tied the flap with a particular knot that was still in place when he'd come back. With a faint smile on his lips, he looked at Bill's face.

Bill paused, realizing the boy had been testing him. Bill roared with laughter and slapped his knee. "Damn it, Robb. I think we're going to get along just fine. Tell me, what made you leave a steady job and your family?"

Bill sat and listened to Robb's story. He saw the misery on Robb's face as he spoke of Emma, her suitor and his dismissal by her father. *He's just a lovesick pup.*

"What about you?" Robb asked, as he found his little bag of salt and cleaned his teeth with his hog's hair toothbrush before settling into his sleeping bag.

"My wife and kids died in a house fire five years ago. I hit the trail, had some luck in California but not great. I've met some interesting people. I'm hoping to meet them again somewhere along the way," Bill replied. "I used to be in the cavalry but there's war brewing back home and I don't want any part of it. I might settle up here if I like the country."

Robb realized Bill was armed when he saw him remove a small gun from the back of his belt and place it under his pack, where he could quickly grab it if he needed to. Having been up since midnight, Robb was exhausted with all the excitement of the day and fell asleep as soon as his head rested on his backpack, too tired to think about Emma, his family or what could lie ahead.

Chapter 10

The *Enterprise* started to load around five in the morning. Some two hundred men managed to get on board, but only a few from the *Eliza*. Gathering their belongings, Bill and Robb shuffled ahead in the lineup. "There's about sixty ahead of us," Robb said, counting heads. "We should be good for Friday's run, if we can hold our spot."

They took turns going to the fort and walking about town. Leaving Bill to guard their packs and their position in line, Robb went down to the riverbank where he could see Indian canoes. The dugouts looked different from the Songhees' canoes; they didn't have the high front prows. He spoke with the men and found they were Salish but a different tribe. While the language was not the same, there were similarities. Many of them were taking miners up the river by canoe to Yale. He stopped at the fort and purchased flour, beans, jerky, rubber boots and soap. Bill indicated that jerky would be lighter to carry than bacon and didn't need to be cooked, making it less attractive to bears. That was a good point, but Robb planned to use bacon grease to make his biscuits. *It's a trade-off.*

"I see you managed to keep our place," he said when he got back.

Bill nodded. "They're pretty orderly at the moment. What did you find out this time?"

"Quite a lot. The big island across the channel is McMillan Island and there are three local Indian tribes in the area. Some of them are taking men up the river at two dollars a head. They catch a lot of fish, particularly when the salmon's running. Apparently, it's salted and shipped in barrels to Hawaii, of all places. Who'd have thought that? Apparently, we trade it for some plant fibre called pulu, that's used for stuffing mattresses here. A lot of wood gets shipped too, like those cedar shingles," he said, looking at the stacked pallets sitting at the dockside.

"I'll take a walk around," said Bill and sauntered off towards the fort. "I need ammo and I want to see if I know anybody. We need to team up with another group, at least four other men, I think."

Robb took a chunk of bread and piece of beef from his backpack, savouring the food and watching the activity around him. He had enough left for his meal that night. He'd try to buy a piece of fish tomorrow and some bread to get him through to Yale. No women were in sight. His thoughts turned to Emma, and he could envision how she'd looked that last day in church. Any time he thought of her, somehow Jackson's face got in the way. He shook his head in disgust. *Am I on a fool's errand here? Will I ever have enough gold to be able to go back and face everyone?*

Bill came back a couple of hours later carrying a burlap bag of food. "We won't bother with the tent until we're on the trail. The tarp's enough to keep us dry but portable enough we can move in a hurry if anyone butts in the line."

"Bill, I really miss my musket. Should I be buying one?" Robb asked.

"With the new rifles out, I wouldn't be bothering with a musket. Winchester's putting out a good carbine, and Sharpe's have got a buffalo rifle that's a real beauty. They're a lot more accurate at a distance and it's easy to reload without having the bother of black powder and balls. You can even do it while you're on a horse. Most of our troubles will be other miners, close contact, so the derringer type pistol can be quite useful. Why don't you wait and see if we team up with another group? If we've got a couple of rifles between us then that would be plenty."

"I was thinking we'd need one for hunting. The packs are going to be heavy enough as it is without taking a ton of food along. Did you see anyone you knew?"

"Yeah, see the guy in the black hat over by the tavern? Take a good look at him. He's one to stay away from, real bad dude. He cheats at cards and he's killed a few men. So far, he's managed to avoid the law. His name's Quinlan; quick tempered and quick on the draw, and he carries a knife. If you're going to play cards, he's one to avoid."

Robb eyed the man. *That's an easy face to remember with that scar over the right temple.* "Did you see any of your old buddies?"

"I saw some guys I knew but not the ones I wanted. I'd join up with Dunlevey if I could find him. He's got good business sense and he's more honest than most. He headed up here late last year. You need a group to work claims together – larger area to work and a better chance of finding gold. In some places they've dug tunnels down to bedrock. It would be a real bonus if I could find a geologist."

"Don't think I've ever met one. What do they do?" Robb asked.

"They know the lay of the land and how it formed. The gold is in quartz rock in certain formations. It would be a real asset to know where to look in the first place," Bill replied.

It didn't look like rain, so Robb decided to wash a few things. He decided not to bother shaving, as he rubbed the stubble on his chin. *Mother would have a fit.* He changed his shirt and socks and went down to the river, pleased he'd bought a couple of bars of yellow soap. He gave his clothes a quick scrub and rinsed them in the river. Wringing them out, he hung them up to dry on the tarp poles.

It was early evening and they hunkered down under the tarp. Robb ate the last of the bread and roast beef. He thought about his family a lot and realized how lucky he was. A lot of these guys didn't have family, or like Bill, had lost them. He'd picked up a lot of skills working for the Bay dealing with the miners and Indians. That could be very useful to him out here. He thought about Emma and felt a deep sadness. She was so beautiful, and he wanted her badly he could almost reach out and touch her.

In the darkening gloom, they watched other men in the lineup settling down under tarps to play cards by candlelight or firelight. Robb could feel the air of impatience and tension. Some went off to the tavern while others disappeared into what apparently was the local brothel, a small, nondescript wooden house. They reappeared later looking pleased with themselves. The militia patrolled periodically. It seemed quiet and orderly.

In the dead of night, they were abruptly awoken by shouts, the sounds of things falling over, bodies knocking down tents, two shots fired and the sound of someone running. They were both on their feet trying to sort out the chaos of dark shadows. The rumble of running feet and the flaring of burning torches emanated from the fort as soldiers rapidly approached.

Their torch lights revealed the two men lying on the ground, one still and the other groaning and clutching his right arm. The flattened tent half-covered them; their packs, contents and playing cards were strewn around, and everyone else in the lineup was on their feet wondering what had happened. Neighbouring tarps had been knocked down too, much to the confusion of the occupants who had been beneath them and trampled in the melee.

"What the hell?" said Bill, watching as more soldiers scurried down from the fort, including an officer. The one man on the ground was obviously dead when the soldiers checked him, but the injured man was now sitting up while a soldier examined his arm.

Robb saw the officer talking to the man and to bystanders who pointed in the direction the fugitive had taken, the south road, by the look of it. *They know who they're looking for and they'll be after him in the morning. He won't get far on foot. If he's guilty, he'll hang for it, especially if Judge Begby's in the area.* A cart was loaded with the body and the injured man, and lumbered off to the fort, fading into the darkness. Silence descended again, and the miners went back to bed.

* * *

Daylight revealed scant evidence of the fight, except for a few playing cards trampled in the dirt. A party of soldiers had ridden out early on the south road, accompanied by a large hound. The empty space in the lineup quickly disappeared. Bill left to find breakfast. Robb hoped he'd find some fresh bread, as he needed enough to last him to Yale. He watched out for the Indians too. They would be along some time with fish for sale.

Later, a young Native with his son came down the lineup carrying a pole between them loaded with dried smoked salmon. Robb examined the fish. They were last year's catch but still good. He bought two large ones, wrapping them in a piece of tarp. He thought about getting another knife, knowing he'd be in real trouble if he lost or damaged the one he had.

The miners were more restless and impatient that morning. *Everyone wants to get going, including me.* He noticed Bill moving around talking to people. For a time, Bill disappeared inside the fort. It was over an hour later that he reappeared with three other men. The fourth, an older man, was holding their place in the lineup about a hundred feet further down the line. As they approached, Robb carefully looked them over. Three were in their late thirties or early forties and looked experienced and confident.

Bill introduced them to Robb, and they all shook hands. "Robb, this is George Sutcliffe, Melvin Franks and James Harwood. Back there in the line is their partner, Henry Jessop. They're 49'ers too and have been working up the Columbia. George here is a geologist," he said with a grin, dropping a bag of bread under the tarp.

"I'm mighty glad to meet you," said Robb with enthusiasm, knowing they were just the sort of men Bill had been looking for.

They stood and talked for a while then Robb left Bill to guard the goods while he went back with the others to meet Henry. He was the oldest of the group, probably in his early fifties, but he looked tough and fit. They seemed to be an educated bunch. George had a university education and the others were all businessmen; it sounded like they'd been successful. He also noticed the four rifles propped up on their backpacks. He wouldn't need to buy a rifle if they joined forces. After talking to them for a short while, Robb went into the fort and bought another knife and a spare toothbrush. There weren't going to be any conveniences out in the bush. He figured he'd be using twigs for toothbrushes soon enough.

At supper, the *Enterprise's* whistle had everyone on their feet. Robb knew they wouldn't load passengers until dawn, but he couldn't keep still. The evening passed slowly, and Robb was so excited he barely slept.

The *Enterprise* started loading passengers at 5:00 a.m. Captain Wright stood on the head of the gangplank collecting the four dollar fares. Robb and Bill had no difficulty getting on board, and together they waited to see if the other four would make the cut. On hefting his backpack, he realized just how heavy it was. Everything in it was essential. There was nothing he could do to lighten it. The trail was going to be hard going with that load. Slowly, the lineup moved and they both heaved a sigh of relief when the foursome finally came on board. They grinned at each other over the heads of the standing-room-only crowd on deck.

The gangplank was hauled in, and with steam belching from the stack and the engines throbbing, the waters boiled and foamed as *Enterprise* moved out into the channel. Robb watched as Fort Langley faded behind them, leaving disgruntled miners on the wharf waiting for the next trip.

Mid-morning saw them at Chilliwack, stopping only long enough to drop off the mail and exchange supplies, and then the channel started to narrow, the current increasing. The low, marshy areas disappeared, replaced by gravel bars and low areas of pines with mountains on either side getting progressively higher and closer as the river narrowed. Some of the distant mountains still had patches of snow but the nearer ones were tree-covered. There was hardly any sign of habitation other than a few cabins and occasional smoke inland. Lots of small boats and canoes were taking miners north. It was wild country. He looked around and saw the young Brits looking at the scenery with some trepidation, their previous smiles reduced to frowns. They were just starting to realize what they were up against. A light rain started to fall, so they all backed as far under the upper deck as they could and pulled their tarps over their heads and packs. Robb made a sandwich, and he found the bread almost as good as his mother's and the salmon a deep, rich pink. It was so good he made himself another one. The boat would stop at Hope overnight and get into Fort Yale tomorrow.

"Everyone's quiet. I think they're figuring out that this really is wilderness. Don't think you're going to see anyone playing cards or fighting tonight," said Bill. It was a tight squeeze on the deck as the men hunkered down for the night, packed in like pigs in a sty.

Robb curled up, his tarp over him as darkness and quiet descended. He lay there listening to the current lapping against the boat, the creaking of her beams, and the snores of the men around him. He thought back to the day in Craigflower School, where Reverend Staines acted as both the post chaplain and schoolmaster. They had been practising their letters when the door had opened and Henry Freeland appeared, escorting his twelve-year-old daughter Emma for her first day in class. Every child in the building stopped what they were doing and stared. The girl was tiny, her blonde ringlets hanging down over an immaculate frilly, gingham dress, a satin ribbon in her hair, and dainty leather ankle boots. She was so unlike the other girls, including Jane and Emily, who were dressed in plain cotton dresses. Some children were barefoot. Very few families could afford to educate both their sons and daughters. His sisters were lucky.

Emma cast her blue eyes around the room, ignored the other children, then smiled at Reverend Staines. Fourteen-year-old Robb was immediately hooked. He thought of her as his darling and could still see her smile, her eyes and loving face. He fell asleep with visions of Emma lying beside him as he confessed his love and kissed her.

Chapter 11

Dear Robb,

I'm hoping this letter reaches you at Fort Yale but you've got a head start on us and the *Eliza* won't be back in town for mail pickup for another two days. I wish you had talked to us before you left. We might have been able to talk you out of it.

I am heartbroken. The thought of you out there with those ruffians is a nightmare. They are so crude and sinful. It goes against everything we brought you up to be. They're not the kind of people you should be involved with and it is so dangerous. Emma is now formally engaged to Captain Jackson, but the wedding will not take place until next summer, when she turns sixteen.

Sir James told Father he was going to ask you to be his personal courier. He will be moving to New Westminster shortly in his new role as governor of New Caledonia. Will you please consider this offer?

Your father has been deeply distressed by all this. Jane and Emily send their love. Your brothers are still working hard. They've had to hire someone else to help in the licence office. You are sorely missed around here. We have to buy beef now since there's no one to hunt venison or bring fish home. You have no idea what I have to go through with Ivy every day. Please take care of yourself, keep safe and come home as soon as you can. Love Mum

Chapter 12

It was noon before the *Enterprise* docked in Fort Yale. The town lay on a gravel bar between two steep, forested hills, little more than a niche carved out of the hillsides hemmed in by the river. The miners poured off the gangplank like a tidal wave, filling the muddy streets as some sought the northbound path out of town, while others headed for the Branch or Bennett saloons.

Bill and Robb helped each other get their packs on and adjusted their loads while waiting for the others to join them. Robb found the pack heavy as the harness bit into his shoulders. He felt awkward with the handles of the pick and shovel dangling through the loops.

It was Melvin who mentioned picking up mail at the fort. "I'm going to check for mail before we leave. My wife sends letters regularly. We might not be able to get mail further north." He trudged off towards the fort with the rest of them tagging along behind.

Robb figured it was too soon to have mail from home, so he watched the carpenters putting the finishing touches to a new church, St. John the Divine. He decided he needed all the help he could get on this venture and stood outside the unfinished church, silently praying for success.

Robb hoped he'd get used to the load. As they walked about town, he looked at the older men. Their packs were as heavy as his. Even Henry was carrying his pack and rifle with relative ease. Robb noticed an advertisement in a store window for rubber boots at ten dollars a pair, more than in Fort Langley. He couldn't believe how the prices were jacked up. He quickly penned a letter to his parents.

> Dear Mum and Father,
>
> Arrived at Fort Yale this morning. The view is very different from home. Can see high snow-capped mountains in the distance. The boat ride has been interesting.
>
> Have met a good group of miners, experienced business men and one of them is a geologist. They seem decent, educated and are well armed. They're my safest bet. Conditions will get worse as we go north. From Yale, we will be heading for Cache Creek. Give my regards to everyone.
>
> Love Robb

Robb put the stamp on his letter and Melvin nudged him. "Who's the woman on your stamps?" he asked.

"That's Queen Victoria," said Robb. "Since we're a British colony, she's our head of state. Who's on your stamps?" he asked.

"George Washington's on ours; he's our president." Melvin and Henry opened their letters from home, which they read quickly, hungry for news of their families. They wrote immediate replies.

"We've only got a few hours of daylight, but we may as well get started," said Henry and the eighteen-mile trek to Spuzzum began. They walked single file on the well-trodden pathway between the pines. The thunder of the Fraser running a hundred feet below them drowned out all conversation.

As he walked along, Robb concentrated on the path. It was rocky, about six feet wide, enough to accommodate his back-pack, but it was just a notch in the steep hillside, meandering near the cliff edges. No one spoke. He could only hear their breathing, the sound of the river and a few birdcalls. Bill was following him at the end of the line. At times the boughs of the tall pines were dense enough to block the light, what little light there was near the bottom of the canyon. Robb could see George, Melvin and James strung out behind Henry, who was setting a steady pace. Robb admired the man immensely. He made it look effortless, and there he was, half his age, huffing and puffing like an old mule. He hoped he'd be able to keep up with him.

After an hour and a half, they caught up with some stragglers from the earlier bunch, including the four Brits who were sitting at the side of the path with their packs off, panting and sweaty. Robb felt sorry for them. At least at home he'd had an active outdoor life. They'd come halfway around the world to find gold and they weren't prepared.

They came to an area where a recent landslide from higher up the slope had torn a slice out of the hill and slid right down to the water's edge. A hundred feet of the path had been obliterated, denuded of trees that had fallen in a frenzied pile of broken trunks, roots and branches near the bottom. The path narrowed sharply and had loose gravel and large boulders. Henry stopped and surveyed the options. "Others have been across but go slow, and one at a time. This could still be unstable. George, let me get across first before you start. Going together could set this gravel sliding."

He walked carefully, one step at a time, testing his weight with each foot. A few pebbles rolled to bounce downhill and splash into the river. He made it across. George was the next to cross, then Melvin, then James. Finally, it was Robb's turn. They were losing the light now and he was very aware that Bill had to cross after him.

Robb kept his eyes on the ground, afraid to look down the slope. One foot in front of the other. He froze when a pebble rolled under his right boot, but the path held and with a pounding heart he continued. It seemed like forever before he got across to the safety of the treeline and James.

"There, you made it!" said James, grabbing his arm and pulling him to firmer ground. They both turned to watch. Bill was already halfway across, moving at a steady pace. "The others have gone ahead to find a campsite for the night. If anyone else tries that in the dark, they are complete idiots."

A noise behind them made Robb jump but it was Melvin coming back along the path carrying a brush torch that he'd cobbled together. It didn't throw much light, but it was a beacon for Bill, who made the last few steps towards them as they each grabbed his arms. They stood for a moment, letting their tension ease, then turned and followed Melvin through the trees.

Henry had found a relatively flat spot a short distance away beside a trickling spring that was seeping down the hill. George had a fire started and put a pan of water on to boil. James had their tent strung up, the fire creating dancing shadows over the camp. Robb slipped off his backpack, thoroughly glad to be rid of it. He'd been so scared back there, he'd totally forgotten he'd been carrying it. He wasn't used to heights; all he wanted was to get across without sliding into oblivion.

Bill unpacked their tent and together they got it up quickly, gathering sticks, pinecones, anything that would burn for the firepit. It was a quiet evening as the men sat around the fire eating their simple meals and prepared to bunk down early.

Robb was exhausted. They'd only been on the trail for a couple of hours, but he was tired out. He lay on the ground in their tent and listened to the night, glad that at least his tarp was keeping the dampness out of his back. The cold enveloped him and he snuggled under his heavy blanket. He needed his clothes to keep in the warmth. He wasn't even going to take his boots off. Below, the river pounded and roared over its rocky bed. A light breeze whispered through the pines. Nearby small animals rustled in the dark and occasionally an owl hooted. The soft melancholy sound of James's harmonica suddenly had him longing for home; it was the only human sound in the wilderness. At their next camp he thought he'd set out some snares, try and catch a critter or two – make the meat last. If they were working that hard, they needed to eat well. He put up his collar, pulled his hat down over his face to keep the bugs away and fell into a deep, dreamless sleep.

* * *

George took the lead the next day, maintaining a steady pace. Henry brought up the rear. The path went up, down, over fallen trees and around boulders. There were makeshift bridges of felled trees over some of the deeper gullies. Robb caught occasional glimpses of the other groups. Apart from the tramp of feet, there was silence. They splashed through tiny torrents that flowed downhill. They only stopped long enough to scoop a mug of water. Following a curve in the river, the scenery started to change as sunshine revealed bare, vertical rock faces in glowing layers of sandy brown, deep reds and dark browns. The canyon itself narrowed slightly with the river remaining continuous white water, surging and splashing over broken rocks the size of cabins, constantly tearing at the canyon walls.

They took a break around noon and sat on a fallen tree, eating their lunch. Robb was stiff, aching all over, barely aware of the stale smell of his own sweat. No one said much. It felt so good to have the pack off for a while. George had finished his meal and was looking at the scenery and writing in his notebook.

"What do you see, George?" Robb asked.

"See the layers over there?" George replied, pointing to the canyon walls. "Those are old layers of mud and sediment that have hardened into rock over time. But further up there, see that diagonal black seam? It's volcanic."

Robb could see the different layers George referred to. "What does that mean?"

"Volcanic rock is liquid deep inside the earth, and under pressure it can break through to the surface. The black stuff used to be red hot lava that flowed like water. It cooled a long time ago. Gold is often found in those white quartz veins we've been looking at. Sometime pyrite is found in that too. Pyrite looks like gold, but it isn't ... it's fool's gold," said George.

Robb pointed to the forest. "The trees are different too. In Victoria, we don't have pines like that tall one. These ones here look like Douglas fir but they're much shorter than the ones on the coast. It must be drier here."

Melvin spoke up. "In Washington state, we call those lodgepole pines; nice and straight if you're building a cabin or a rail fence."

Break over, they re-shouldered their packs and plodded on. Several times, they stepped aside to allow southbound miners to pass. The men looked haggard and it was obvious they had not been successful. He still wondered if he was doing the right thing as he followed the descending path. Through a break in the trees, he caught glimpses of a creek up ahead. He recognized the cattails immediately in the swampy area and pulled out an armful by the roots. Long Feather's words echoed in his head that the roots and stems could be boiled like potatoes. He was tired of not having proper meals.

"Why are you bothering with weeds?" asked James.

"Because they're edible and could be really useful to us if we run out of food," replied Robb, thinking of being stuck in a small cabin with three-foot snowdrifts, no money and no supplies. James looked skeptical.

"This creek's barely forty feet across but it's too deep for ordinary boots," said George, changing into his rubber ones. He looked at the gravel bars upstream and pointed. "Looks like some of the others are trying their luck upstream. They probably aren't going to find much. These sandbars have been worked before, by the look of them; the river didn't make piles like that."

Robb could see five men on the far sandbar bent over, working their gold pans. *Soon we'll be doing that too.*

It took another two days of steady trudging to reach Spuzzum. It was such a tiny place, with a church, a couple of cabins, a blacksmith shop, stores and the saloon, but it looked like civilization to him. Every muscle in his body ached and he was stiff beyond belief.

Two young women were standing at the saloon doors, inviting the miners to come in. Most of the men were watching them, and a few broke from the crowd and headed for the saloon. He was too tired to respond. The blonde one looked a bit like Emma, but she was definitely no lady. Moving on, he followed the others to the edge of the tent encampment, where they gladly rid themselves of their backpacks and pitched their tents beside the other weary men around them.

Everyone was too tired to fight or argue. Robb was amazed how a few days of tough hiking could change a man. "What are we doing about food?" he asked.

George said, "I'm going to the store to get the lowdown on the local streams and rivers. I don't think we need a guide yet, but we do need meat. There should be some local Indians around to bring in game. The path's pretty clear, by the look of it," said George. "They've been finding gold here since '58 around Boston Bar and near Kamloops east on the Thompson river."

As Robb followed him into the store, he looked in the store window and was startled by the stranger reflected back at him. He rubbed his beard and laughed as the apparition did the same.

"What's funny?" said George.

"I just got a good look at myself. My mother wouldn't recognize me with this beard, untidy hair and dirty clothes; I almost didn't myself." He wandered around the store, talking to the other miners. He could hear George questioning the store master. It sounded like some were heading for Lytton but no big finds so far. Two guys were heading south – they'd run out of money. There was talk of Sir James continuing the wagon road from Lytton right up to Quesnel. *There will be jobs on the road crew.* The Royal Engineers would be building it, so he hoped he wouldn't run into Jackson. A brief image of Emma danced in his mind, then was gone.

"Melvin, I've eaten most of the salmon; just got a little bit of jerky left. Do you think I should pick up some more?"

"Wait 'til morning. We'll see if any locals come in. According to the owner, they'll bring stuff to sell tomorrow," Melvin replied.

They had fallen into a regular routine once they had pitched their tents. Three went off to gather wood for the fire and the other three took care of the cooking. They used their gold pans as both plates and pots. That night it was Robb's turn to do the bread, so he took six handfuls of flour, mixed it with water until it was a thick paste and let it sit for a bit before dividing the dough between two pans. He added some pine seeds he'd found along the way for extra flavour.

James sliced the venison into thin strips, setting them out in three pans. Once the fire got going, the venison was fried, the greens were boiled, and finally the bread was baked. It came out like a pancake and only took five minutes to cook. Everything was divided six ways. The inner bark of the trees was a tasty snack for dessert.

Robb had a habit of setting his snares whenever he had the opportunity, and occasionally caught a rabbit, raccoon, groundhog or skunk. He hadn't had any luck fishing. Melvin had managed to shoot a duck and a goose so far.

He even tried to boil up some spruce needles to make a makeshift tea but wasn't impressed. However, it did make a nice warm drink on a cold night.

* * *

With morning light sliding down the canyon walls, Robb awoke and crawled out of his tent. Tent town was quiet, and he seemed to be the first one up. He saw a group of Native men dressed in buckskin, quietly waiting at the edge of the trees. They had a deer carcass strung on a pole between the trees. "Bill, get up. The Indians are here with meat." Rooting through his backpack, he found his money wad then walked over to the other tent to wake Henry.

Robb looked at the Natives. They were quite different from the Songhees, being taller and wearing decorated buckskin shirts and pants. He noticed the intricate quill beadwork on their shirts. The trader had said they were from the Nlaka'paxum tribe – interior Salish. Choosing the elder as his contact, he paused in front of him and spoke the traditional greeting. The old man's head came up, and the brown eyes looked him over thoroughly. Robb waited. As the old man spoke, Robb listened to the words, but the language was different from the Songhees. "I don't understand," said Robb and resorted to the hand signs he was used to and a mixture of English/Salish. The old man led him over to the carcass and responded with more hand signals and guttural words. It looked like a good fresh kill; a nice buck. Robb indicated the haunch he wanted, and the man hacked it from the carcass. Robb also looked at a cedar basket of smoked salmon. He selected two fish and started dickering.

Bill and Henry joined him. They examined the venison and agreed with him on the meat. "This should last us to Lytton."

Robb continued dickering with the elder, their fingers flashing signals back and forth until they both nodded. The old man took his money then started dealing with the next miner. Robb noticed that Bill and the others ignored the fish. He didn't know why they weren't interested in fish; it lasted so much longer than fresh venison.

Back at their campsite, James was restarting the fire. Henry was preparing the morning's bread. "You got a good deal on that, Robb. Could you understand what they were saying?"

"No, it's different from the Songhees' language, but you can get by with hand signals. I'm used to that." His eyes kept track of the procession of miners. Soon the meat was sold, and the Indians simply disappeared into the woods. It was obviously a good strategy to get up early.

"Now what, Henry?" Bill asked.

"We'll follow the path to Lytton. It's about sixty-five miles from here, so it'll likely take us about four or five days from what the storekeeper was saying. We'll be able to have a look at Hell's Gate. No choice but to go around it."

Robb scanned tent town. He noticed the Chinese group dismantling their tents. The four young Brits were notably absent. He guessed they hadn't made it. He recognized many others from the boat. After breakfast they broke camp and headed north on the path. While his muscles were still very stiff and sore, Robb found that the pack didn't seem quite so heavy.

* * *

Two days out found them strung out in a long line along the rim of the canyon. Robb stood there in complete amazement, looking down into the depths of Hell's Gate. The jagged, vertical dark-gray walls of the canyon were over five-hundred-feet high with the sides only a hundred feet apart. He was used to the ocean but had never seen such a volume of water moving so quickly in such a confined space. The surface was a roiling mesh of foaming eddies and whirlpools, totally impassable to a canoe. Bill poked him in the ribs and pointed at the narrow ledge barely visible on the canyon wall.

85

Dear god, that ledge is only two feet wide! How did Simon Fraser ever go through it? It would have been handholds all the way. He couldn't imagine carrying a backpack and keeping his balance.

The journey continued, one day much like the rest. By day four of steady walking, Robb noticed the landscape changing. The hills weren't as high and were farther apart. Walking was much easier except his feet were starting to hurt in his boots. The country now had open areas of greening bunch grass, with trees in the gullies and ravines. Robb could see dandelions starting to poke through the grass in some meadows and what looked like camas plants. That was a good thing. Once they flowered, he could dig them up. *The blue ones are safe to eat but the white ones aren't.* He needed to remember everything Long Feather had taught him about edible plants, and it would help him save the little money he had.

They were getting into a good routine, and Robb was slowly getting to know his companions. He found them to be reliable and knowledgeable men, willing to share their knowledge. Their comradery was melding them into a close, almost family, group. Robb listened to their tales of the California gold rush, what they had done with their lives and their dreams for the Cariboo. They depended on each other for everything, including safety.

Next day, he took his turn as leader, keeping a steady pace as the others had done. The river was wider and shallower here, the roar reduced to a steady rush of water. They could see tiny dots of men below them working the sandbars that formed on the curves in the river as far as the eye could see.

Every day was getting a bit warmer. The snow was limited to the peaks now. Leaves were coming out on the maples and oaks. The country was much drier than Victoria; they hadn't had rain since they'd left Hope. He paused and picked a leaf from a shrub that looked like huckleberry – good eating by the end of summer. Buds were full on the crab apple trees too. He thought about Emma and his family constantly. Memories of faces and events popped into his head as he walked along. At night, he still felt like he could reach out and touch her.

Chapter 13

Dear Robb:

> I can't believe you've been gone over three weeks. Your letter arrived yesterday on the *Anderson*. We are all really glad you'd got that far safely. Did you get Mum's letter? Father's been in touch with Thomas Elwyn, the gold commissioner at Fort Yale, but I guess he didn't see you go through. Mum has been sick for the past week. She's got herself in quite a dither about the whole thing.
>
> There's lots going on in Victoria. Sir James is moving to New Westminster and John Wood is taking his place. They are starting to dismantle the palisade around the fort and are expanding the Hudson Bay store now there's a lot of competition from the new general store. It has some wonderful dress material, so every woman in town

is sewing like mad. Father's not too happy with us spending money on that. Nothing has changed with the miners. Boatloads still coming in every day. We're still baking bread for the booth.

Rumour has it that measles is killing a lot of the Indians. They're banned from town. No one in town has been sick so far.

Matt and Edna are having another baby. She's due in late October. We all miss you, dear brother, especially Emily. You're her hero. Come home as soon as you can. I'll send this to Cache Creek, as we don't know where you are. Love, Jane.

Chapter 14

The path crested the hill and Lytton lay before them. In a broad river valley between low hills was a knot of log cabins, corrals and shop fronts. Robb looked at the river and saw the demarcation line where the clear waters of the Thompson River merged with the muddy waters of the Fraser. From their vantage point two paths were visible leaving town, one angled north-northeast along the banks of the Thompson and the other headed due north along the Fraser. A long train of mules was being unloaded for the night at the far end of town, their braying fracturing the air.

The men pitched their tents, leaving Robb to guard the campsite while the others went off in search of supplies and information. He noticed that the two exit roads had been cleared to a twenty-foot width; the surveyors' stakes were clearly evident. *The Royal Engineers have started the wagon road already. It's wide enough for two wagons to pass. That will make walking a whole lot easier.* He also noticed miners on the southeast route to Kamloops. They were probably heading back to the States or maybe the silver deposits George had mentioned.

The backpack no longer bothered him. A month on the trail had honed his body, leaving his shirt and pants baggy. His long black hair curled down to his shoulders and the beard was at least an inch long. He'd tightened his belt by two holes and it still felt loose.

He watched the line of miners continuing to come into town. The Chinese group came down the hill at a steady pace. There were still ten of them, moving easily. They were doing well. He recognized several other groups from the boat. There were only five of the card-playing group now. One of them looked pretty banged up and Robb wondered if it had been a fight or an accident. They still looked mean and shifty. He never saw any sign of the Brits again. He looked back at the way they'd come to the tiny dots of colour that were miners still on the trail.

When Bill and Melvin returned, Robb took the time to go down to the river and strip off his shirt and socks. His feet were blistered from his boots. As he scrubbed himself clean with his hands and the coarse soap, goosebumps spread all over him from the ice-cold water. He flicked his head a few times to get rid of the excess water in his hair and finished up by cleaning his teeth. He felt better after that and wondered if he should pick up a bit more salt and another pair of boots. He was cautious about spending ten dollars for a pair of boots, though. Shivering, he was glad to pull on his clean shirt and socks, then washed the dirty ones in the river. There was so little moisture in the air that he was sure his shirt would be dry in the morning.

He returned to the tents and draped his wet clothes over the tent poles. "Bill, do you want me to get some firewood?" he said as Bill was sorting his gear. "This valley's been stripped bare up to the ridge." He looked at the mud and stumps all the way up the hills around town. To him, it looked just plain ugly. *One good rain and all the soil will wash downhill.*

"Yeah, Robb, I guess you'd better get some. We need to finish up the venison tonight and get some more in the morning," Bill replied, sniffing the lumps of meat in his backpack.

Robb walked through town chatting to the locals and found two young boys who delivered wood to the campsites with a horse-drawn wagon. He watched as groups of Natives traded fish and root vegetables, their canoes drawn up on the riverbank. Their buckskin moccasins caught his attention. The shoes looked comfortable, and they'd be silent if he was hunting. He spoke with one Native man who was about his height and pointed to the moccasins. The man pulled his moccasins off and offered them to Robb. He tried them on, and they fit well when he tightened the rawhide thongs. They felt great too. They were well made and sturdy, stitched with sinew, and the insoles are cushioned with something soft. Robb bargained with him and was pleased with a two dollar price tag for the shoes and the vegetables. He had to conserve his savings. He noticed again that the canoes were very different from the ones the Songhees made. While the Songhees hollowed out one of the big Douglas firs to make their sea canoes, the Shuswap made a wooden frame and covered it with birch bark and pitch. That made sense, as it would be lighter to portage between the many lakes.

"What have you got there?" said Melvin when Robb got back to camp.

"A new pair of shoes, and some vegetable roots – they call it bitterroot."

Later they all sat around the fire discussing the next move. "Well, George, where do we go from here?" Robb asked, slurping up the mix of venison and boiled roots, which were indeed sharp, but tasty and filling. The others were now accustomed to Robb adding strange things to their stews.

"I think 150 Mile House will be our destination. It's about one hundred and fifty miles north of here. There's a gold commissioner's office in Williams Lake not far from there. From what they told me in the licence office, Dunlevey's group is near a place called Horsefly. I've heard you have to be careful when you go into the claims office to stake your claim. Some folks have been followed back to their camp by guys looking for easy pickings. There are reports of some being ambushed and killed near the mile houses for their tools and packs. We need to watch our backs."

"When we find gold, how do we go about establishing our claim? What's the process?" Robb asked.

"The gold commissioner will test our finds to make sure they are gold. The size of the lots varies from place to place but are usually around fifty acres per person. Once you have your certificate from the commissioner you have to go back to your claim and put posts at all the corners with the name of the claim and the date on each post. Most places limit you to, say, one-or two-hundred-foot frontage on the river. We can have an individual or a group claim," said George.

They left the next morning as soon as fresh venison was available and followed the northeastern route. Robb and Bill chatted briefly with the mule packer as he supervised loading the mules, dodging the frequent piles of manure. The man was about thirty and quite a charismatic, flamboyant character dressed in a white shirt, woolen pants, a broad-brimmed hat and riding boots. His long, dark hair hung loose to his shoulders and he sported a thick, luxuriant mustache. His voice was loud and heavily accented as he gestured to his mules and packers.

Robb couldn't tell if the man was French or Spanish.

"My name is Cataline Caux, and I'm the best mule packer on the trail. We make the trip to Quesnel a couple of times a season. Each one of these mules carry well over two-hundred pounds of freight. I know every item on every mule, and Castillo, my partner, and I have never lost one single load," he boasted. "If someone wants anything, I will deliver it."

Robb looked at the packs with amusement. He could believe it. There were parts of a piano on one mule and some metal parts for mining equipment on another one. Cataline Caux could be the right man to get his gold out on his trip home.

Two riders passed them with a pack horse. The leading rider looked familiar. For a few moments Robb couldn't place him, but the man's voice brought instant recognition. It was Judge Begby and his assistant. Robb had seen him on one occasion when the man had been visiting Sir James in Victoria a few years earlier. Begby was the law – six-foot-five inches of authority! He had a graying hair and beard but a dark moustache and was formally dressed in a hip-length jacket, a shirt, tie and vest, riding britches, spotless leather riding boots and a flat-topped black felt hat.

Robb's companions were surprised when Robb greeted the man by name. "Good morning, Judge Begby. Haven't seen you since you were in Victoria. My father works at the Hudson Bay Post there. Where are you heading?" There was no hope of Begby recognizing him dressed the way he was.

Begby reined his horse and looked down at him for a moment or two. "One of the McDonald boys?"

Robb was flabbergasted. "I'm surprised you remembered," he said.

"Well, despite the beard, you all look alike. I'm heading up to Williams Lake right now. They've got a murder suspect in jail. He can cool his heels until I get there. Justice will prevail. Good luck to you. Stay out of trouble," were his last words as he tipped his hat and rode on.

Robb told his companions of the judge's courageous solo administration of justice in the gold fields. "He sets up his tent in a field, a barn, or a bar, wherever he can. He puts on his robes and can be the judge, the jury or the prosecutor when he has a case. He's not afraid to tackle a mob either. Amazing man. My father told me he's fluent in Shuswap and Chilcotin, and the Natives call him 'Big Chief'. If a man gets a guilty verdict for murder, then he hangs. He's a one-man police force."

* * *

Whenever they came to a stream, George took the time to venture down it and look at the rocks. Robb donned his rubber boots then joined the others. He dipped his gold pan into the gravel of the stream bed, letting it fill with water and the fine sand mix. Bill showed him how to angle the pan's rim downward, swirl the water and flush out the bigger pieces of gravel, leaving the very fine material on the bottom.

"Keep swirling the water, Robb. The gold is heavy and will sink to the bottom. Gradually work the sand out. Let's see ... yes, there you are. Just a few flecks, but that's gold."

Robb looked at the few tiny glints of gold, no bigger than a pinhead, and with shaky fingers went back to panning with a grim determination. *This is how I'm going to get Emma back.* They panned for about two hours.

"I think that's enough," said George. "Let's see what everybody's got." They gathered on the stream bank and looked at their finds. Between them all it didn't amount to more than a teaspoon of gold flakes. "Not enough to be bothered with. Let's get back on the road."

Borrowing George's brass tweezers, Robb carefully placed the minute flakes into a leather drawstring pouch, put his pack back on and followed the others out. He didn't think that tiny bit would even buy him a loaf of bread.

* * *

Robb could see some cabins had been built here and there, with snake-rail fences to contain the horses and a few cows. "Settlers must be coming in now that the road's opening up. That must be awful hard on the women and children; no stores or schools yet. I wonder how much an acre the land is going for?" he said to James, who shrugged and they moved on.

Stopping frequently to sample the rivers slowed their progress, so it took them nearly two weeks to reach Cache Creek where Moody's Royal Engineers were widening the road. As they passed the work crew, Robb snatched up some spruce bark from a freshly felled tree and peeled off the soft, white inner lining. He cut it into strips with his knife and chewed on it, finding it sweet and tasty. He collected enough bark for everyone and put it into his pack for supper later.

There was an officer on horseback supervising the crew. In his red jacket and pillbox hat, astride a well-groomed bay horse, he was easy to pick out. Robb looked to see if it was Jackson, but it wasn't. *Maybe it's just as well he isn't here. I might have been tempted to do something stupid.* The road ahead of the work crew tapered down to the single-lane path again until it came to a rocky hill. Dust and large rock fragments were scattered over a wide area from a recent dynamite explosion, leaving a gap in the massive rock walls wide enough for the road to go through. The workers were bringing in a team of horses to clear the bigger pieces.

George was immediately on the prowl, sorting through the rock debris as they continued on the path, as were a lot of the work crew. He stooped from time to time, looking at samples then discarding them. "I don't see anything worthwhile here," he said and took the lead again, but everyone froze as an audible rattle reverberated in the air.

There on a chest-high rock ledge was a large, coiled rattlesnake, not two feet from George's face. The rattling tail was a blur of motion. George twisted sideways as the snake drew back into a tight s-shape, its mouth gaping, ready to strike. A shot rang out and the rattler's head disintegrated into pulped, thrashing flesh, with George falling sideways out of harm's way. Bill stood in the gunfighter's stance, the smoking derringer in his hand. "Are you okay, George?"

Robb helped George to his feet, his unwieldy backpack making it awkward for him to get up and keep his balance.

"Thanks, Bill. It was so well camouflaged I didn't even see it on that rock," replied George. He was pale and a little shaky. "I must be getting complacent about the dangers out here. I should know better."

Robb was amazed at Bill's speed and accuracy with the gun. The shot had been impressive. He had no idea Bill was so good. He changed out of his moccasins into his leather boots. They'd be better protection for his legs in snake country.

He watched as Bill picked up the now-motionless serpent and slung it across his backpack. Seeing the question on Robb's face, he said "There's a couple of pounds of meat here, and it's good eating."

George slowly got the colour back in his cheeks and they continued on.

* * *

Cache Creek was the overnight stopping point. The sun was setting when they finally walked into the tiny village where the saloon was overflowing with thirsty miners. Two girls were outside flirting with the men. Robb looked at their dresses and the amount of exposed ankle and bosom. His eyes were riveted to them. Part of him was interested, and part of him was surprised. Emma would never dress or behave like that. He had been too tired to even think about it in Spuzzum, but not now.

Melvin laughed and gave him a shove to get him moving. "Your Emma wouldn't like you looking at that kind of woman, now would she?"

Robb grinned sheepishly, "I guess not."

"Of course, we'd never tell, and she'd never know," Bill chimed in, slapping him on the shoulder. "It would cost you a dollar to lay with one. I can't see you squandering a dollar like that. You're good at bargaining; maybe you could charm her into giving it for free."

"Enough, you guys," said Robb, laughing. "Let's get the tents set up." They knew darned well he'd never been with a woman, and they sure enjoyed making fun of him for it.

Chapter 15

Over the next two weeks the journey continued. They sampled stream beds along the way, finding traces of gold but not in quantity. Robb still had less than a quarter of a cup of gold flakes in his pouch. They stopped at the road houses: 50 Mile House, 59 Mile House, Clinton, 100 Mile House, 108 Mile Ranch and Lac La Hache. He'd bought a couple of good used flannel shirts, some trousers and socks at the ranch dirt cheap.

Finally, they came to 150 Mile House. "These places are simple – good food, a dry place to sleep, a chance to catch up on the news," said Henry as they entered the large, two-storey log house with its wide veranda to be greeted by the Chinese cook, who was for some reason called Hank.

There was a store, a barn with a blacksmith shop and a few stalls, plus fenced fields for cattle and horses. Robb looked at the land, a vista of long, low hills, thick with lodgepole pines and miles of firs, dotted with glistening lakes and rivers. He looked at Bill and could see the longing on his face. "I can see you ranching here when you're done with the gold."

"You may be right about that. It's good country," said Bill. "I'd need to raise the money for at least a couple of hundred acres. I could run a roadhouse and make money off it like these guys do or simply raise cattle. There's always a need for fresh meat."

Hank was busy stirring pots of stew on the woodstove. The aroma of fresh biscuits had Robb drooling. They feasted on the simple meal provided by Tom Davidson, the owner. Although the table and benches were primitive, just rough-sawn lumber, even sitting at a table instead of sitting on the ground felt like a luxury. Having beef stew, fresh biscuits, potatoes and coffee with milk seemed like heaven to Robb. That evening they joined the other strangers on the veranda. With their diversions to sample stream beds, they had lost track of their acquaintances from the ship.

James was playing his harmonica. The soft, lonely melodies floated out over the pastures into the hills, but men made requests and soon they were humming or singing "Far from Home" and other familiar songs like they'd known each other for years. The card players were deep in their game in the corner. It was a pleasant, relaxed evening; lonely, driven and worn-out men taking a moment's respite. Twenty of them bunked down on the upstairs floor, which was just an open room. Robb slept a deep, untroubled sleep.

The following morning they gathered around Tom Davidson, seeking information.

"We're heading to Horsefly. We need a Native guide. Do you know anyone local and reliable?" said George.

"If you follow the main road another couple of miles, there's a pathway on the right that heads east. Follow that to the lake. There's a Shuswap village along there and you can ask for Long Baptiste. He's done guiding before. Secwepemc is the chief up there."

"Long Baptiste? That's a funny name for an Indian; is he French?" asked Melvin.

"No, I think his Indian name was too complicated to pronounce," said Tom.

Melvin asked another question. "How far are we from Williams Lake? I'd like to send some letters home."

"It's about fifteen miles; pretty much a full day's walk," replied Mr. Davidson. "It's the biggest local town. It has stores, and Phillip Nind is the gold commissioner. If you find any gold up in Horsefly, you're going to have to register your claim with him. They have a full-time constable too, Bill Pinchbeck. He's pretty good at keeping the miners and the Indians in line. Governor Douglas has promised to build us a government house as soon as the road goes through, hopefully with a proper jail. Judge Begby comes up here occasionally so there's a hanging tree in town. A lot of supplies come in from the west coast along the Bella Coola River route as well as the one up the Fraser."

"Well, that's useful information. We met Begby on the trail. He was heading to Williams Lake. I guess we'd better get going and see if we can find this Long Baptiste feller," said Melvin, and they were back on the road. It looked like they were the only ones taking that route. The rest of the miners were staying on the main road to Williams Lake.

***

Sure enough, two miles from the roadhouse, a pathway rutted with wagon tracks branched east. They followed it. The land was much the same as what they'd passed through, but the biting flies were out in full force. They were swatting the bugs so much that Bill pulled out his bandana and covered the lower part of his face with it, bandit-style, and pulled down his hat as far as he could with his collar up to protect his ears. "Geez, I can see why they called that place Horsefly."

They stopped at several streams to sample the gravel beds. Robb found not just flakes but a couple of tiny nuggets as did the others.

"That's encouraging. I think we're getting into a better area," said George.

The scenery didn't look any different to Robb, just low hills, open meadows, rocks and lakes, as he swatted at the flies and scratched the welts on his arms and neck. The flies were a constant nuisance.

It was late afternoon when they reached the lake. Robb could smell wood smoke, but he couldn't see the village. It had to be close by. He had the sensation of being watched but hadn't seen anyone. Coming to a fork in the footpath, they met a Native man carrying several trout. He had a long bow and a beaded quiver of arrows slung across his shoulder.

"We are looking for Long Baptiste. Do you know him?" asked George

"I am Long Baptiste," the man replied in broken English.

"Tom Davidson gave us your name. We're looking for a guide," explained George.

Robb was fascinated with Long Baptiste; the Native man was clad in plain buckskin, looking quite exotic with tattoos on his dark sculptured face, and his ears pierced with copper loops. Around his neck was a rawhide pendant strung with abalone shells and six curved, four-inch-long animal claws. Robb guessed the man to be in his mid-thirties, slim and no taller than himself. *Those aren't black bear claws. I wonder if they're from a grizzly.* He'd never encountered a grizzly and wasn't sure he wanted to.

George discussed their needs, and finally Long Baptiste nodded, agreeing to their terms. "Continue on the path and camp by the lake for tonight. I will find you in the morning and we'll go from there." In the blink of an eye, he was gone, melting silently into the forest.

After they'd put up the tents, started the fire and cooked supper, Robb went out into the underbrush to set snares. A light rain started to fall, and they quickly went into their tents and closed the flaps to get away from the mosquitoes and flies. Even then, his sleep was broken by the whining of mosquitoes around any exposed skin. His thick beard didn't protect him much either. He pulled his blanket over his head, undecided about if it was better to suffocate in his sleeping bag or be eaten alive.

Chapter 16

Early morning brought a tentative sun with light cloud, creating a halo effect of rosy, red gold behind the black-shadowed eastern mountains. The far western mountains, miles away, shone in the light. Robb found a marmot in one of his snares and quickly gutted it. He heard Henry calling his name and headed back to camp to find them packed up and ready to move out.

"Long Baptiste, do you know a man called Peter Dunlevey? He's a friend of mine and I'd like to meet him again. I believe he has a mining claim near here," said Bill.

"I know him. They have a gold claim about half a day's walk southeast of here, closer to Horsefly."

"Good, we're looking for the same sort of rock formations he wanted, a valley with a good strong flow of water, gravel beds and the rock walls straight up and down; hanging walls. Do you know a place like that?"

Long Baptiste thought for a few moments. "There is a place less than a day's walk from here. I've never looked for gold there, but the hunting is good, and it has the straight walls you have described."

Everyone nodded and followed his lead away from the lake and back out to the wagon track. Robb felt his enthusiasm start to build again. There were bunchgrass meadows with dense stands of trees in the gullies, a mixture of willow, pine, elder and larch. No cabins or other habitation were visible, but periodically footpaths that looked well used angled off the road and disappeared into the valleys. Robb assumed these went to other mining claims.

The road branched and Long Baptiste pointed to the right-hand wagon path. "Horsefly is down that road, about an hour's walk. They have a small general store, a blacksmith shop, a lumber mill and a saloon. They take the wagon into Williams Lake every week or so to get supplies. The place I want to take you is on the left-hand path." It was a mere footpath heading northeast. Close to noon, they crossed a creek that looked like it had been worked by miners. The banks were bare of trees and irregular mounds of gravel extended several hundred feet up the creek on both sides.

"Guess this place didn't work out," muttered Henry.

"They did well for about six weeks, but then no more. They moved on, north toward Soda Creek or maybe Alexandria," said Long Baptiste.

Something would be better than nothing, Robb thought. Later, in passing a dry meadow, Robb noted blue daisy-like flowers about waist high blooming in the lightly wooded areas. Catching up with Long Baptiste, he asked, "Are those camas plants? The ones that are safe to eat?"

Long Baptiste looked at him with surprise. "You know that?"

"One of the Songhees I knew at home was teaching me about plants. He told me the white flowered ones would kill me, but the blues were good eating, if I didn't eat too much at once."

"He was right. Never eat that plant unless you can see the colour of the flowers. These can be harvested now as the flowers have almost finished blooming, but you should only take the big bulb and leave the smaller ones to grow for next year." Long Baptiste was surprised to find a white man who was interested in plants.

Robb lagged behind the others to dig up some camas. Using his knife and fingers to remove the soil, he pried out a three-inch brown bulb. Separating it from the small bulbs, he packed the soil back in place, carefully reburying the smaller bulbs. When he had seven bulbs, he tucked them into his backpack and caught up with the rest of them.

"Long Baptiste, when we camp tonight, will you show me how to cook these? I caught a marmot in my snare this morning, so we can eat that too." He seemed eager to learn, and Long Baptiste nodded, absent-mindedly swatting at the ever-present flies.

* * *

The footpath had disappeared, and they were now moving into virgin bush. Long Baptiste was marking trees with his knife every hundred feet or so as they moved from stream to stream, panning as they went.

"You will follow these marks when you want to get back on the main road, so you don't get lost," he said as he moved effortlessly through the bush. Near the end of the day they came to another creek and several ponds. The hills opened up into a wide, green valley. The creek was shallower here, fanning into islands on braided gravel beds. George gave a shout and they looked at the hills, which formed sharp cliff faces with vertical sides several hundred feet high. A scree of shattered rock had accumulated at the base.

"This is grassy valley," said Long Baptiste to George.

George had his eyes fixed on the far end of the valley where he could see a landslide had partially blocked the creek. The water was gushing through one channel, creating a cascade of white water about ten feet high. "Okay, guys, that's where I want to go."

That high feeling of expectation flooded through them as they splashed through the shallows at a brisk pace, flushing nesting ducks as they went. The mallards resettled after they had passed. A large dark shape moved out of the water and into the trees. Long Baptiste pointed out the disappearing shape of a moose and her long-legged calf. "Never get between a cow and her calf. Dangerous animal if she feels threatened and very quick on her feet."

They stopped periodically to pan on some of the sandbars and were rewarded with a few pea-sized nuggets. Robb picked one out of his pan and stuffed it in his pocket. His fingers shook, he was so excited. Weeks of trudging, carrying heavy packs and hoping now came down to this place. His whole future depended on what they would find.

They finally reached the waterfall. They struck camp and got the tents up as quickly as they could. George was already doing a preliminary scout, and when he returned to them he opened his right hand, revealing two pearl-sized, rounded pieces of gold. "This is the best prospect we've had so far. I suggest we approach this systematically in the morning; the light's fading now and I don't want to miss anything. We'll each take a section on this side of bank and work it. Then we'll work on the other side. There might even be some good stuff above the waterfall. We've got to check it all out."

They sat around the campfire eating their meals, the excitement palpable. Robb was aware that every one of his senses was on high alert. The air smelled cleaner with the scent of pine; he could hear birdcalls, the splashing of fish somewhere in the creek, an occasional hoot of an owl. The moon was a pale-yellow crescent casting a faint swathe of light on the treetops with the overhead panorama of the star-dotted night sky.

Long Baptiste had disappeared earlier and now returned with the carcass of a yearling doe over his shoulder. He dropped it on the ground near the campfire and quickly gutted it before hoisting the carcass into a tree until it was about fifteen feet off the ground. "That should do you for a few days, and this will keep it out of a grizzly's reach," he said.

They thanked him for the venison and started to talk business.

"George, I want to make sure I have the claim thing right. From what you told me before, I could have my own claim and work it, or we could all go in together on the six lots and do a six-way split on whatever we find," Robb said.

"That's right," said James, cutting in. "Some claims might not be as profitable as others, so this is a good way to even things out."

"What would happen if I wanted to get out of the deal and go home with my share the gold?" said Robb.

"We'd divvy up what gold we have – six-way split. You'd get your share and we'd have first option of buying your claim," said Melvin.

"Let me think on it," said Robb. "How much does it cost to put in a claim?"

"Five dollars a year," replied James.

Robb didn't sleep a wink that night.

* * *

All of them were raring to go in the morning. Long Baptiste sat on a log and watched as George counted out fifty paces on the rocky north bank; Henry took the first section; Melvin took the next plot, then James, Bill and Robb took the rest. George kept the last section for himself, then all of them started shovelling the sandy gravel into their gold pans, either squatting or bent over in the shallows, swirling the water. It seemed to

Long Baptiste that this group of men were much more methodical in their search in comparison to other groups he had guided for. Occasionally there would be a shout as someone found something.

By the time the sun was high overhead, they had been working steadily along the banks for about three hours. Robb felt tired already and the day wasn't even half done. He had worked about ten feet of his section, roughly twenty pans full, piling the sifted material at his perimeter line. He paused and stretched his aching back.

George called out, "Time for a break. Let's see what we've got."

Each of them had at least a tablespoon of flakes; Melvin and Henry had each found a pea-sized nugget. It was better than they had done anywhere else.

After grabbing a quick snack of bread and leftover venison, they all returned to the creek and continued their work, intent on the gold flakes in their pans and oblivious to all else.

Long Baptiste approached George. "Do you still need me?"

George paused and thought for a minute. "If you could wait one more day. We've had a very promising morning. I'll have a better idea by tomorrow. If this is the place, I'll have to register the claim in Williams Lake. Is there a shortcut to get there, or do we just go back the way we came in?"

"It would be safer for you to go the way we came in. There is a shortcut but I'd suggest you avoid it. Make sure you have your rifles. There are thieves along the way. Some men have been killed," replied Long Baptiste, seeing the thoughtful look on George's face.

"Thanks for the warning. We were told that at 150 Mile House too."

Long Baptiste nodded and disappeared into the woods. He'd collect firewood while the others worked the river. He decided that when he got back, he'd spend some time cooking and drying the venison so it would last a while. The fly-covered carcass had been hanging overhead. He stripped off the hide, filled it with the ashes of the fire, rolled it up and placed it in the creek to soak. It was the perfect size for his wife to make a buckskin shirt. He then set about cutting and cooking some of the venison.

* * *

They finished panning as the sun was setting. Robb had never been so tired in all his life. Even the hard days on the trail with a full backpack didn't compare to the pain he felt now. He couldn't imagine how Henry was still on his feet. The older man sat, clearly exhausted. His face was a haggard maze of deep creases, his skin dusky. He looked more like a corpse. Melvin, Bill and James didn't look much better.

They sat around the fire and opened their pouches, displaying the gold they had collected all day, and compared the results. George rummaged through his backpack and removed a small mahogany case with brass hinges that Robb hadn't seen before. Inside was a tiny set of brass weigh scales. Robb was fascinated as he watched George pour Henry's gold into the pan.

"You've got just over an ounce there. That's worth twenty dollars."

They eagerly took their turns getting their finds weighed. It became obvious by the time they got to Robb that the further downstream they were from the waterfall, the less gold there was. Robb's haul was three quarters of an ounce. Even so, Robb was stunned. While he knew an ounce of gold was worth twenty dollars, to actually see and feel what an ounce looked like somehow came as a surprise. He had panned fifteen dollars worth of gold. That was more than two weeks' pay as a clerk for the Bay and would greatly supplement the few dollars left in his savings. He'd been getting increasingly concerned he was running out of money. The fee for the claim would have cleaned him out.

They ate the venison strips, too tired to make any bread or coffee.

"Tomorrow we'll do the same thing across on the south bank. I am going to check above the falls in case any bigger nuggets have collected back there," said George, measuring out his own pouch, which weighed the same as Robb's.

They all crawled into their tents, oblivious to the stench of their own sweat or the hum of the ever-present mosquitoes. Bill collapsed onto his sleeping bag and didn't bother to get in it. He was snoring within minutes. Robb was too tired to take his boots off and instantly fell asleep, not even thinking of Emma.

* * *

Robb awoke at the sound of James's voice and the rattling of the tin mugs. He was so stiff from bending all day yesterday that he had trouble getting to his feet. Henry seemed to be moving better than he was, which surprised Robb. He couldn't believe the man's resilience. Soon they were across the creek working their sections.

In the meantime, George, carrying his backpack and pick axe, climbed the dark-coloured rocks around the falls. Long Baptiste followed him. Robb could hear them moving through the pine-covered slopes above. The canyon seemed to re-direct birdcalls that echoed, but it was hard to pinpoint direction. With the rising sun, the sheer canyon walls took on an orange glow. It looked like the middle of the valley had dropped down in ancient times, leaving the vertical sides impossible to climb. The rock debris from the landslide was dark gray, almost black, and looked fairly recent. The foliage of tumbled pines and cedars was still green. Some trees lay right across the creek, partially blocking the water. The flow was strong enough to move up and over, under or through the branches in a frothy spate.

They worked until lunchtime. The rhythm of their work had changed from the frantic scrambling of yesterday to a slower, steadier, more sustainable pace. As they sat around the firepit, they compared their finds.

"Well, Robb, how did you do?" asked Melvin, sitting on a log to stretch his legs.

"Probably about the same as yesterday, so far," said Robb.

"Me too."

"I found one of those pea-sized nuggets. I hope there's more of that around," said Bill, holding the glittering stone up to the light. Henry and James came over and examined the nugget.

"I think we've found our place," said Henry. "I'm interested to see what George finds above the falls. If we can get this kind of quantity even for a couple of months, it will set us up nicely. There's no guarantee on how long it lasts; could be a few weeks or a few years, if we're lucky."

Robb was squatting on a flat rock beside the creek swirling his gold pan when there was a shout. They all turned and there was George on his way down from the waterfall, waving his arms. Although Robb had picked out some more flakes, he was only too happy to get up, move around and see what George had found. The others joined him.

George had a grin on his face and took off his backpack, lifting out a handful of small nuggets, including one the size of an egg. There was dead quiet for a few moments as they all looked at the spectacle, then Bill let out a war whoop and they were slapping each other on the back and jumping up and down.

Long Baptiste stood there with an amused smile on his face. He still didn't understand why a shiny rock made them act that way.

"Where did you find them?" Robb asked.

"Caught in the roots of a fallen tree. I haven't had time to check out the rest of the area, but this is enough to stake a claim. Tomorrow I'm going to head into Williams Lake and register the claim. We've got a lot of things to do before then. We've got to decide which areas we are going to keep. Robb, are you going to join the group or go it alone?" asked George.

"Seeing that the gold can vary from claim to claim, it's probably better if I join the group. It evens out overall. We can help each other out that way. There's too much I don't know; I'm learning from you all the time," Robb replied.

They sat around the firepit and debated which sections to keep. After much discussion, they decided to keep three sections on each side of the river, two sections above the falls and four sections below.

"If we do it that way, then we have control of the waterfall, and that's critical for panning. Someone could stake claims higher up the valley above our claim. We can set up a sluice and process more gravel than panning. Once this is registered, you can bet that word will get out and this valley will be flooded with miners. They will be everywhere," said Henry.

"George, can I go with you to Williams Lake?" asked Robb.

"I think there should be three of us. We need to bring in a lot of supplies. We're almost out of flour, beans, sugar and just about everything else. We'll need ammo too. Once other miners are working this creek, it won't be safe to leave the place unprotected. We're going to need some lumber to make a sluice box, but I think we can do that later and get it from the sawmill in Horsefly. Henry, I think I'll keep you here to get the staking started. That piece of rope I have is twenty feet long, so you can use that for making measurements. You know the dimensions of the marker posts, so we can carve our names and the date as soon as I know what the date is. When we get back then you and the others can go to town."

"I'll stay with Henry," said James. "Now, is there some place we can hide our gold? With other miners coming in, the risk of theft increases tremendously. We need some place to cache it."

"I haven't seen anything yet, like a cave or crevice, but we all need to keep our eye open," said George. "Melvin, will you come with us or stay here?"

"I'll stay for now and work with Henry and James. I need to write to my wife, but I can do that when you get back."

Bill grinned with the thought of going to town with George and Robb to make the claim.

Long Baptiste kept himself busy scraping down the deer hide he'd retrieved from the creek. The pieces of muscle and membrane separated under the skillful strokes of his obsidian blade. "I'll leave with you in the morning and go back to my village. You know the way back to the main road from there," he said.

"We thank you for finding this place," said George, paying him in cash.

Chapter 17

Dear Robb,

We've had no news from you in over a month now. Are you getting our letters?

It is such a worry. Nothing much has changed here. Sir James and his family have moved to New Westminster and things seem very quiet without them.

Everyone is keeping well. No spread of the measles in town. Haven't seen any Natives at all.

Billy Robertson has asked your father for permission to court Jane. They have been friends most of their lives and it is a good match for her. Billy is working in the store with your father now, and occasionally helps James in the licence office, taking over what you were doing. I doubt if the wedding will be until next spring.

That will give Billy a chance to save some money to build a house. He has his eye on a building lot just outside town close to Finlayson's Point. He wants to buy it now before the land prices get too expensive.

We all miss you. Stay safe and write as soon as you can, so we know where to send the mail. Love, Mum

Chapter 18

George, Robb and Bill moved along at a quick pace to keep up with Long Baptiste. Robb was excited to get this phase of the venture done. He was looking forward to establishing the claim, opening a bank account and writing home. His step was lighter now that his backpack was limited to spare clothes, his gold pan and mug and enough food for three days. The load was a lot lighter without the pick and shovel. He'd left his tent set up back at the camp and only carried his tarp and knives. The trail Long Baptiste had marked on the trees was easy to follow. They made good time, and evening found them near the junction of the road to Horsefly. Here they camped under the cover of the lower branches of an old pine tree, in a deep bed of dry pine needles. Robb set his snare, hoping for a rabbit or maybe a groundhog.

Long Baptiste left them there and continued on his way as the sun started to dip below the horizon, turning the sky to a mass of red and purple clouds. His distant figure disappeared into the forest, leaving the trio alone beside the wagon road.

"The wagon must have passed here sometime today; the horse manure is still fresh," Bill said, looking at the rutted tracks.

Robb knew the next few days would change his life, one way or another.

* * *

They were on the road early, keeping up a steady pace when they saw shadowy figures in the bush. Ahead, a long line of Native men and women were walking in single file, heading north across the wagon road, following a very faint footpath. Robb looked at the pack dogs, some just carrying packs, others harnessed to a v-shaped contraption of two poles slung with a piece of buckskin. The sleds were loaded with bundles of buckskin, furs, pots and other goods.

"These must be Long Baptiste's people," he said to Bill.

Bill had a strange expression on his face and was staring intently at one particular woman.

Just then, Long Baptiste came into view. He came over and acknowledged them. "These are my people, my wife and family. We are heading to our annual tribal gathering. It is a time when we trade for many things with the tribes from the coast and the north. Our young people have the opportunity to seek partners."

Bill interrupted him. "Long Baptiste, who is she?" he asked, pointing out the shy, black-haired woman standing beside Baptiste's wife. The woman was dressed in a beautifully beaded buckskin dress, leggings and moccasins. She appeared to be in her late twenties.

"That is my sister-in-law, Helen Raven Wing. My brother died in a hunting accident two years ago, so she lives with my family. I wish you good luck with your journey. I must be on my way; we too have far to go. Keep safe," said Long Baptiste as he moved on, herding his family in front of him.

They walked along in silence, with Robb bringing up the rear. He was puzzled by Bill's reaction to Helen Raven Wing, especially when Bill periodically looked back over his shoulder in the direction the Indians had taken, his eyes scanning the hills for any sign of them.

Late afternoon brought them out to the Cariboo wagon road. There was no one in sight. Once again, they camped under the trees, finished off the venison and talked.

"I can hardly wait to have a bath and get rid of this beard and these clothes," said Robb.

"I'd keep the beard and clothes if I were you," said George. "We look like a bunch of miners. If we get all cleaned up, we'll stick out like a sore thumb. I want to stay as anonymous as possible. There'll be people watching the gold commissioner's office to see who comes and goes. I'd rather not be followed back to camp if we can avoid it. Whatever you do, don't tell anyone we've found gold or flash it around. We may have to sneak out of town very early to avoid being followed."

"I hadn't thought of that," said Robb. "Bill, you seemed very interested in Helen Raven Wing."

He left the question hanging.

"Well," replied Bill with a wistful sigh. "It's just that she looks a lot like my wife; same build and black hair. My wife's parents were Italian and had the same dark hair and skin. Even after five years I still miss her and the kids." He sat there, eyes downcast, looking at the ground, deep in thought.

Robb had no idea what to say to him. Bill had obviously cared for them very much.

* * *

There was a fair amount of traffic on the wagon road, mostly small groups of miners. They passed a pack train of horses heading north. Robb looked to see if it was Cataline Caux, but it wasn't. The man said he was Michael Brown and he was using horses, not mules. Robb wondered if horses would be as tough and sure-footed as the mules. He felt safe, seeing the rifle George was carrying, and knew that Bill had the derringer tucked in his belt. As soon as he had enough money, he was going to buy a rifle. He missed having his own weapon.

Robb was musing about the businesses he could run. A pack train could be a good money maker, or maybe running a general store on a seasonal basis. He realized he'd have to leave Emma in Victoria, as he couldn't picture her putting up with the rigours of life in the bush. If there was enough gold, he could always run a hotel, but that was a business he knew nothing about.

By late afternoon, the road became crowded with more wagons going both directions, southbound ones loaded with bags of flour, lumber and others supplies. The northbound ones were mostly empty.

The landscape hadn't changed much. The surrounding hills were tree covered near the river, rising as high as eight hundred feet, but distant rock-tipped hills several thousand feet higher flanked them to the east. The river was wide and shallower here, allowing canoe and boat traffic. The next bend showed a broad floodplain with many buildings. They all picked up the pace, heading down the slope into town.

The road sign read *Williams Lake, population 800.* The town had a broad dirt main street still rutted from the recent rains, with two saloons, a couple of small hotels, a bank, two general stores, one of which had a sign in the window for the post office, a Chinese laundry, two stables, a blacksmith's shop and a lumber mill. There were many small log homes, a larger home with the doctor's shingle at the gate, a tiny one-room schoolhouse and one small church. Tent city was on the outskirts, just like in every other waypoint. Robb thought it unusual to see women and children out and about. The town must have been relatively safe. There were a large number of miners, mostly near the saloons and the general stores.

George was looking about and finally saw a plain, whitewashed building that looked governmental with the Union Jack fluttering on the flagpole. The town hall sign outside detailed the public offices: the mayor and council, the sheriff, surveyors and the gold commissioner. A bunch of miners were lounging around town leaning on hitching posts, just watching.

There was a large tent set up under a tree beside the building, and the two horses hitched outside looked familiar to Robb. He recognized Judge Begby's horse but didn't see the man.

"I think it would be prudent to walk down the street a little further then go down an alley to the back streets. There must be a back door," said George quietly; a few shifty eyes monitored their progress. Closer to the north end of the main street, they slipped into the space between two buildings and started to nonchalantly double back. The back yards were full of empty wooden shipping crates, woodpiles, several outhouses, some wooden storage sheds, wagons and garbage dumps, but no people.

On reaching the back door of the town hall, George tried the handle and pushed it open. They were safely inside and noted several miners lined up outside the gold commissioner's office. They joined the lineup. George went to the clerk's desk and asked for paper and pen to draw a site map. He was still busy with his drawing when a miner came out of the office and the next group went in.

The man didn't look happy. "Damn it, it's just pyrite," he said, heaving a handful of rocks out the door as he was leaving.

Twenty minutes later, the other group left and the three of them went in, closing the door behind them.

The gold commissioner was a man in his mid-forties in a white shirt and vest. He had thinning black hair and a well-trimmed moustache. On his desk was a weigh scale, a microscope and a geologist's loupe. He indicated that they sit, and they promptly removed their backpacks and sat in the wooden, ladder-back chairs facing him. "I'm Phillip Nind, the gold commissioner. Who are you and what have you got to show me?"

George was the first to answer. "I'm George Sutcliffe; I'm American. I'm also a geologist. We have found a promising area northeast of Horsefly, near Quesnel Lake, and we want to register a group claim. There are six of us; the other three remained in camp." He rummaged in his backpack and produced a small buckskin pouch containing the nuggets he'd collected and handed it to Nind. He quickly dug into the side pouch to find his free miner's licence. Bill and Robb followed suit.

Nind took the pouch, loosened the rawhide thong and poured the contents onto a sheet of paper. The nuggets and flakes glittered as the sun shone through the windows onto the desk.

George, in the meantime, had finished the rough site map and handed it to him. Nind was checking the nuggets individually, with the loupe in his right eye, assessing them under its magnification.

"This site is part of the Quesnel Highlands. What's your bedrock up there?" he asked.

"Mostly quartz, but a lot of magnetite for the coarse black sand in the gravel beds," said George.

Nind took the largest nugget, weighed it, then scratched the surface with a clear crystal that left a mark on the surface of the nugget. He placed a magnet beside the gold but there was no reaction. Finally, he took out a small vial of clear liquid and placed one drop on the nugget, which fizzed with a clear foam. He recapped the bottle and carefully wiped the nugget clean while inspecting the rest of the nuggets and flakes.

"Well, what's the verdict?" asked George.

"It's not magnetic, it is easily scratched and there is no colour change with the acid test. What you have here, my friend, is gold. Congratulations," replied Nind. He looked carefully at the map. "No surveying in that area yet, I take it?"

"No, the Indians call the place 'grassy valley,' no settlers yet. It's half a day's walk from the junction to Horsefly."

Nind funneled the gold back into George's pouch then repeated the process for Bill and finally Robb. "I'm from Victoria," said Robb, handing over his licence and his stash of gold. The results were also positive. Robb could hardly believe it. They had done it; found real gold! *Now to find enough to make me rich.* Nind entered their names in his register. Glancing up, he said, "I need the names of the others in your group, but they must come in personally with their certificates as soon as possible, no delays. What are you calling this claim?"

"How about the Green Valley claim – keep it simple," said George.

"Now, I understand all of you have been miners in the States, except Robb here. I'll explain our claim sizes and the requirements for the size of the marker posts that must be at the corners of your claim." He proceeded to give George the measurements of both the claim and the posts. "You now officially own the Green Valley claim. It's good for one year and the fee is five dollars for each of you annually. The date today is June 14, 1860; that must be marked on the posts as well. Good luck."

Robb was stunned – June 14. They'd been on the road over eight weeks. He had to get a letter to his parents. He handed over his last five dollars, thankful that he had his pouch of gold flakes to carry on.

As they were getting ready to leave, George asked, "Are there any indications of copper or silver deposits in this area?"

"Yes. McLeese Lake north of here on the way to Quesnel has had some copper assayed and down in the Slocum area they have struck silver. Why do you ask?" said Nind.

"Well, the placer deposits of gold will run out sooner or later, and copper and silver are always in demand, although they usually need more investment for a proper mining endeavour. It's something to consider for the future," said George.

They went out the back door, keeping an eye open for trouble, but nobody was paying any attention to them, or so they thought as they came out on the main street and headed to the bank. They were ushered into the bank manager's office. Each of them opened up a bank account. Their gold was weighed out and Mr. Briggs gave them cash for their gold to the tune of twenty dollars an ounce. Robb looked at the ninety dollars in his hand and decided to deposit twenty-five. Three days of panning had netted him the equivalent of three months' pay. He couldn't get his mind around it. Now he understood why the miners were so crazy. A man could make a lifetime's wages in just a few months, if he was lucky.

He watched as George's nuggets and flakes were weighed, coming to a hefty six and a half ounces. George banked half of his take. Bill's haul came to one hundred dollars.

"We need a place to eat and bunk down for the night," said Bill, eyeing the buildings. "How about we try the boarding house? It would be a real treat to sleep in a proper bed."

The faded sign on the wall read *Mrs. Hall's Boarding House*. Bill rapped on the door and it was opened by a tired-looking older woman in a dull gray dress. "Ma'am, we're looking for a place to sleep for the next two nights. Do you have room for the three of us?"

"There will be no swearing, smoking, loose women or drinking in this house, you understand? Will you be wanting meals as well?" she said primly, giving them the once over. A younger woman came out of the kitchen.

"Yes, ma'am, if it's available," said Bill politely.

"I charge a dollar a night," she said.

Bill got the nod from George. "That will be fine, ma'am." They introduced themselves.

She led them upstairs to a large room that had been divided into four tiny rooms, each with a wood-framed bed, rope woven and knotted between the planks to support the thick soft mattresses. The pillows were feather filled, and the gray blankets were thick and smelled fresh. The fourth room door was closed.

The savoury aroma of stew permeated the house, so they left their backpacks on the beds and headed downstairs. The front parlour was bright with the light from two coal-oil lamps, revealing a long bench table and chairs; the corner was occupied by a fireplace but the grate was empty. Two other miners were already seated.

"Mrs. Hall, I'd like to wash up first," said Robb.

"Go out back, there's a pump and wash basin," she replied, handing him a towel and directing him down the back hall.

He noted two other rooms leading off the hallway. He assumed the other guys were bunking down there. Outside on the stoop there was a small table with an enamelled tin washbasin, a large bar of brown soap and a scrub brush. He noted the outhouse along the back fence beside the woodpile but headed for the well in the middle of the yard. He pumped a full bucket of water and quickly scrubbed his face and hands, unable to get the dirt out from under his nails. The water was cold. He dumped the water and hurried back inside to find everyone else seated.

Bill was talking to the two other men when both Mrs. Hall and the younger woman appeared carrying tin plates loaded with steaming stew. Conversation ceased.

"Gentlemen, you seem to have forgotten your manners. Remove your hats," she said. Hats were hastily dropped on the floor. "Mr. Sutcliffe, please lead the prayer."

There was a ghost of a smile on George's face as, duly reprimanded, he bowed his head and said the blessing. Robb was reminded of his mother scolding his father for some breach of etiquette and almost laughed but managed to keep his face straight. Eight weeks of camping rough had eliminated etiquette; survival had been more important.

The women disappeared back to the kitchen, returning with two loaves of fresh bread. Soon Robb's mug was brimming with dark, steaming coffee as Mrs. Hall circulated with the coffee pot. The stew was delicious, with big chunks of beef, potato, carrots, onions and green beans in a thick gravy. A dish of fresh butter and a jug of milk were passed from hand to hand accompanied by the licking of lips and sighs of satisfaction.

The plates were soon wiped clean and the women returned with two pies. The crusts were thick and flaky with a filling of sweet, juicy berries. Before long the plates were empty, and everyone's lips were stained purple. Robb brushed the crumbs from his beard.

He stuck his head into the kitchen where the two women were washing dishes. The big cook stove was still emanating a glorious wave of heat.

"Thanks, Mrs. Hall. That meal was as good as my Mum's cooking," he said. He found himself talking about her and the church food booth. It struck him again how much he missed home. He thought about the sparse furnishings of the rooms and wondered how these two women were managing, obviously on their own, and if it was safe for them to be running a boarding house alone.

"You're welcome, Robb," she said, somewhat taken aback by his compliments.

"Isn't your husband here to help you with all the work? I wouldn't have thought it would be safe for you to run a public place by yourselves with the likes of some of the miners I've seen," he said.

"Ted's not here at the moment. With Ann, my daughter here, I can manage with some help from the neighbours. Most of the miners stay in tent town, so we haven't had much problem. The sheriff's deputy stays in the other room upstairs, so he keeps an eye on things."

"I'm glad of that." He paused, thinking that Henry, Melvin, and James had left their wives behind too, but wrote regularly. "Is there somewhere in town where a man could have a bath and get his laundry done?" he asked. "We'll be heading back into the bush and there's nothing out there at all."

Mrs. Hall looked at her daughter and there was an unspoken decision. "Ann and I can do your laundry, if you leave it for us. It will cost you a dollar. There's a bath house behind the saloon down the road," she said.

"That's grand. I'll do that. We have to go to the general store in the morning, so I'll pick up another shirt. It's dirty work and my clothes are worn out," he said, smiling as he returned to the parlour. The men spent the rest of the evening talking and going outside for smokes. Robb caught sight of the women eating their evening meal now that the men had been taken care of.

One of the other men staying there, Tom by name, gave them an interesting piece of information.

"There's a trial tomorrow. Some guy named Quinlan shot a man during a card game at the saloon. Sheriff Pinchbeck nabbed him before he could worm his way out of town. Begby's the judge, so I think we'll have an afternoon hanging. Begby doesn't mess around."

Robb said to Bill, "Wasn't that the guy at Fort Langley with the scar on his face, the one you warned me not to play cards with?"

"I wouldn't mind seeing that guy swing; he's a slimy bastard," said Bill.

Later, lying in the luxury of his soft mattress, Robb took off his clothes and dropped them on the floor. It was a delight to sleep without his boots. It actually felt quite odd. The upper rooms were warm, as the ornate metal floor vents allowed the heat from the cook stove to rise and the days had been warm enough that an overnight fire wasn't necessary. He snuggled under the soft blankets, not missing the bugs, and listened to the subdued voices of the men in the back bedroom downstairs, then slept right through the night.

Chapter 19

Mrs. Hall provided a quick breakfast of coffee, bread, fried eggs and bacon. It smelled so good, Robb was salivating. The two strangers were off early, heading north to Quesnel.

Robb could see a big pot of water on the stove. Ann added some shavings of soap from a yellow bar on the counter and stirred it into the water with a big wooden spoon. His filthy clothes went into the pot, the foaming water instantly turning brown. She shyly smiled at him. Robb looked at her a bit closer and estimated she was in her early twenties. Like most of the women he'd seen out here in the wilderness, she went about her business with a quiet efficiency and could probably handle just about everything. She kept her eyes on the pot as she stirred the shirts, her dark-brown hair tied back in a neat bun. Her slim figure was almost hidden by her plain clothes. They were so plain that Robb had momentarily compared her to Emma, then totally dismissed the thought.

His first stop was Cullen's General Store with the post office. Robb wrote a letter to his parents, remembering what George had said about keeping the site secret. George was busy writing his own letter home to his brothers. Bill had wandered off into the depths of the store to explore the shelves and counters piled high with various merchandise.

> Dear Mum and Dad,
>
> Am sending this to you from Williams Lake. It's the nearest town to our campsite about thirty miles from here. We have registered our claim, so will be here for awhile.
>
> We were just about out of food but will stock up while we're here. We'll probably be coming to town once a month so will check for mail then. I am keeping well.
>
> It is rough, hard work, dangerous at times. So far, so good. How are the girls? I sure miss your cooking. We had a good meal at the boarding house last night – made me think of you. My partners are great, like big brothers, and I'm learning a lot from them. Hope you and Father are keeping well. Love, Robb

Over at the general store, Robb was surprised that Mrs. Cullen was the postal clerk while her husband Gilbert was looking after the supplies. It seemed unusual to have a civilized woman working so publicly. She was young and pretty, easy on the eye with her dark hair and fair complexion. She seemed unaware of the stares from the miners in the store. He told her he'd be staying in the area and to hold any mail for him and his partners. She smiled pleasantly and took down his name.

He asked her if it was possible to check on letters that might still be at Fort Yale or Cache Creek now that they were staying in one location. She said she would try. Then he wandered around the store. Bill gave him a nudge and pointed to the rifle on the wall, the brass spotless and wood gleaming. "What's that?" Robb asked Gilbert Cullen, the owner, who noted his interest.

"That's one of the new Henry lever-action repeating rifles. Beautiful, isn't it?"

"Lever action?"

"Yes, you pull the lever down and it loads a cartridge into the chamber. It's a .44 Rimfire. Holds fifteen cartridges," said Gilbert, taking the rifle down and running his hand over the smooth, glossy stock. He handed it to Robb, who looked at it in awe, getting the feel of the weight. When he raised it to his shoulder to stare along the barrel, it fit snuggly.

"So no messing around with black powder and balls, no reloading every shot?"

"Right. The barrel's rifled so it's accurate at a distance," said Gilbert, placing it back on the wall.

"I wouldn't mind one myself," said Bill, admiring it over Robb's shoulder.

"How much?" Robb asked.

"Thirty-five dollars."

Robb did some quick calculations. Flour was eight cents a pound, beans a dollar a pound, salt seventy-five cents a pound, bacon a dollar a pound, and tea ninety cents a pound. He wandered around looking at the clothes. A couple of shirts, pants and socks, that was another ten dollars. Then there was the laundry and the bath. That left him with less than thirty. *I can't afford the Henry.* He eyed an old musket with a five-dollar price tag.

"I can't afford the Henry right now, Mr. Cullen, but I will take a look at that musket. Bill, I think I'm going to get that. I'd be happier with some sort of gun out there. We're going to need meat, and I want my own. I don't want to be bear bait carrying bacon home."

He watched Mrs. Cullen tending to the town's women who were shopping for food and household items, and from the sound of it, the local gossip, while her husband and a younger man took care of the miners. "It seems strange to me that he lets his wife work in the store. Father wouldn't allow that, of course, though the Bay sets the rules," he said to Bill.

The familiar ka-ching of the old cash register reminded him of his childhood fascination with the one at Fort Victoria. That model had been a shiny, ornate, silver-metal creation with four rows of lettered and numbered keys. It had given him great amusement to press one of the keys and see the number tab pop up at the top, hit the total button and ka-ching, the wooden drawer would fly open. He'd driven his father crazy.

"Well, she's looking after the womenfolk, plus it saves him from having to pay another clerk," said Bill, being the practical one. Robb hadn't thought of that.

"George, do you want me to buy a saw or axe?" Robb asked.

"It's okay, Robb, I'll pick up a few tools later. We'll need some short planks too," George replied, mindful of the line of listening miners in the queue.

Gilbert Cullen's assistant measured out the flour, beans and other food items into small linen bags and passed them over so Robb could arrange the weight in his backpack. Robb estimated his pack weighed about fifty pounds and he felt a whole lot more comfortable now he had a musket. They went back to the boarding house and took their packs up to their rooms. The door to the fourth room remained closed. From the small window at the end of the hall, he could see the back garden and his clothes drying on the gently swaying clothesline. *They haven't been that clean in weeks.*

They joined the gathering crowd around Brennan's Saloon. Robb could hear Begby's penetrating British voice emanating from inside. Court was obviously in session. Begby was questioning the bartender who had been serving the night the shooting had occurred. The crowd both inside and out were silent, not wanting to miss a word. Most of the crowd were miners who had delayed their exit north to attend the event. Several witnesses, regulars who had been in the saloon that night, said their piece. Then Begby questioned Quinlan directly.

Robb could hear Quinlan stridently defending himself. "That man was cheating ... he reached into his jacket. I thought he was pulling a gun on me ... I was defending myself. I have every right to defend myself."

"But we know full well, don't we, Mr. Quinlan, that John Cameron was unarmed? You deliberately shot an unarmed man and you were using a marked deck, the very deck I have in my hand. Three witnesses here could see his hands and yours. You are not going to get away with that in this town. I am your judge and these six men are your jury. Gentlemen, what is your verdict?"

The jury conferred for a few minutes and the foreman announced, "We find this man guilty, your honour."

"You have been found guilty of murder, Mr. Quinlan. In this country there is only one penalty for murder, and the law states that is hanging." Robb heard the smack of the judge's gavel on the table. A rumble went through the crowd.

Sheriff Pinchbeck strode outside the saloon to where the horses were tethered. Quickly mounting, he rode down the street to where Begby's tent stood and swung a rope over a thick branch of the maple. He then dismounted and firmly secured the rope around the tree. Women were scurrying down the street, driving their children in front of them, not wanting to witness wilderness justice. The crowd waited. Pinchbeck rode back to the saloon and headed inside. A few moments later the doors of the saloon swung open, and the sheriff and his deputy emerged on either side of a handcuffed, clearly terrified Quinlan.

Robb looked at Quinlan, the scar obvious against the man's ashen skin. He didn't look very much like the man he'd seen in Yale; that confident, swaggering man was gone.

"I don't think it ever entered his head that he might get caught," said Bill.

Quinlan was led to the middle horse and assisted to mount, his white-knuckled, cuffed hands gripping the saddle horn. Then Pinchbeck and the deputy mounted and slowly walked the horses down the street straight toward the noose, Quinlan riding bolt upright between them. The crowd filled the street, moving slowly behind. Robb could see the local minister standing by the tree.

Begby strode out of the saloon, his judge's gown flapping. He quickly removed the gown and handed it to his assistant, then mounted his horse to join the party under the tree. The crowd parted like the biblical Red Sea to let Begby ride through then closed up again. The minister was speaking quietly to Quinlan, but the doomed man was silent.

The deputy moved aside as Begby manoeuvred his horse into position and placed the noose over Quinlan's head. Robb was close enough to hear Quinlan's ragged breathing. There was a sharp slap as Begby swung his riding crop down hard onto the rump of Quinlan's horse. It spooked instantly and took off at a gallop, leaving the thrashing body dangling under the tree.

Robb thought for a moment he was going to be sick, but he was fascinated and couldn't take his eyes from Quinlan's face, which was now turning purple.

Begby rode out in front of the crowd and addressed them, his eloquent voice booming. "This is a warning to all you miners. It doesn't matter what country you come from. I don't care what your laws are at home. If you break the law here, if you steal or kill, you will be dealt with according to our laws, as this man has been. It is my duty as a judge to punish any law-breakers, and that is exactly what I will do. I have the power and the authority. I am the law. Remember that," he said and rode back to the saloon.

The thrashing slowed and finally stopped. Robb looked at Quinlan for the last time, at the unrecognizable face with its bulging eyes and protruding tongue, still feeling nauseated. The crowd was now abuzz with conversations and slowly started to disperse. Most of the miners were leaving town now that the entertainment was over.

Sheriff Pinchbeck and the deputy cut Quinlan down and slung his body across the saddle of the recaptured horse. It was led away in the direction of the town cemetery.

* * *

"I'm heading for the bath house," Robb said as the three of them walked down the street. He followed the sign on the building housing the saloon, indicating the alley.

"We'll go in and have a beer while we're waiting," said George.

Robb knocked on the back door of the saloon, which was opened by a middle-aged woman in a rather revealing dress. "How much is it for a bath?"

"One dollar," she said with a provocative smile on her face, showing more leg than he was accustomed to. "You go in the bath house and I'll bring out the water," she said, handing him a bar of soap, a scrub brush and a towel.

Robb sat on the bench and took his boots off, but he wasn't about to take his clothes off until she'd filled the tub. The old tin tub was big enough for him to sit in.

"I'm coming in," she called as she opened the door, pouring two buckets of steaming, soapy water into the tub. There was another younger woman behind her, a blonde who also carried two buckets. They returned several times to fill the tub, then grinned and left him to it. Robb closed the door when they were gone but there was no lock. Stripping off, he climbed into the tub up to his chest in warm water. He let out a huge sigh of contentment and scrubbed himself all over.

It wasn't five minutes later, when he was enjoying just lying in the cooling water, that the young blonde returned and slipped inside. "Your friends thought you might like me to wash your back," she said.

Robb was not only startled but speechless. The soapy water covered up his private parts, but she was quick to stand behind him and start soaping up his shoulders. He found out several important things very quickly – two people could not fit in the tub, the floor of the bath house was cold and female secret places were delightful. His fingers fumbled through her blouse to feel the softness of her breasts. Her name was Cassie. It was over much too soon. He lay on top of her on the floor, elated, short of breath, his heart pounding. She coyly suggested that in future, a bed in the room above the saloon would be a lot more comfortable, and it would be better for both of them if he slowed down. "A woman gets more pleasure, you know, if it's done slowly and gently," she said.

"This is my first time, Cassie," he said, looking at the pretty yet hard face of the young woman. Although she was blonde, she bore no resemblance to Emma at all. The thought of Emma quickly brought him back to the real world. He couldn't for the life of him picture Emma lying on the floor under him, but then again, Emma wasn't a whore.

Straightening up her rather damp clothes, she slipped out the door, leaving him naked on the floor, tired but exhilarated.

* * *

George and Bill were sipping their beer when Robb walked into the saloon a short while later. "Did you enjoy your bath?" asked George, as innocently as he could. The look on Robb's face was priceless, and both men burst out laughing.

Robb flushed bright red, then he heard Cassie giggle as she went upstairs with another customer. The older woman winked at him and had a chuckle too.

"I'm glad everyone's having a good laugh at my expense," said Robb. Even the other men at the bar were grinning at him. He downed his beer quickly and the three of them returned to the boarding house. Mrs. Hall had specified that supper was at five o'clock.

Robb borrowed a pair of scissors and trimmed his beard and his hair by a couple of inches. The face in the hall mirror looked a little older, a little wiser, but certainly a lot cleaner and a bit more civilized. Mrs. Hall had left his clean clothes stacked neatly on the stairs with new patches on the elbows of his shirts and the knees of his trousers.

"Thanks, Mrs. Hall, for patching them up. They'll last a bit longer."

"You're welcome," she said.

They were not alone for supper. The other man at the table was Deputy Sheriff Ryan O'Connor, the regular boarder.

"Well, you've had an eventful day. Begby's quite the character, isn't he?" said Bill as they sat at the table.

"It's never dull when he's here. He always does the speech to the miners; it does help to keep things under control. With no real police force in these parts, it's up to him and the Royal Engineers to keep the peace as best they can, especially since all the American miners are armed and most of the others aren't. He'll be gone by morning. He has to go to 108 mile Ranch. Apparently, the rancher and his wife have been murdering the miners and stealing their belongings, burying their bodies in the woods. They don't know how many they've killed."

"Robb, isn't that where you bought those cheap shirts?" said George.

"You mean I've been wearing a murdered man's shirt?"

"Sounds like it," said Bill. "Didn't I tell you it was dangerous to be on your own on the trail?"

"Don't know if the judge has ever hung a woman before but it will be interesting to hear about it," said O'Connor.

Mrs. Hall and Ann brought in the meal and conversation instantly stopped as the four hungry men demolished the afternoon's cooking. The evening was spent pleasantly sitting on the front porch watching the parade of miners from tent town to the saloons. Music and laughter could be heard even at their end of the street. As the sun went down, lamplight showed in the windows of the houses, curtains were pulled, and children were ushered in from playing. Williams Lake settled into quietness, with the smell of wood smoke from tent town lingering in the air. George went and spoke quietly to Mrs. Hall, letting her know they'd be heading out early to avoid detection by the miners.

"I'll make up some sandwiches and leave them on the table for you."

"Thank you. We'd appreciate that," said George.

Robb watched him pack a hammer, a chisel, a saw and a bag of nails into his backpack and tie up a bundle of four-foot-long wooden boards. "What's that for?"

"I'm going to build a couple of rocker boxes. They're a lot more efficient for sorting the gravel than a gold pan. You can do four to five times as much in a day with one of those."

Robb went to bed early and just lay there for a while. He couldn't remember a day so full of surprises. He was tired, and eventually nodded off, not even hearing the others come up. He felt he hadn't been asleep very long when Bill shook him awake.

"Time to go, buddy."

He tiptoed down the stairs, carrying his backpack and musket, trying hard not to wake Mrs. Hall and Ann. George tossed him a packet of sandwiches, which he slipped in his shirt as the pack was full. They went out the back door and kept to the shadows. There didn't appear to be anyone on the street, and tent town was dark and quiet. A dog started barking in one yard, but they kept going and were soon on the outskirts of town. The rope was gone from the big maple and the space beside it where Begby's tent had been was empty, the grass trampled.

They walked in silence, with just enough moonlight to see the road. George was listening for any signs of company. "Anybody out at this time of the night is likely up to no good." There were animal noises and the rustling of leaves in the bush. A distant wolf howled to be answered by a pack on the far side of the valley. An owl flew through the pines on silent wings, startling them all. There was a scream of a small animal, then silence.

They had been on the trail over an hour, when Bill whispered, "Stop!"

"What is it?" said George when they all froze.

"I saw a small light just ahead, only for a couple of seconds." They moved off the path into an area of rocks and trees in deep shadow and waited.

Robb sniffed the air. "Tobacco smoke." He loaded his musket, George was ready with his rifle and Bill had the tiny derringer in his hand. They were patient. There was the occasional sound of a voice.

An hour later, the eastern horizon was starting to lighten, leaving the landscape in varying shades of grey, with a faint staining of pale pink on the undersides of the clouds. Robb nudged Bill and pointed. Just down the road two men were visible with the occasional flare of their cigarettes. George put his finger to his lips, and they waited again.

Finally, the sun was up, the greys changing to greens and browns on the rock walls around them. The two men got up and were walking back along the road heading to Williams Lake. Robb took a really good look at them, memorizing the faces, just in case he ever saw them again.

The men were talking. From their accents, they sounded American. "Damn it, I was sure they'd be heading this way. This is the way they came in. Do you think they went north?"

"Maybe they didn't leave this morning. We'll have to check it out. When we were in the gold commissioner's office, they were careful not to say anything about their claim."

"Yeah, and they went to the bank immediately afterwards."

The voices faded as the men moved out of sight on the trail. George finally relaxed. "Let's have our breakfast then get a move on." The bacon sandwiches were right tasty.

It took them until noon to reach the junction of the Horsefly road, meeting northbound groups of miners, then another two days to get back to camp, with very little traffic on the wagon road. There was no sign of Long Baptiste or his people. The track into Green Valley didn't look any more disturbed than when they'd come out.

Chapter 20

Robb couldn't believe the amount of work Henry, Melvin and James had done the week they'd been away. Cairns of rocks marked the western boundary from the water's edge up the north-sloping hill. Many trees had been felled along the northern back boundary and Henry was just completing the measurement on the eastern boundary above the falls when the trio walked into camp.

Henry scrambled down the rock pile, eager to hear the news. "Well?"

"Gold it is, Henry. We were right about the boundary dimensions for the claim. I've registered it in all our names as the Green Valley claim. You guys will have to head out in the morning. The gold commissioner wants you there as soon as you can," said George.

"You're going to have to be real sharp 'cos we almost got waylaid on the way back by some guys who'd been watching us, even though we left at three in the morning. If Bill hadn't spotted their cigarettes, we could have been killed," said Robb.

Soon they were sitting around the fire with the beans boiling and the bacon frying. Bill pulled a bottle of whiskey out of his backpack, and they each took a good swig to celebrate. George told them all about Begby and the hanging and shared the information on the 108 mile Ranch.

"Don't think Quinlan'll be missed much; nasty individual, from what I saw of him," Bill muttered.

"So, what's the first thing we tackle in the morning?" asked Robb.

"I'm going to work on chiselling out our name and date on the corner posts. You can dig the post holes, put the posts in and stack rocks around them," said George. "We'll keep the straight trees they've cut down in case we need to build a cabin for the winter. Depends on how long this claim holds out. The rest we'll use for firewood."

"By the way," said Melvin, "check out behind the waterfall. There is a cavity there; it's not big, mind you, but might be a good place to put our gold out of sight. Haven't seen anything better yet."

Robb was showing them the old musket and telling them all about the Henry rifle.

"There were mule deer across the river a couple of days ago. They'd be good eating. Best time is early in the morning and late evening," Melvin replied.

Back in the tent, Robb crawled into his sleeping bag, boots and all, wishing for the soft mattress at Mrs. Hall's. Williams Lake had been an adventure in more ways than one, but now it was back to work. He pulled the blanket over his head to fend off the hordes of flies and mosquitoes, hoping all the aggravation was worth it.

* * *

As soon as breakfast was over, Henry, Melvin and James were off to Williams Lake. All three had their rifles. Their backpacks were almost empty, except for a change of clothes, enough food for three days on the road and the gold they had collected so far.

Watching them disappear down the river behind the wooded hills, Robb hoped their journey would be a safe one. They'd been very lucky to avoid the bandits, despite how careful they'd been in town. He proceeded to dig a good-sized hole for the marker post, pausing to remove tiny flakes of gold. He shovelled the sandy, gravelly soil to one side to sort through later.

George sat on a log, trimming the sides of the post square with his axe. Later, he started to carefully use the chisel and his knife to incise "Green Valley Claim" and "June 14, 1860" on each side. By lunchtime, he had finished the first one and Robb planted it in the three-foot-deep hole. After tamping the soil back in the hole, he packed the flat stones around the base to fix it firmly in place even if the waters rose. He moved up the hill to locate the northwest corner. The soil was rocky higher up and it took Robb over an hour to get post hole #2 dug. The sweat was dripping off him, but it didn't seem to deter the mosquitoes.

Bill was panning all morning above the falls and had collected about two ounces of flakes and tiny nuggets. "Hey, Robb, you've got a rabbit in your snare."

Looking down from the waterfall, the view of the valley was spectacular – rounded, green hills with the wide valley and the creek winding through. Robb finished digging posthole #3 on the northeast corner noting gold specks in the dark soil, then collected the rabbit, gutted it and reset the snare. Moving up to the eastern corner at the creek, he got post hole #4 dug. *Thank the Lord that's finished,* he thought, his back and leg muscles aching.

Bill gave a shout. He'd been working a section of the creek outside their boundary but stood there ankle deep in water grinning, a nugget the size of an egg in the palm of his hand. "That must be at least two ounces. Makes the day worthwhile."

They climbed down the rock pile, the waterfall gushing past them, and looked at George, who was setting post #2 in the hole.

"I'm done for the day," said Robb. They gathered branches, pine cones, the shredded bark from the corner posts and dry needles to get a fire started. Robb peeled off the inner bark and added it to the beans and wild onion simmering over the fire. The flour and water biscuits were sizzling in the pan with a few slices of bacon for the grease and the rabbit was on a spit when George finally came down the hill looking worn out. He was sniffing the aroma of the bacon.

"We've done well today. If I can get the last two posts finished tomorrow, then we only have the south shore section to do. Hopefully we can get that done before the others get back."

Bill showed him the nugget and he weighed it out. "That's four and a half ounces in total. Good haul. Switch over tomorrow while I'm working on the posts. We'll work each part of the claim systematically then move to the next one."

"I found that nugget beyond our claim. Figured I'd take what I could get while the going was good," said Bill. "Won't be able to do that once someone else has a claim there."

"Where are we going to store the gold?" asked Robb, turning the rabbit, the juices dripping and sizzling on the hot rocks.

"I looked at the hole under the falls, but I don't think it will work. It's not stable and could wash out after a storm. There's a big fallen pine up the hill, half buried in the dirt. It's hollow inside and that might be alright. Keep looking. Once there are other miners in this valley, we'll be at much higher risk of theft. We'll save the flour bags. They'll come in handy for storing it."

In the fading light, Robb noticed several deer feeding in the shallows about a mile away. There were a few ducks, and a lot of bird calls, mostly songbirds. So far, he hadn't seen any fish. They sat on logs around the fire eating their meal, tired but content.

* * *

The next day it was Robb's turn to pan, so he continued working above the falls while Bill crossed the river and dug the post holes. Henry hadn't had time to cut any trees on the south side and the area was boggy. They kept a sharp eye open for snakes and saw a few turtles, small ones with green and red markings.

Robb was rooting around at the base of one the fallen pines that lay half submerged in the creek. He estimated that the tree was thirty-to forty-feet high. The ball of bare roots was huge, clawing the sky like bony hands high over his head. He poked the dirt away to expose the underside when a gleam of yellow caught his eye. Using all his strength, he swung the pick, breaking the clods of dirt and pebbles away, and gasped as a handful of good-sized nuggets fell out, landing in the shallows. It took his breath away. Quickly, he plunged up to the top of his rubber boots and groped around until he'd recovered them. He removed his hat and put them inside.

He looked around but didn't see any more under the tree. He noticed the grooves in the soil made by the pine when it had tilted down the hill during the landslide and followed the marks upward. The tracks ran about fifty feet to the area above the slippage where the soil wasn't disturbed, and grass was growing. Carefully, he started examining the soil and gravel for any signs of gold. There didn't even appear to be any flakes up higher as he poked around, examining every rock and crevice.

He yelled for George to come up.

"What did you find?" said George, clambering up the slope.

Robb showed him the contents of his hat and George whistled.

"They were in the roots of the tree where Bill got that nugget yesterday. I haven't been able to find anything up here and you can see where the tree came down. Should I be looking somewhere else?"

Together they scoured the hillside then examined the tree and removed the rest of the dirt from the immense root ball, with no results.

"Robb, work along the edge of the creek above the dam. Some nuggets may have been washed down from higher up. I'll need to get back to doing the posts," he said, scrambling back down the spray-drenched rocks.

The end of the day found them sitting around the fire eagerly weighing their take. The total weight, including flakes, was nineteen ounces. Grins spread over their faces. "That's three hundred and eighty dollars for one day's take! Hell, I don't believe it ... the best day I've ever had," said George. "Listen, both of you work up there tomorrow. I've finished the posts for the north side, but it's going to take me another two days to complete the south side ones."

The bacon, beans and biscuits never tasted so good. George wrapped the gold in a used flour bag and stuffed it inside the hollow log, blocking the hole with a large rock. It looked so natural that an outsider would never notice, or so he hoped.

* * *

Five days later, with the boundary markers complete, all three of them systematically panned the two sections above the falls. There had been no more large nuggets, but the total daily take of gold flakes was averaging six to ten ounces, a huge amount.

"The others should be back any time now," said George when they took a break, scanning the other end of the valley for any signs of their friends. By late afternoon, they still hadn't appeared.

"I'll build a rocker box tomorrow."

They had finished off most of the bacon, leaving only beef jerky, so Robb decided it was time to go hunting. Taking his musket, powder and balls, he gave George and Bill a wave and headed south across the river into the swampy area by the lake. Among the cattails there were plenty of ducks and geese, so if he didn't get a deer, he'd hunt the birds.

He'd been sitting quietly at the base of a tree, keeping his eyes on a nice young buck that was grazing out of range of his musket. The buck suddenly brought its head up on instant alert, ears forward, poised, and in one swift, elegant motion vanished into the trees, the white tail out of sight in seconds. Robb hadn't heard anything but turned around, listening intently. Above the noise of the creek, he couldn't hear anything unusual. He wondered if the guys were back. He shot a duck that had been paddling in the shallows then waded out to collect the bird. It wouldn't feed six of them.

By then the light was fading, the sun a distant crescent in the west. Once he crossed their southern boundary line, he had a good view of the valley and stopped short, eyeing not only a couple of men at the campsite but a whole string of strangers along the path. *Damn it. We've got company.*

He hurriedly crossed the river, finally making out the features of the two men talking to George and Bill. It was Melvin and James, but they looked awful and where was Henry? Robb clambered up the hill to meet them. He looked at Melvin's black eye, bruised face and torn jacket. "What happened?"

"We were ambushed on the way out. Two guys jumped us on the Horsefly road. In the tussle, Henry got shot in the right leg by one guy and I got knocked down by the other one. He hit me in the face with the butt of his rifle. James shot the one hitting me and killed him. The other one took off.

We were lucky! James was carrying the gold. The supply wagon came along shortly afterwards and took us all into town. Lucky for Henry it was a through and through. The bullet didn't break any bones. Doc patched him up and we left him at Mrs. Hall's. When we described the guys, Pinchbeck said he knew who they were. He agreed it was self defence and we didn't get charged, but I'm sure he'll be letting Begby know. The deputy must have buried the body. I didn't see it on the way back in."

"We've got company now, I see," said George, eyeing the other miners setting up camp downstream.

"Sorry about that, but couldn't avoid it trying to get Henry tended to."

"Were you able to get all the registration stuff done?" asked George.

"Yeah, James and I saw Nind right away, but he actually came over to Mrs. Hall's to see Henry. We're legal now."

Both him and James sat down on the log, looking haggard. After stashing their backpacks in the tent, they were content just to sit and eat the supper of duck, biscuits and potatoes. All of them knew that life was going to be different now that they had neighbours.

* * *

Robb lost track of time. Each day was the same, pan, pan, pan until George built the rocker box. It looked like a two-layered cradle with a handle. George showed him how to shovel dirt in, add water and rock it back and forth. Gold particles were heavy and fell through the holes along with fine dirt into the bottom tray, which made it easy to sort.

The mounds of discarded gravel started to pile up along the western edge of the claim where he'd been dumping it. It took two of them to use the rocker efficiently, one rocking and the other shovelling in the dirt, but the results were rewarding. They were processing much more gravel together than they would ever have been able to do by panning. By the end of the day he was too exhausted to think of Emma or anything else.

Evenings were spent around the campfire. Even collecting the wood for the fire seemed a chore. Hunting was limited.

They had very little to do with their neighbours, who appeared to be having moderate success and for the most part kept to themselves. Voices, sometimes raised in anger, carried clearly down the valley. There were occasional fights. It got lively one night when he was awakened as all hell broke loose with shouts, screams and shots fired as a bear raided someone's cache of bacon. With men stumbling around in the dark, yelling and swearing, the crashing through the undergrowth indicated that the bear had got away with his prize.

"We need to go to town soon for supplies. I wouldn't mind going to Horsefly, as it's closer, but I think we need to see how Henry's doing and get this gold in the bank," said George. Robb volunteered for the trip.

The following day as George and Robb headed out, they were joined by five young men, each from different camps. Robb wasn't sure it was a good idea, as they were outnumbered. George took the lead. Robb positioned himself at the end of the line so he could keep an eye on everyone. His musket was loaded, just in case.

Over the course of the next few days on the trail, he got to know each of young lads better. They asked all kinds of questions about registering their claim, which he was able to answer. One lad, Christopher, was from Chilliwack and like himself was seventeen, a farm boy with no mining experience. The rest were Americans who had run into the Indian wars south of the border and bore the scars of their battles. He realized again just how lucky he'd been to have experienced partners. He also realized that if these men were as decent as they seemed, that combining forces to go in for supplies might actually be a good way to do it. There was safety in numbers, if they could be trusted.

Several days later they arrived in Williams Lake. George sent the young lads off to the gold commissioner's office while he and Robb headed to the bank. The manager was happy to see them and measured out their gold. It came to a whopping ninety-six ounces, converting to three hundred and twenty dollars each! Quite a haul for a month's work. George deposited that amount into each of the bank accounts for the others.

Robb felt overwhelmed with that much money, equivalent to a year's pay at the HBC. He decided to deposit two hundred and seventy five dollars, giving him a balance of three hundred in his account. He kept enough to purchase supplies and just maybe get that Henry rifle, if Cullen still had it.

They arrived at Mrs. Hall's boarding house and were delighted to see Henry sitting on the front porch, his right leg resting on a bucket and a makeshift crutch leaning on the wall behind him. Henry's face broke into a grin as broad as their valley as he hobbled to his feet. Robb was happy to see him up and moving but wondered if he was going to be able to walk all the way back to camp. He grasped the older man by the shoulders, looking up into his face. "Henry, it's so good to see you. We've been really worried."

"You and me both. Mrs. Hall and Ann have been taking real good care of me. They've changed the bandages every day. I've been practising walking all week, hoping you'd come soon. No infections so far and they've been feeding me real good too," he said, indicating he'd had to put an extra hole in his belt for his expanded waistline.

Mrs. Hall appeared at the door and a big smile appeared on her face when she saw them.

"Good morning, Mrs. Hall. Have you got room for two more?" George asked, tipping his hat to her and greeting Henry with a firm handshake.

"I've got two rooms upstairs. You know my rules, so you're welcome," she said, calling to Ann to put extra food in the pot.

"Henry, we're going over to Cullen's to get supplies, then we'll leave in the morning," said George.

"The wagon from Horsefly is here, so maybe I can cadge a lift with them as far as our turnoff," said Henry. "I'll come over to the store with you and have a chat with the driver. I don't want to slow you down."

"We've got company in the valley now. Some of them came in with us to register their claims, but I see now they're heading for the saloon and not the bank. Hope they'll have enough cash left to buy some food," George said, watching their trail mates being greeted by Cassie and two other buxom young women. He turned and looked at Robb, who shook his head.

"Not this time, George." Robb knew exactly what George was thinking. As much as he would have loved

163

another session with Cassie, being fourth or fifth in line didn't impress him much, and even if his body wanted it, it would have cost him a dollar. The thought occurred to him that she was probably making more money than he was, though she probably had to pay the saloon owner a fair chunk of money for her room and board.

Sure enough, the wagon was outside Cullen's with two men hefting hundred-pound bags of flour, beans and sugar. Henry limped over using his crutch, and Robb could tell he was still having some difficulty walking. The right leg looked stiff.

Robb stopped at the post office counter to check his mail. Mrs. Cullen remembered his name and brought out a wad of envelopes from one of the boxes. "You've got quite a stack."

They must have forwarded them from Yale. Quickly, he put pen to paper.

> Dear Mum and Father,
>
> Received a whole stack of letters from you today but haven't had a chance to read them yet. We are doing well and have been working hard on our claim. I've finally got some money in the bank. There are other miners in our valley, so we have to keep an eye on them. Henry was shot but has been recovering in Williams Lake. He'll be coming back to camp with us tomorrow. Don't know how long this claim is going to

> last. We've got two or three months left before the weather will start getting cold. If we're still pulling out gold, then we'll have to build a cabin for the winter. I've heard the snow gets about three feet deep out here. Love, Robb.

"Thanks," he said, paying for the stamp. The postmark on one of his mother's letters was April. Then he looked around the shelves, searching for the Henry rifle. The place on the wall where it had hung was empty. He was disappointed. *Somebody must have bought it.* He got in the lineup for supplies. George was filling his backpack with the smaller bags, same old stuff, flour, beans and beef jerky. Some of the miners were paying with gold dust, which Gilbert Cullen was carefully weighing out.

Robb bought an extra bag of flour, figuring Henry wouldn't be able to carry a full load. He paid in cash. "Will you be getting any more rifles in?"

Gilbert looked at him. "You really want the Henry?"

"Yes, I do."

Gilbert pulled the rifle out from under the counter and handed it to Robb. "People have tried to steal it a few times, so I took it off the wall."

"I'll trade the musket," said Robb, laying it beside the Henry. They dickered for a few minutes, but Robb was quite happy to get the Henry and four boxes of ammunition for twenty five dollars. Robb loaded it and walked out of the store feeling on top of the world. George was talking to the wagon drivers.

"Well, what's happening?"

"They've agreed to give Henry a ride as far as the cut-off. I was asking them if they could deliver supplies to us on a regular basis instead of us having to come to town. Every time we come here, we're wasting a week's work. That adds up to a lot of gold. If they could deliver even as far as the cut-off, it would save us a heck of a lot of time. They drive for Michael Kelly in Horsefly, so they'll have to talk it over with him."

"We wouldn't be able to bank the gold, though."

"No, but we could pay in gold like everyone else does."

"At some point, we'd have to get the gold to the bank. Letting it pile up in camp could be a real problem with the other miners around," Robb said, thinking of the constant prying eyes.

They headed back to the boarding house. Robb decided to clean up, and he filled the washbasin on the back porch.

Ann poked her head out the door. "Do you want some hot water?"

"Sure," he said, taking the bucket from her and adding some to the basin. He stripped off his shirt and started to wash his hair and beard. She blushed and disappeared back into the house. He finished his scrub down, revelling in feeling clean.

The evening was spent exchanging the past month's news and savouring the meal Ann and Mrs. Hall had prepared. He sat and slowly read his mail. He had obviously missed a good opportunity to work for Sir

James. Who knew if it might be an option later. Edna was going to have that baby in three months, and he wasn't sure he was going to be there to see it. He really wanted to attend Jane's wedding. He just didn't know if the gold would hold out, requiring him to overwinter in the north. *Life in Victoria is going on without me.*

Later, Robb lay in bed thinking about Emma, wondering what he would do when he got back to Victoria. There'd be no point in working at the Bay again. A dollar a day working for them wasn't going to be good enough. Billy was doing his job anyway. He would need to open his own business. He still had no idea what that would be. He felt an aching loneliness for his family, the good times he'd had with his sisters, playing with his nephews, even arguing with his father. He missed his mum's smiling face. He longed for the day when he could go home and face Emma's father as an equal. He wanted to be clean-shaven and dressed in a good suit and boots. He wanted to look like an important business man. He could envision Emma looking up at him with those blue eyes and finally fell asleep with a smile on his face.

It was raining the next morning. Mrs. Hall gave them a hearty early breakfast and sent them on their way. The last view Robb had was Mrs. Hall and Ann standing on the porch waving them goodbye. They helped Henry climb on the loaded wagon. With a flick of the reins from the driver, the horses moved off with George and Robb trudging behind. The trotting horses soon pulled ahead out of sight, quickly outpacing them. The road was busy with northbound miners and a mule train, but Robb felt much safer with the Henry rifle under his arm and was hoping he'd have an opportunity to get a deer closer to camp.

It was late afternoon when they reached the turnoff for the Horsefly road. The rain had stopped but it was still cloudy, and the mosquitoes remained a constant nuisance. They met a few outbound miners on their way in, none from their valley. Nightfall found them camped under a big fir, sharing the quiet.

Robb was awakened by a snuffling, shuffling sound. He sat up and nudged George, who was already awake. Robb slipped out of his bedroll and crouched, rifle in hand, looking and listening.

"We forgot to hang up our backpacks. The bacon's in there," he whispered.

There was very little moonlight and the woods were shades of black. The snuffling grew louder and came from the north. It didn't sound human. "Bear?" he whispered to George. They backed up behind the tree, peering out at the darkness in front of them. There were pauses but the snuffling continued, and whatever it was came closer.

Robb cranked the lever, hearing the cartridge click into the chamber, feeling the fear but praying he'd have enough light or luck for a good shot. Their backpacks were twenty feet away under the other tree, the light-coloured leather just a shade of pale grey in the shadows. Something came out of the woods. It wasn't so much a shape but something huge that blocked the outline of the tree. It sniffed and went to the backpacks. It made a rumbling noise and Robb saw the grey patch move. George whispered, "Be prepared to climb this tree in a hurry." Both of them opened fire.

There was a roar, a terrible screaming, angry roar. They'd hit it! Robb knew he had fifteen shots, so he kept cranking the lever and firing. In the flash of his rifle he'd seen a shape, but now the shape was moving. George was climbing the tree. The screams, roars and thrashing noises continued, seemingly closer. Robb fired again then started to climb the tree, fighting the branches and trying to climb one-handed, not wanting to drop his rifle.

He could hear George above him, reloading. The noises from the beast continued as it seemed to circle the tree. He knew bears could climb and his hands were shaking. He was balanced about fifteen feet up the tree, his back against the trunk, his feet wedged on two puny branches. He was unable to climb any higher without using both hands and realized how vulnerable he was.

The thrashing and roaring slowly tapered off. The whiffling noises stopped, and it was quiet.

"Do you think it's dead?" whispered George.

"I don't know, and I'm not about to get down from this tree until it's light enough to see it," said Robb.

It was a long, tiring night balanced on the branches, trying to stay awake, holding his rifle. He thanked his lucky stars for buying the Henry. *It probably saved my life tonight. I'd never have had time to reload the musket.*

The lightening of the early morning sky revealed the scene. There, not twenty feet from the base of the tree, was the body of a brown grizzly. It was massive. The ground was torn up in all directions. The bear was curled up facedown. Cautiously they clambered down. Robb looked to see if it was breathing but didn't see any movement. He moved closer, counting the bloody holes in its hide. George poked it. There was one swift grunt, a roar and then a gaping mouthful of teeth and a massive paw that swung through the air, knocking Robb sideways. Flung to the ground, he landed hard, striking his head. He heard the deafening blast of George's rifle and for a few brief moments the world blurred.

He sat up, with George beside him, and focussed his eyes. The right side of his back was a searing mass of throbbing pain, and there was a warm trickle down his back. When he removed his jacket, the rip down the right side of it was was bloody and about a foot and a half long. George took off his bandana to put pressure on the wound. "You're lucky he didn't take your head off. Not all that blood's yours," he said, looking at the bear beside them. Robb's rifle was on the ground a few feet away where he'd flung it.

A voice called out from the road, and Long Baptiste and two other Native men came through the trees. Robb was relieved to see them. They all looked at the bear.

"What do you want to do with it?" Long Baptiste asked.

"I want a haunch of meat, but otherwise you can have it," said George. "It's too much for us to take back to camp. The hide won't be much use. We've put a few holes in it. How did you find us?"

"You're not far from our summer camp. We heard gunfire when it was still dark, but enough to tell us the direction. We were looking for the source when we heard your last shot." Long Baptiste said something in Shuswap and the other two men started gutting and skinning the bear.

Long Baptiste helped Robb to his feet, removed the bandana and looked at the wound. "His claws caught you. You're a lucky man," he said as he put pressure on the wound. "Come back to camp with me. My wife can clean that up and stitch it closed."

Robb nodded and said, "Long Baptiste, I'd like a bear's claw necklace, just a single claw, the longest one. Can you make one for me, one like yours?"

"I can do that. George, your man Henry is alright. We met him on the trail yesterday. He is walking back to your valley. He said he was slow but able to do it. Robb and I will go back to my camp then catch up with you on the trail."

The bleeding had eased off, so Robb picked up his rifle and found his backpack, which was still intact. He carried his pack instead of wearing it, but felt quite shaky, and the pain was worse if he took a deep breath. He glanced back at the tree that had been his perch all night. He'd only been fifteen feet up. That bear could have reached him easily without even climbing. It was a sobering thought. He turned and slowly followed Long Baptiste out to the road.

Chapter 21

Robb found himself in the Shuswap's camp sitting beside the firepit, surrounded by children of all ages plus their parents. They solemnly stood in a semi-circle around him, their dark eyes curious about the stranger. The old chief sat nearby, watching him. If the pain in his back hadn't been so bad, he would have interacted with them more, but he was more interested in watching Long Baptiste's wife add pieces of hemlock bark and a couple of pieces of hardened fir sap to a pot of heating water.

Long Baptiste dispatched two younger men to help the others transport the bear meat. Robb could see a group of women and girls in the meadow gathering fruit, and further down the hill there were boys fishing in the creek. He thought he could see Helen Raven Wing among the women. The tents of the summer camp was minimal, merely deer hide supported by branches and poles.

A tiny, very old nut-brown woman walked over to him. She had an abalone shell full of dried leaves and a long feather. She lit the leaves using a burning twig from the firepit and fanned the feather over the shell, producing a pungent white smoke. Fascinated, Robb stared up at her as she moved around him, chanting as she wafted the smoke over him with the feather. He'd seen this before in the Songhee camp and knew she must be very important, one of the healers, maybe even the shaman of the tribe. This was part of the healing ceremony, so he sat quietly. When she was finished, she handed Robb pieces of dried tree bark from a small leather pouch and motioned for him to chew them. It felt strange to be included in their rituals, and he was grateful.

Long Baptiste spoke up. "That is willow bark. Chew on it; it will ease the pain." Robb stripped off his shirt and lay on his side .Long Baptiste's wife removed the pot from the fire and knelt beside him. She took handfuls of soft, downy plant material, dipped them in the water then squeezed out the excess. She carefully cleaned Robb's back, discarding the bloody, soiled swabs into the fire.

The pain came in waves, but Robb gritted his teeth, trying to keep still. He closed his eyes, afraid to show his fear, concentrating on not crying out. *They'll think I'm a coward.* She said something but Robb didn't understand the language.

"She's going to sew the skin back together now," said Long Baptiste.

Robb opened his eyes long enough to see her dip the bone needle and one of her own long, black hairs into the pot. Then she threaded the hair through the needle.

He quickly closed his eyes as her fingers sought the raw edges of the wound and started sewing. He felt every stitch. It was agony. Then finally it was over. She washed his back again. She said something to her husband and stood up, wrapped the remaining clean, damp material in some plant leaves, placed it in a leather pouch and offered it to him.

"What do I do with this?" he asked, sitting up with difficulty to accept them from the gentle, brown-eyed woman who turned to her husband and gave a list of instructions.

"She says to take the stitches out in seven days. Get one of your friends to wipe the plant fluff on your back for the next few days, then leave the scab alone. The hemlock and fir water helps to stop infection. We often use it on cuts or wounds," said Long Baptiste.

"I'm very grateful for your help," said Robb, nodding to Long Baptiste's wife and the old woman.

"How can I repay you?"

"Don't worry about it. We will eat well. It's not often we get bear, and there'll be enough meat to feed all of us."

"Don't forget there'll be some bullets in that carcass. I don't know how many. I just aimed in the dark. I'd better get going and catch up with George," said Robb. Long Baptiste helped him to his feet. Robb reloaded the Henry, which fascinated Long Baptiste, slipped the pack over his other shoulder and nodded to the chief, the old woman and Long Baptiste's wife as they left camp.

* * *

It didn't take long to get back to the wagon road. Long Baptiste eyed the pathway, pointing out fresh tracks on the ground. Robb looked down, noting the moccasin and boot prints. He would have missed them. They caught up with George and his guide in about an hour. The haunch of bear meat was strapped to George's shoulders.

They parted company with the Native men and moved on towards Green Valley. There had been so much foot traffic that the path was much easier to follow. They caught up with Henry just as they were entering the valley. He was limping along, maintaining a slow and steady pace with the crutch for support. It was a constant surprise to Robb how strong Henry was. He was thankful he hadn't run into trouble alone on the path.

Robb stared at the barren hillside. Many trees had been felled, leaving wide-open spaces and jagged stumps on the northern slope where the miners were working, and the gravel piles were extensive. It would be a waste of time to set traps from now on. No small animals were living near the camps. There was no doubt in Robb's mind that it was ugly. As they passed by the other camps, he saw Christopher busy panning and thought he recognized the other young men he'd met on the outbound trip, so they had got back safely. Some were still working on the corner markers on their claims.

Finally, they made it into camp where Melvin, James and Bill were waiting for them. It was like coming home.

"What happened to you?" said Bill, looking at his torn jacket.

"We had a disagreement with one big bear last night. Long Baptiste's wife stitched me up," Robb replied, dropping his pack on the ground with immense relief. He was just plain tired, and his back hurt like hell. Henry, too, looked happy to shed his pack and sat down on the log beside the fire. It was obvious his leg was giving him grief.

George slipped out of his backpack and untied the haunch of bear meat. "We brought supper. I'll get a spit put together and we'll roast it. Are you still working up top?"

"Yes, output's been pretty consistent, a lot of fine flakes but no more big nuggets," said Melvin quietly. "It makes a huge difference using the rocker. We've moved at least three feet of gravel from the north bank for roughly thirty feet."

"I built a storage box out of logs. Figured we needed a safe, dry place to keep the flour and stuff," said James, pointing up the hill.

Robb dragged his backpack up the hill and stacked the bags inside the box. He gathered all the beef jerky they'd bought and hung it high in the tree, having learned his lesson the hard way. He felt the stitches pull when he stretched, so he moved more carefully. The bear meat was excellent, a tasty change from jerky. All of them were exhausted, especially Henry, who went up to bed early. Robb offered him some willow, which he was happy to take. Later, he pulled off his shirt and had Bill wipe his back with the moist fluff Long Baptiste's wife had provided. He put a notch on the tree with his knife to keep track of the days and was content to tuck into his bedroll. He curled up on his good side, chewing on some willow.

* * *

Midweek, George headed into Horsefly alone, his destination the general store to get more boards for another rocker box and to see if supplies could be delivered to them. "I'm also going to try to contact Bill's friend, Peter Dunlevey. He might have suggestions for other claims." Their daily routine didn't vary. Henry manned the rocker box, since it gave him a chance to rest his leg, while the others shovelled sand and mud. Henry noted that it must have rained upstream, as the volume of water seemed higher than the previous week and was eating away at the muddy creek bed, undermining it in places.

Robb gathered a lot more willow bark; thankfully it grew in abundance near the swamp. He had to adjust his style of digging to prevent his back from giving him too much grief. Sometimes he relieved Henry and worked the rocker box with his good arm.

James was monitoring the dam, as some of the smaller stones had shifted and were carried downstream. The water going over the dam was silty. "We'd better get our drinking water from further up. I don't want to drink that muck." From his vantage point, he could see the other claims being worked, the landscape gradually changing. They were very careful to wait until dark to place the daily gold take into the log by their tents.

Three days later, George returned to camp heavily laden with planks, a saw and nails.

"How'd it go?" asked Melvin as the rest of them gathered for the news.

"Good. The track has worn down with all the traffic in and out of here; there are enough people to make it worthwhile for Michael Kelly to bring in some pack mules with supplies. He said he'd come in a couple of weeks. And, more important, I met Peter Dunlevey. He's as interesting as you said he was, Bill. He's going to visit sometime. We've got a lot to talk about. He overwintered last year, so it will give us a good idea of what to expect. I did tell the rest of the miners about the deliveries on the way in. They seemed happy with it."

As they all sat around chowing down the bear meat, beans and biscuits, Henry broke the silence. "Talking about the future, I think I will be going home in the fall. I'm still having trouble with my leg and I really miss my family. I ain't getting any younger, either. It's time. Are you folks interested in buying out my claim?"

There was total silence for a moment or two as the others considered his declaration.

"What kind of price are you asking?" asked James.

"That will depend on how things are going. We're taking in six to ten ounces a day. If that continues and looks like it will extend into next year, I was thinking of three thousand."

What am I going to do now? Robb thought. He needed to get back to Victoria with at least two thousand dollars in his pocket, although he'd been hoping for more. He needed to see Emma before her marriage date was set. He had to change both her mind and her father's. His share of Henry's claim would be six hundred dollars and he'd have to commit to working the claim next year.

"It's the end of July, so that gives us six or eight weeks at most before snow and ice hit us," said George. "I'm willing to buy you out, Henry, so we'll work it through. If we're staying, we need to get that cabin built and a good supply of wood cut to last us 'til April. The rest of you think about it." The days passed, and the bellowing of rutting bucks and a light show of yellow on the aspens, as well as cooler temperatures at night, heralded the coming of fall.

Chapter 22

Dear Robb:

> I'm glad you finally got all your mail. It was an anxious time for us not knowing where you were. So glad to hear your claim is going well, although it worries me that your friend got shot. I understand there are no police out there. Doesn't sound very civilized.
>
> Not much has changed here. I think your father is planning to retire at the end of the year from his current job, as he is now sixty-nine and finding the lifting a bit much. I think he is considering taking over the licensing office. I don't know what I'll do with him under my feet all day during the winter months. James will apply for his job at the Bay. They have finished the new Bay store. It is much larger than the old one, with big windows and more shelf space.

Jane has finished school now, and is helping me more at the food booth and around the house. She also helps Mrs. Cameron down the street with the housework and the children. She is sewing skirts in her spare time and selling them at one of the new stores in town so she can save some money for her wedding dress. Anderson's store has some lovely satin, but it's very expensive and plain linen would be more practical. She and Billy will make a fine couple. They haven't set a date for the wedding yet, probably in early spring. He's saving every penny to get that building lot.

Miners are still coming in with every ship. I'm looking forward to the end of August when it tapers off for the winter. We've got enough money from the food booth now to get the foundation of the church started.

Emily sends her love and wonders if you are coming home for the winter. Edna's getting quite big. They're hoping for a boy this time. Stay out of trouble.

Love, Mum.

Chapter 23

With the second rocker box finished, they worked both sides of the creek above the falls. George also built a sluice box and placed it under the waterfall. The water fell straight in, washing the gravel away so only the fine material fell through the mesh screen for them to pick through. It was still hot, sweaty work, but well worth it.

With seven notches in the tree, Robb knew it was time to get the stitches out and asked Bill to do it. Bill found it awkward getting the tip of the knife under each stitch but managed by keeping the blade flat on Robb's skin. One by one they came out.

"Well, how does it look?" Robb asked, moving his shoulders around, glad to be free of the pulling sensation of the stitches. The pain had eased off quite a bit but still bothered him at times.

"It's healed really well, but it ain't pretty," said Bill.

"No one's gonna see it much, anyway," said Robb, putting his shirt back on. He needed to repair his jacket if he got the chance.

* * *

It was a couple of weeks later that supplies were delivered by pack mule to the camps. Michael Kelly was a middle-aged man, clean-shaven and about six feet tall, with a broad Irish accent. Robb looked at the younger man carrying a Sharps rifle who was accompanying Kelly. The men looked so much alike that they had to be father and son. Kelly set up his weigh scales on a convenient rock, and the miners stopped their work to get supplies. The father weighed the gold and the son weighed out flour, jerky and beans to each customer. They'd even brought a few bottles of whiskey.

While Robb and the others were in the lineup, another figure appeared on the path. Robb didn't recognize the man, but Bill and George immediately waved and set out to meet him.

They greeted the man with firm handshakes and brought him back to camp. Bill did the introductions. "This is Peter Dunlevey."

Dunlevey was younger than Robb expected, probably in his late twenties. He was medium height with dark hair and a quick, lively expression. He spent the evening with them. Robb was enthralled. The man was clever and a real business man. He had an eye for opportunities and apparently had the money to back it up. He described how he intended to set up a series of general stores along the route the miners were taking north to Quesnel once his group were done with their claim.

"The Royal Engineers will be continuing to build the road all the way up and maybe further," he said. "More settlers will be coming in all the time. It'll be a great opportunity for stores and hotels."

Robb looked at him, an idea tumbling around in his head. "Will you be wanting an experienced man for your store? I've worked for the Hudson Bay Company in Victoria for the past three years with my father and brothers. I'm used to working with the Salish people trading furs, and I have a fair knowledge of their language. I've been trying to figure out what to do once this claim runs out."

Dunlevey looked at Bill, who nodded. "Robb would be a good man for you. He's proved his worth here."

"Bill's word is good enough for me. Come and see me when you're ready. I'll likely be north of Williams Lake in the spring, probably around Soda Creek," he said. They shook hands. They talked long into the night, with Robb and Bill discussing the possibility of raising cattle or even pooling their resources. Melvin and James hadn't made up their minds on what they were doing either.

Dunlevey informed that them that if they were going to spend the winter here, they'd need to get a cabin built by the end of September. "There'll be ice on the creek by then. Snow in October is a possibility. We had over two feet of snow here last year by December. It doesn't get better until early April. If you're staying, you'll need food, wood and meat to last you through."

"Is it safe to leave from October to the end of March?" asked George.

"More than likely. Your claim markers look solid. With the ground and the river frozen, no one can pan. The problem is, where do you go? The winters are hard if you stay."

"What's the safest way to get the gold out of here?" asked Melvin. "We've been attacked before. Henry's still not able to walk properly from the last encounter."

"They've got an armed stagecoach running from Yale to Williams Lake now. It's expensive, but you've got guards to protect you. Of course, it will only be running from April to late September. Change the gold dust and nuggets for cash at the bank or get them to give you a bank draft you can cash at one of Victoria's banks. Don't carry a lot of cash on you and wear your miner's clothes. Don't be dressing up fancy. Thieves are watching all the time. If you're on that stage, they'd know you're well heeled."

Robb listened to the discussions, still undecided. "George, we haven't even finished with the two claims above the waterfall. How much gold do you think the four claims below are going to bring in? Is it worth our while to come back in the spring?"

"The tests we did show the further away from the falls, the lower the amount of gold we got out. We've got a month of panning time left for this season. We could always sell off the lower four. If the two top ones are still producing like they have been, we could finish them up in the spring."

"I'm going to spend the winter here. I'll likely try to get a place in Horsefly so I'm nearby," said Bill. "I'm not going back to the States. I want to set up a ranch for beef cattle. Robb and I have talked about this."

Robb suspected Bill was thinking of getting to know Helen Raven Wing better too. Bill was always watching for her when the Natives were around.

"There's no point in me going back to the States for six months just to turn around and come back here," said Melvin. "Panning is damned hard work. I want to see my family again, but it makes more sense to finish up next season then go home for good."

Peter looked at George. "Well, what's your plan?"

"I think there's enough gold in the top two for us to clean up quite nicely next season if it continues producing the way it has been. I'm interested in moving up the Fraser north of Soda Creek. There's the possibility of silver and copper deposits there. But that's real mining, not panning. I think I'll be staying in the general area too."

"I'd like to go back home for a while," said Robb. "My sister's getting married in the spring and I'd like to be there for that, and my brother Matt's baby is due in October. I also need to see Emma and figure out what the future's going to hold for us. But I'll be back. I'd like to have my own general store or road house. This gold rush isn't going to end anytime soon, and I can make a lot more money here than working for the Bay, especially if I own the store."

The embers of the fire finally died down and the men turned in for the night. Robb pulled George aside and whispered to him, as voices carried far in the silence of the darkness.

"I'm concerned about the amount of gold we've got stashed in the log. What do you think if I go out with Peter in the morning and catch a ride with the supply wagon to Williams Lake? Maybe I could ride back with them too."

"I'm worried too." He motioned for Peter to come over an join them. "Peter, Robb wants to go out with you as far as the Horsefly Road, to do a bank run. We got a large amount of gold here. Would you be willing to go along with that?" said George.

Peter thought about it for a few moments. "Yeah, I don't see why not."

Robb slept outside in his sleeping bag, giving Peter his space in the tent.

* * *

It was barely daybreak when Robb woke up. George rolled the stones away from the log and pulled out several of the flour bags full of gold, mostly fine flakes with a few small nuggets. Robb tried on his backpack. "Give me one more," he said, taking it and stuffing it in the pack. "How many more do we have in the log?"

"Eight," said George.

Robb just shook his head. "That's over twenty-five thousand dollars!"

"Yeah, I know."

"Then I've definitely got enough to buy my share of Henry's claim. Count me in for that."

They carefully replaced the stones around the open end of the log, brushed away their footprints and repositioned the fallen tree branches to make it look natural.

Robb gathered a change of clothes, covering up the bags in his backpack, and checked his rifle. It was loaded and ready to use. Melvin was cooking a breakfast of biscuits and jerky, which everyone wolfed down. In the faint morning light, the sun peeped over the horizon beneath the pink and gold-tinged clouds. It looked like a good day to travel.

Robb and Peter gathered their belongings and were quickly on the trail out to Horsefly road. They quietly moved at a brisk walk past the other claims. Robb judged from the snores that most of the tents still had sleeping miners except for a couple getting water from the creek. Hours passed as they made their way to the Horsefly road.

"This is Monday," said Peter. "The supply wagon usually goes to Williams Lake today. I'll walk with you as far as the turnoff for Long Baptiste's camp. The wagon should catch up with you by then."

Robb nodded and they continued west. The weight of the gold didn't bother Robb. It was half of what he'd hauled in the first few months on the Fraser trail. He hoped he'd meet up with Long Baptiste; he felt a sort of kinship with the man and his family for the help they'd given him. The scar on his back didn't bother him at all now. He wondered if Baptiste had made the bear claw necklace.

About an hour later, the rattle of wagon wheels and jingle of harness broke the silence as the team came behind them. Robb flagged them down and was pleased that the driver recognized him and Peter.

"Can I get a ride with you into town? I'm willing to pay," said Robb.

"Mr. Kelly doesn't usually let us take passengers, but if you're willing to pay, why not? I know you."

Robb put his backpack on the empty wagon bed and pulled out a small leather pouch containing two dollars worth of gold dust from his pocket. "Will that do?"

"You bet," said Patrick, tucking it into his own pocket. "Hop on, then."

Robb climbed into the back of the wagon, waving goodbye to Peter, who turned back the way they'd come, heading for his own claim. Robb sat cross-legged on the wooden slats with the rifle in his lap, looking at the passing forest. "When do you come back from town?" he asked.

"We usually stay overnight and load early tomorrow morning."

"I'd like to ride back with you. I can ride shotgun on the top of your load."

The man thought for a few moments and looked at his partner, who nodded. "Mr. Kelly doesn't need to know … right? Same price?"

"Sure. I'm not going to tell. I don't want to be away from camp for very long. I just need more ammo for my rifle, and I've got to send a letter home," said Robb.

The horses kept up a steady trot, stopping only to drink at one of the streams. It wasn't a comfortable ride, as he bounced with every rut. Robb watched the woods intently for anyone who might be a threat and realized he was suspicious of everybody. All the locals knew the timetable for the wagon, but then again at the moment it was empty – nothing to steal. They paused at the main trail, allowing the horses to graze briefly at the side of the road.

The men got a quick drink from the stream and ate their lunch. Robb had more biscuits and jerky in his pack and ate that as he watched the traffic on the trail.

There were a few miners heading north, a pack train of mules loaded with supplies, some riders and a dusty ox cart with several families of settlers. Robb mentally wished them luck, knowing they only had a month at most to get a cabin built and prepare for winter. He couldn't decide if it was courage or foolhardiness, but they amazed him. He couldn't imagine the challenge of survival with women and children involved.

It was mid-afternoon when they arrived in Williams Lake. Robb clambered off the wagon feeling stiff and watched the drivers go into the general store with their long list of needed supplies. He headed for the bank. There were a few customers, and he waited until he saw the manager, who immediately nodded in recognition and called him into the office. With the office door closed, Robb unloaded his backpack onto the desk. Briggs did the acid test to confirm the gold. Each bag was opened and the gold weighed with great precision.

"Well, Robb, you've done very well. That's four hundred and seventy-four ounces in total; at twenty dollars an ounce, that's nine thousand four hundred and eighty. Divide it six ways, that's one thousand five hundred and eighty each. Into each account as usual?"

"Yes, and I need a receipt for each one to take back with me. How much will I have in my account now? I'd like to keep thirty dollars cash. I'm in dire need of some shirts."

"Certainly. Let me just get the entries done," said Mr. Briggs going out to the front desk. Ten minutes later, he returned with a handful of receipts, the thirty dollars in bills, and a slip of paper with Robb's account balance: one thousand nine hundred and forty dollars!

He sat there mesmerized. He had almost two thousand dollars in his bank account! *That's five years work at the Bay.* With eight bags still to come, he could have more than six thousand by the end of the season.

"Mr. Briggs, I'm thinking of going back to Victoria for the winter once the panning season is over. What's the safest means of taking some money home?"

"A bank draft's the best way. You can cash that at any bank. Gold is too heavy to carry in quantity, and some stores don't take it. Cash is risky too. The stage is carrying passengers now. We ship our gold with them for processing in San Francisco and haven't had any problems so far. I'd be really happy if someone built a stamp mill up here. They've got four armed riders riding shotgun. It runs weekly. I think it's ten dollars to get you to Yale, a lot quicker than walking. They stop at the road houses to change horses along the way, so food and lodging would be extra. You can get the boat from Yale to Victoria, same one you came in on. You still have to be cautious, no matter what."

"Thanks for the information," said Robb, shaking Mr. Briggs's hand. With that, he placed all the paperwork in a hide pouch and put it in his backpack. Having safely deposited the gold was a great relief, so he crossed the street to Cullen's General Store. Nothing much had changed; Gilbert was busy weighing beans and Mrs. Cullen was sorting mail. Robb leaned his rifle against the counter and asked for paper, pen and an envelope.

> Dear Mum and Father,
>
> We don't have much time left for panning before the bad weather sets in. It is much cooler at nights now, and the leaves are starting to change colour. I am hoping to come home maybe early October. Can't give you a specific date yet as I don't know how long the trip will take. I'd really like to be home when Edna has the baby. Has Jane set a date yet?
>
> By the end of September, I'll have a better idea of whether we'll be continuing in the spring or not. I really like the

area, and stand a much better chance of buying land up here than in Victoria. It's a lot cheaper. Will have to wait and see.

Henry has decided to go home, so five of us are buying him out. His leg is still bothering him and he is the oldest man here. I'm exhausted at the end of the day, so I don't know how he keeps going. I'll keep in touch when I can. We don't come into town often. Love, Robb

He put the letter in the addressed envelope and handed it to Mrs. Cullen to put the stamp on.

"There's no other mail for you right now, Robb, but you can take the mail for the others while you're here," she said, gathering a bundle of letters from one of the pigeon holes behind her.

Robb thanked her and tucked the bundle in his pack. Walking around the store, he picked out a couple of shirts and a pair of heavy twill pants. His clothes were in tatters and seriously beyond repair. He almost forgot to get some toothbrushes.

"Gilbert, I need a couple of boxes of ammo for the Henry," he said. He completed his transactions and slipped his backpack on. A woman's scream outside the store caused everyone to turn and look. He heard Mrs. Cullen gasp, "Oh, no!" Through the window he could see several miners harassing a young woman and one of them grabbed her by the arm, slamming her up against the building. Both Gilbert and Robb headed for the door on the run. Gilbert pulled the woman inside. Robb slipped past him and confronted the miners, firing a shot in the air. He knew that would bring Sheriff Pinchbeck.

The three scruffy men just stood there. One was unsteady, reeking of booze. They all stared at Robb. The one on the left made a move for the gun in his belt. "Grab that gun and you're a dead man. You don't rough up women in this town," said Robb, his finger on the trigger.

There was a clatter of hooves and Sheriff Pinchbeck and Deputy O'Connor reined their horses to a dusty, sliding stop. "Robb, what's going on here? Did you fire the shot?" he demanded, dismounting with his rifle in his hand. O'Connor dismounted with his pistol in hand and covered them from the other side.

"I did, to get your attention. They attacked a woman right here. She's inside," said Robb.

"Hell, we didn't attack her, we just wanted to get acquainted, like," said the middle man with a grin. "She has a nice ass."

"Wipe that grin off your face, mister," the sheriff said. "Ryan, pat these guys down then put the cuffs on them. We'll take them to the jail to sober up after I check on her."

The deputy cuffed each of them to the hitching post despite a spate of grumbling protests of their innocence and a lot of cursing. He removed the knives and guns the men were carrying.

NUGGETS

Robb followed Sheriff Pinchbeck into the store. Mrs. Cullen was consoling the weeping woman. It wasn't until she turned to look at them that he realized it was Mrs. Hall's daughter Ann. With her bonnet on, her face hadn't been visible. To see her abused like that filled him with rage.

Sheriff Pinchbeck took her aside and quietly talked to her. Robb stood back and waited. With the excitement over, the customers lost interest and business continued as usual. Ann slowly regained her composure, looking in Robb's direction from time to time. Meanwhile, Mrs. Cullen filled Ann's basket with the usual supplies. Finally, the sheriff was finished with her, and got details from Robb, Gilbert and Mrs. Cullen. He then left the store to deal with his three prisoners. Robb's last view was the three being herded down the street in the direction of the jail.

Robb walked over to Ann, who was finishing her shopping. "Are you okay?" he asked, his arm around her shoulder.

She took a deep breath and looked up at him. "I'm alright now. He scared the daylights out of me," she said. "I wasn't expecting that. I'd walked past them and didn't hear him coming up behind me."

"I'm glad you're alright. I'll walk you back home," said Robb. "I was heading there anyway. Have you got a vacant room? I need one for tonight." He opened the door and escorted her out.

"We've got the back room available. Mum will be glad to see you," she said, her eyes surveying and assessing

195

everything and everybody on the street. "All the years I've lived here, I've never had a problem. I thought I was safe; it's only three blocks from home and it's broad daylight. I dress properly and didn't talk to them. He really took me by surprise. Other than walking around them, I didn't pay much attention to them."

Mrs. Hall met them, took one look at Ann and said, "What's wrong? You've been gone a long time."

"She was attacked by a miner outside the store. It took a while for the sheriff to sort it out," said Robb.

"I heard a shot but didn't think anything of it," said Mrs. Hall, opening her arms to give Ann a hug. Robb removed his pack and sat down at the table, giving the women time to talk. After a few minutes he went out back and scrubbed himself clean, putting on one of his new shirts. He cleaned his teeth and trimmed his beard. He was pleased that he still had all his teeth. He looked in the mirror, but the wild man still stared back. He was looking forward to getting back to Victoria and really getting cleaned up.

Back inside, Mrs. Hall came up to him and thanked him. "I'm deeply grateful for you taking care of her like that. You'll be staying with us tonight?"

"Yes, please. Ann said you had an empty room."

"You can have the one here on the main floor," she said, opening the door behind the kitchen.

Robb pulled a dollar out of his pocket and gave it to her.

"No, Robb, not after what you've done," she said.

"Mrs. Hall, take it," he said, closing her hands over the coin. "It still costs money to feed me. I'd spend that at the saloon for a meal and it wouldn't be half as good as your cooking." He sniffed the air at the aromas emanating from a large pot simmering on the cook stove. He went into his room, knowing he could at least guard them that night. He had no idea if Pinchbeck would keep the men in jail or not. He could hear the other guests moving around upstairs. It worried him that the women had nobody other than O'Connor to be there for them, and he probably had night duty at the jail if the prisoners were being held over. The vulnerability of the women bothered him.

Supper was excellent. The other three boarders were heading up to Slocum. O'Connor did not come back to the house. Robb kept his eye on Ann, but she seemed to have regained her composure and was back to normal, serving the meals with steady hands and helping her mother.

He sat on the porch for a while as dusk fell, pondering his future. He figured that when the creek iced up, he'd take the stage to Yale then the boat home. He'd stay with his parents over the winter to sort out his arrangements with Emma and come back to work the claim in the spring until it ran out. The prospect of working up in the Soda Creek area with Dunlevey made a lot of sense to him. If Emma was going to be with him then she needed to change her ways a bit and help him out, just like Mrs. Cullen did for Gilbert. There was also the possibility of starting a beef ranch with Bill. Still lots of options. He went to bed contented and slept well.

Chapter 24

The next morning, after saying goodbye to Mrs. Hall and Ann, Robb was out early to catch the wagon back to the Horsefly road. Ann gave him a sandwich to put in his pack. He looked down at her, their eyes locking for a moment. "Take care of yourselves and be careful," he said.

Both women waved goodbye as he went back up the street where the two drivers and the store clerk were loading the wagon, the horses waiting patiently. Robb tucked his pack and rifle under the back of the wagon seat and pitched in with carrying the sacks of flour and beans. The wagon was soon full, and Robb arranged the sacks so he could sit facing backward, watching the road behind them with the Henry in his lap.

As they headed out of town, Robb noticed the stagecoach parked outside the bank with four armed riders waiting. "Pat, stop for a minute, I'd like to talk to those guys."

Pat slowed the horses and came to a stop. Four rifles immediately pointed at him. Robb put his hands up. "I just wanted to know what days you pick up here and how much it costs to get a ride to Yale. I'll be going home in about a month."

The driver turned to him and said, "We run four stages on this route, so it's a weekly run out of here on a Monday. It's ten dollars to Yale. We will stop mid-October or when there's more than a couple of inches of snow on the ground."

"Thanks," said Robb. "Okay, Pat, let's go." Four sets of ice-cold eyes never left his face and the rifles remained aimed directly at him, only lowered as the wagon passed the town line.

Sitting on a sack of flour was infinitely more comfortable than sitting on the bare boards when the wagon was empty. He had a good vantage point from the wagon and noticed things he hadn't seen when he'd been walking. Footpaths snaked into the woods in more than a few places and smoke was rising through the trees. Some trees had been felled and the sound of hammering rang clearly. There was definitely a cabin being built, although he didn't see any survey stakes.

By early afternoon they had reached the Horsefly road. They only met a couple of miners coming out, but none of them were from Green Valley. There was no sign of Long Baptiste or his people. Robb suspected the young lads went to Horsefly to the saloon, as it was closer. He doubted they'd ever have much gold to take home if the tales of gambling, whiskey and girls were to be believed when they sat around their campfires bragging. They probably didn't realize how sound carried, or maybe they didn't care. He thought about the girl

Cassie in Williams Lake. Part of him wanted to have a drink and see her again, but he didn't intend to squander the money. He realized he was the same age or even younger than some of the Green Valley crew, but he'd been brought up differently. His father had taught him to be frugal, and maybe those old Scottish ways weren't so bad after all. The money he was saving could buy the status he needed to regain Emma's affection and her father's approval.

He noticed the deepening yellow of the maples now, in sharp contrast to the green spikes of the evergreens with their burgeoning crop of cones. The sun was dying on the horizon when he stumbled into camp. He'd been fortunate to have an uneventful return with no ambushes or bears. The temperature was dropping rapidly as the sun set. His hands and feet were cold. His mates were surprised and pleased to see him. He rummaged through his backpack and handed the receipts to everyone.

"What's new in Williams Lake?" asked Henry.

"There's a weekly stage that runs to Yale with an armed escort. Might be a good way for you to start your trip home. Costs ten dollars, and it would be a whole lot easier than walking. I'm seriously thinking of taking it myself," said Robb. "It does stop running in October once the weather's bad."

"Good to know," said Henry.

"How's the panning going?" asked Robb.

"We only took in six ounces today," said George. "We'll have to see what tomorrow brings."

NUGGETS

* * *

Over the next three weeks, they worked to the point of exhaustion. Temperatures dropped sharply after the sun set, and it was cold enough that Robb slept fully dressed under his blankets. Every morning now there was ice on the creek, which melted during the day. Bull elk were bellowing across the valley and the geese were in long vees, heading south. Some of the golden leaves were now littered on the ground and squirrels were busy burying things. No doubt winter was coming.

James and Bill had done a run into Williams Lake to deposit the gold, accompanied by some of their neighbours on a whiskey run. One group of youngsters was going to stay the winter and were frantically putting the finishing touches to a small log cabin.

The daily take of gold dust had dwindled to six ounces a day. Robb mused to himself that while an ounce a day for him seemed paltry in comparison to what they had been getting, it was still a month's pay back home. George stacked the rocker boxes. The campsite looked bare.

George, Melvin and James intended to stay at Mrs. Hall's, which was a huge relief to Robb.

"I'm so glad you're going to stay there. I've been worried about them since Ann got attacked. I think I'll go with Henry on the stage and head home too."

One day the ice on the creek didn't melt and was strong enough to stand on. The time had come to leave. They had completed all the money arrangements with

Henry, and he'd signed off his portion of the claim to the five of them. He'd sold his pick, shovel and axe to one of the young lads and gathered his gear together. Bill had found a room with a local family in Horsefly recommended by Mike Kelly. Christopher and some of his buddies were also going to stay there.

The Green Valley crew left the camp fully loaded with the tents, tools and backpacks. As they marched down the valley, a sharp, cold wind blew from the northwest with a promise of snow. Robb wished he had gloves; his fingers felt numb. He looked down the valley at the bare hillsides one last time and realized it would be six months before he would see it again.

Bill parted company with them once they reached the Horsefly road. They shook hands and wished each other luck for the winter. The rest of them continued on to the Cariboo Road. A lone figure in buckskin was waiting for them. It was Long Baptiste.

They hadn't seen much of him over the summer. They paused and chatted for a while, and he wished them all well and handed Robb a pendant. It lay in his hand, a plain, rawhide thong with coloured beads, chips of abalone shell and a single, five-inch-long polished grizzly claw. "Thank you, Long Baptiste. I'd totally forgotten about that. You made it. I will wear it for good luck." He reached into his pocket and handed his friend a small, round pea-shaped gold nugget. Long Baptiste accepted it and slipped away into the forest.

The next day saw them in Williams Lake. The town was quieter, with only a few tents in tent town. Few miners were heading north now. They headed to Mrs. Hall's and she was pleased to see them, as her rooms were vacant except for the deputy. George broached the subject of the three of them staying over the winter months.

"I think that would work out just fine, but it depends on whether I can get enough supplies in from the stores, since we won't be getting any deliveries until spring this far north. I won't have enough firewood either," she said.

"James, Melvin and I can certainly get your wood supply, even if we have to cut it ourselves," said George. "We'll check around. In camp, each of us are using about a pound of flour and beans every day. Will your well tolerate the extra use?"

"We've never run out yet," she replied, her brow knotted as she calculated quantities of onions, sugar, apples and potatoes, plus the tea and coffee she'd need. They all stashed their picks, shovels, tents and axes in her back shed.

Robb and Henry headed to the bank to arrange their bank drafts. Robb took out one hundred cash and four hundred as a bank draft, leaving him with nine thousand in his account. Henry closed out his account. He was taking over ten thousand dollars home. They stopped in at the hotel to check on the stage leaving the next morning and bought their tickets. Robb watched for anyone taking interest in them, seeing only locals and two of the armed stage riders he'd seen the last time.

"How long's it been since you left your family?" asked Robb

"Close to two years," Henry replied. "I know it's a terrible strain on my wife to look after the three kids; they've done their schooling. Hopefully they'll be working by the time I get back. She lives close to my brother and his wife, so she's not entirely alone. This has been a very risky venture. I just want to make it back home in one piece. If there's a civil war, I'm too old to go back in the army, so I should be okay."

"Make sure you give me your address. You're in San Francisco, aren't you? I'd like to keep in touch. You've helped me out a lot, you know," said Robb. "If you want to contact me, just address it to me care of my father, William McDonald, in Victoria. It'll get through." Henry grinned.

The rest of the day was spent scrounging for provisions at all the stores. Gilbert Cullen gave them the name of a man up the road as a source of firewood and lent them a wheelbarrow to get the hundred-pound bags of flour and beans back to Mrs. Hall's. He was expecting the last load of supplies to arrive any day on Caux's last mule train and with any luck another shipment via the Bella Coola traders.

Robb started sorting through his clothes, discarding some of the shirts that were too shabby to keep. He trimmed up his beard that night but left his hair long, heeding Dunlevey's advice on maintaining the miner's persona for safety reasons. He looked at the bear-claw pendant hanging around his neck and thought of Long Baptiste. *I'm proud of this pendant.* Somehow it represented the wilderness and the struggles he had gone through. It reminded him of Long Baptiste and his family. The Green Valley crew had worked hard in very primitive conditions. He was proud of himself for having survived it. But the journey wasn't over. The trip home was going to be just as dangerous as the trip inland.

Deputy O'Connor joined them that evening for supper, which was excellent as usual. They traded stories and James played his harmonica. Robb hadn't laughed that much in a long time. He kept his eye on Ann, who seemed her usual self, snapping lively, quick retorts to some of the comments, seemingly no worse for her altercation with the miner. She was a resilient woman and he admired that.

Chapter 25

Mrs. Hall gave them a hearty breakfast. Henry and Robb gathered their backpacks, said their goodbyes and headed up the street to meet the stage. The horses were hitched, and two other passengers were getting on board. The four riders were already mounted, on alert, their rifles in the scabbards. The luggage rack and roof of the stagecoach were crammed full of steamer trunks and carpet bags. Robb and Henry climbed in. They placed their rifles between them, out of the way, and wedged their backpacks between their feet. Robb was excited. This was his first stagecoach ride, and he was going home to Emma.

The two gentlemen sharing the coach were dressed in suits, white shirts and bowler hats. They looked at Robb and Henry with obvious distaste, not impressed with having to share a coach with a couple of miners. Robb was okay with that. It was just the effect they wanted in order to get home safely.

With a snap of the whip, the driver clucked to the team and the coach pulled away from the store, heading south. Robb watched as they passed through town, and then Williams Lake disappeared behind them. It seemed peculiar to just sit looking at the scenery. The bench seats were reasonably comfortable. They passed the time looking at ranches they'd seen on the northbound journey five months ago.

"There's been a lot of building since we were here in June," Henry remarked, pointing to new log cabins and fence lines.

Around lunchtime, when the sun was overhead, they stopped at 150 mile House to change horses. Robb felt stiff when he climbed down, not used to sitting that length of time. Tom Davidson led the fresh team over as the driver unhitched the horses.

"Hello, you two. Heading home?" Tom said, recognizing them.

"Henry's heading home. I'm gonna visit family and come back in the spring," replied Robb.

"How did you do?" asked Tom.

"Barely enough to get by," said Henry, knowing that sharp ears were listening. "I've had enough of the hard work. I'm too old to go on. It's time I went back to my family."

"I see you're limping. What happened?"

"Got shot by some damned claim jumper," said Henry. "James took care of him."

"You folk go on in. Hank has a good lunch prepared for you for two dollars," said Tom, pointing the way up to the ranch house. "I'll just put these horses out to pasture, and I'll be right back." The riders ate outside, separate from the passengers, never leaving the stage unattended. They were a mean-looking bunch, tall and silent for the most part. They looked and behaved like ex-military. They were well equipped with Winchester rifles and good horses. Robb wondered if the bank's gold was in the trunks they were guarding.

Stopping only to change the team every twenty-five miles, they had a quick stop at Lac la Hache, reaching 100 Mile House by nightfall. Robb was amazed at the distance they had covered. It had taken them weeks on foot. After a good meal, Robb and Henry slept on the floor upstairs while the two gentlemen had the downstairs rooms with beds. The riders took turns on night watch.

The sun was barely up when they were on the road again. It was a cold morning with a heavy frost, and the horses were snorting clouds of vapour, the long hairs on their muzzles etched in white. There were rocky places where the riders rode two ahead and two behind the coach. Robb saw them scanning the ridgetops; any place where an ambush was likely. Mid-morning, the coach slowed down to let the mule train move past. Henry stuck his head out of the window to yell a greeting at Cataline Caux. Caux waved back. Robb noted that the mules were loaded mainly with food supplies. Gilbert and the other merchants would be mighty glad to see that delivery.

The constant motion of the coach almost put Robb to sleep, but the potholes bounced him awake. He wasn't used to sitting around all day. The landscape was forested with pines and firs, a relatively flat table land cut with deep river canyons. The steep-sided valleys with their red layered walls reminded him of Green Valley before they'd cut all the trees down.

Henry seemed content to just sit contemplating the scenery too. Sometimes the jolting of the coach caused him to grimace. *He's still having a lot of pain with that leg,* Robb thought, wishing he'd brought some willow.

They changed horses and ate lunch at 70 Mile House. There were three other riders eating lunch there and Robb had an uneasy feeling about them. They reminded him of the bunch of young card players they'd come north with. Their shifty eyes were casting glances at the two business men. Robb was sure they were up to something.

Robb walked up to Garnet Henderson, one of their guards who was standing on the porch eating a sandwich along with the drivers. Not only did Garnet have a rifle, but Robb could see the outline of a pistol under his coat. "I'd keep an eye on those guys, if I were you. I've got a feeling they're up to no good."

Garnet looked over Robb's head and scanned the area. "We often have problems in this section of the run. There are a lot of places just ripe for an ambush. Do you know those guys?"

"No, I don't think so, but they remind me of a bunch we travelled with. Listen, both Henry and I are pretty good shots, so count us in."

The guards put their heads together for a few minutes, obviously discussing the situation, then talked to the drivers. Soon they were back on the road heading for Clinton. Ben and Howard rode out in front, leaving Garnet and Wayne positioned behind the coach. The first hour was uneventful. Robb and Henry sat with their rifles cradled in their arms, peering out at a wild landscape with few signs of habitation. The two businessmen seemed nervous and were fidgeting and looking around.

The driver cracked the whip and urged the horses forward. The coach lurched and bounced, almost unseating everyone. The road was in no condition for anything faster than a trot. The valley narrowed and Robb could hear Garnet order Ben and Howard to ride up onto the ridge. He saw the riders spurring their horses up a steep, narrow path and disappearing through the pines. If he remembered correctly, there was a stream to cross just ahead where the coach would have to slow down. That would be an ideal place for a holdup. The tension was palpable.

Gunfire suddenly erupted from the top of the ridge, with return fire from somewhere close down on their level. Both Robb and Henry were ready for action and he could hear the driver yelling, "Riders ahead!"

Garnet was now galloping his horse alongside the coach. Bullets pinged off the coach, sending slivers of wood flying. He returned fire, the reins loose, riding his horse with his knees. Wayne was right behind him. The spare driver was firing, and Robb could hear yells from Howard somewhere above. The coach was right close to the edge of the road, so Robb wasn't in a position to see anything but the trees.

The coach came to a jarring halt and both Robb and Henry jumped out, their rifles ready. The driver fought to keep the team under control and the frightened animals reared and squealed, kicking up clouds of dust. Ben and Howard came crashing down the hill to join Garnet and Wayne.

There were three dead bandits sprawled on the road, their horses scattered. "They had a lookout posted up top. We nailed him," said Ben.

"I think it was that bunch from 70 Mile House," Howard chipped in.

Robb held the reins of the wheel horse, trying to calm him. The whites of its eyes were still showing, the nostrils flared, and it danced on the spot, sweat and lather dripping from its neck and shoulders around the collar and strapping. "Easy boy, easy, easy," he said, resting his hand gently on the horse's trembling neck. Slowly, the horse started to settle and gradually its breathing slowed and it stood with Robb patting its nose. The spare driver was calming the lead horse as well.

Garnet kicked the bodies over, removing guns and ammunition and emptying their pockets, while Wayne started to round up the loose horses. They all pitched in to throw the bodies up onto the saddles. The guards tied the reins of the thieves' horses to their saddle horns and the procession was on the road again, slower this time. The businessmen never got off the coach and just sat there in silence, watching. As Robb was climbing back into his seat, he couldn't help but notice the outline of a derringer in one passenger's belt as he was turning to talk to his companion. Robb dug Henry in the ribs and whispered, "He's armed." It raised all sorts of questions in Robb's mind. *Why hadn't they tried to help out?* An even nastier thought popped into his head. Were *they part of the gang?*

It was nearly dark when they finally arrived in Clinton. They headed to the saloon for a meal and planned to bunk down over the stable. The businessmen went to a little hotel. Garnet took the bodies down to the Royal Engineers' post since the town didn't have a sheriff.

In the meantime, Robb had a quick word with Ben. "Just to let you know, one of those guys, the one sitting across from me, he's carrying a derringer. I find it really suspicious that they didn't try to defend themselves back there. Would you let Garnet know?"

Ben listened. "So, Mr. Smith is carrying a gun ... that's interesting. I wonder if Mr. Brown is as well. You might be right. Just watch yourself. I'll tell Garnet."

Later, when they were stretched out in the hay mow above the stable, Henry rolled over and said, "I'm glad I'm going home. I've really had enough of all these greedy buggers scheming and killin'. When I get home, I'm gonna stay there. My travelling days are over."

"I'll be going back in the spring to finish up. Bill and I might buy some land and raise cattle, or I might run a store for Dunlevey. Don't know yet. A lot depends on Emma and me. I'll know better once I see her. You're more than welcome to come back here and bring your family if you want to," said Robb.

"Thanks for the offer, Robb, but I'm American through and through, and I wanna go back home," said Henry.

They settled down in the hay and slept to the cooing of pigeons and the rustling of small creatures in the hay. Robb dreamed of Emma again.

* * *

The next day was cloudy, and the north wind blew cold. The far north was covered with slate-blue-gray clouds that hinted of snow and obscured the tops of the mountains. Robb wondered if it was snowing in Green Valley and how the young lads were doing stuck in the cabin. He shivered and decided he'd better get some gloves, as his fingers were numb already.

Garnet was saddling his horse. "Robb, we've got a couple of spare horses here to go along with us, do you wanna ride instead of being in the coach?"

Robb thought for a moment. He didn't have much experience riding, but if he was going to run a ranch he needed to ride better. "Sure, but I don't ride well enough to ride and shoot too," he said, putting the rifle in the scabbard. He pictured Garnet yesterday, low in the saddle, firing with deadly accuracy with the horse in a flat-out gallop.

Garnet grinned. The smile changed his face completely for that one fleeting moment, then it was gone, returning to the stern, calculating expression. His icy gray eyes were always watchful. The men grabbed a quick bite of breakfast at the little café, and then Robb ran into the general store just as it opened. "I need some gloves," he said to the owner. He grabbed two pairs in case Henry wanted some too. Moments later he was sitting on a horse between Garnet and Wayne. Mr. Smith and Mr. Brown remained silent. Henry, meanwhile, had taken a travel blanket and covered up his legs. His rifle lay across Robb's empty seat.

The day passed uneventfully as they headed to Cache Creek. It was a short run for the day with the hills getting higher and the valleys narrower. They passed many miners heading south.

Cache Creek was a tiny place, but to the south stretched the wider, surveyed road; that was as far as the Royal Engineers had got that season.

When Robb dismounted he felt incredibly stiff and rubbed his sore behind, not used to using those muscles.

Wayne laughed at him as Robb exaggerated his bow-legged gait up to the door of the stables.

Again Mr. Brown and Mr. Smith went to the hotel, and Robb and Henry headed for the saloon to get supper. Robb noticed a Chinese laundry on the main street. The oriental man sweeping the outside step sure looked like one of the group they'd met on the northbound trip. He wondered what had happened to a lot of the people. *Had they struck it rich, or gone home empty-handed?*

Garnet took them aside and said quietly, "Just to let you know, Mr. Brown and Mr. Smith are on our side; they're bank detectives. That's our secret, okay?"

"Well, that's a relief," said Robb. "I figured you were protecting the bank's final shipment of gold for the season. I thought they were in with the bandits. If he had pulled that pistol, I might have shot him, you know," said Robb. "I knew they were up to something, but bank detectives ... that never even entered my head."

Henry laughed. "He would have shot them too."

* * *

Mr. Smith and Mr. Brown still didn't speak to them, but both Henry and Robb felt more comfortable knowing which side they were on. The next night they reached Lytton and found the town much changed. Dozens more cabins had sprung up, and there was a barbershop, another general store and a saloon. Word was out, according to the locals, that they were planning to build a schoolhouse and an Anglican church in the spring.

The following day was clear and cool, but not quite so cold. The further south they rode, the milder it got. Robb was getting used to riding, although he was still stiff and sore. He was developing a rapport with his horse and not bouncing quite so hard when it went into its bone-shaking trot. The canter was a lot more comfortable.

There was a skunk shuffling its way across the road, its striped tail waving like a flag as it waddled away into the long grass. "Robb, see if you can hit that," Garnet challenged.

Robb pulled the rifle from the scabbard, levered a cartridge into the chamber, aimed and fired.

His horse exploded underneath him and nearly dumped him. He clung like a limpet and only stayed in the saddle because he had clamped his knees just before he fired. He hadn't been expecting that reaction and quickly gathered up the reins. Steadying the horse with one hand, he circled to see everyone laughing, including the drivers, Mr. Brown, Mr. Smith and Henry. He put the rifle back in the scabbard, taking off his hat in a long, sweeping bow. "I'm so glad to entertain you," he said. He looked around and spotted the motionless skunk in the long grass. "I did get it. You knew the horse would react that way, didn't you?" he said, looking at Garnet.

"Pretty much. I'm surprised you stayed on. Our horses are used to it. If you can stick on him, you'll have no problems handling a horse."

"Where are you guys from?" asked Robb, pegging them as Americans.

"We're from Washington state, ex-cavalry. We took this job for the summer and will be heading back home 'til the spring unless we can pick up work around Yale or Hope."

"Will you come back and do this again?" Robb asked.

"We might; the pay's better than the army. They pay for our food and lodging too. We could re-join our old cavalry unit but haven't really made up our minds. We do all kinds of jobs, working as enforcers with ranchers, bounty hunting, whatever."

By late afternoon they could hear the distant roar of the Fraser River crashing its way through Hell's Gate canyon. A mist hung in the air over the river that could be seen miles away. The wagon road now ran parallel to the river several miles from the rim. Robb was thankful for that. "I'm glad we don't have to walk the canyon again." The memory of the narrow path and the sheer drop into the abyss was crystal clear in his mind. He could still feel the fear it had evoked at the time. They spent the night in Boston Bar.

Robb was getting excited. He knew they would reach Yale the next day and hoped the boat would be there and that there would be room for them on board. Once again they were bunked down in the stable's hay mow. "Henry, are we going to sleep on deck like we did before?"

"I think it would be best," said Henry. "We're just a couple of luckless miners who can't afford anything better. Nobody's bothered us so far; we don't look worth it. I'd like to keep it that way. I'm not going to shave and get into my good duds until I get to San Francisco."

* * *

The coach lurched to a halt in Spuzzum to change horses. Robb noted that this village had grown too; there were more houses but more bare hills and just a few tents where tent city had been. There were more southbound miners as well, looking tired and ragged, walking the old trail. The coach shared the road with many carts and wagons. With the silent and able enforcers guarding them, they were given a wide berth. Cabins and rail fences were evidence of more settlers, and surveyors' stakes were everywhere, marking off building lots and sections. Civilization was coming. He wondered if the Natives are still selling venison like they had been in the spring. The white settlers were encroaching on their land just like in Victoria. It brought Whalecatcher to mind.

Early afternoon found them arriving on Yale's wide, rutted main street. The coach pulled up outside the bank. Robb dismounted, tying his horse to the back of the coach and giving it a friendly slap on the neck. He was glad his riding exercise was over, but overall pleased with his progress. He knew it would be invaluable experience when he headed north next year, especially if he decided to get a ranch. He removed his backpack from the coach and slipped it on after Henry got out. They departed with a wave to the drivers and escorts, leaving them to unload their precious cargo. Mr. Smith and Mr. Brown disappeared into the bank.

They walked down to the dock with no sign of the *Enterprise* but there were maybe twenty miners waiting. Henry asked a bystander when the boat was due and was told it would be the next day.

"I guess we'd better stay in line," said Henry. "I'll go get some grub; be back in a while. I want to send a letter to my wife letting her know we at least got this far. I should be home in a couple of weeks. With the way the mail is, I might even get there before the letter." He took off in the direction of the general store.

Robb took off his pack and sat on the ground, just watching everything around him. He didn't see any familiar faces. He started thinking about getting back into Victoria. Part of him wanted to dress up in a fine suit and go flashing back into town looking like a wealthy man to impress Emma and her father, not to mention his own family. On the other hand, from a safety point of view, once Henry disembarked in Seattle for his connecting boat to San Francisco, he was going to be alone. Until that draft was safely in the bank, it would probably be better to keep up the miner persona. No one was likely to recognize him the way he looked now anyhow. He smelled bad enough to keep most decent folks away. He was very aware of the stench from weeks in his sweaty clothes.

Robb weighed his options. Henry reappeared loaded with fresh bread, jerky and apples, plus a bottle of whiskey. He'd left his gold pan back at Mrs. Hall's, so he didn't have anything to cook with. Robb headed off to the store and picked up bread, a good local cheese, jerky and enough apples to last him to Victoria. At the counter, he carefully counted out his coins, acting like they were the last he had, and handed them over to the clerk, who had a British accent. Robb gave him a closer look and thought the man might be one of the Brits from the trail. He'd often wondered what had happened to them.

Back at the dock, the lineup behind them grew longer but there wasn't the angst, excitement and frustration of the spring trip. All the men in the lineup were tired, beaten men who were going home defeated, their dreams, if not their bodies, shattered. Robb wondered how many died on the trail. *Accidents, murder, starvation? I didn't even understand the risks I was taking. Thank God for Henry and the others, not to mention Long Baptiste. Without their help I wouldn't have made it. Even the plant knowledge that Long Feather shared with me increased my chance of survival.*

He sat there deep in thought about the changes that had happened over the last six months. Images of Emma danced in his head, interspersed with images of the tough and resilient, yet no less feminine, images of Cassie, Ann, Mrs. Hall, Long Baptiste's wife and Mrs. Cullen. He admired the spunk and courage of the pioneer women. The lives they led were tough and at times dangerous in a merciless wilderness that yielded to no one.

Robb put up the tarp and he and Henry slept curled up beneath it, their rifles beside them and their packs under their heads.

* * *

The *Enterprise* docked around noon, her decks loaded not with miners but with burlap bags of food destined for the villages further north. Dozens of men carried the hundred-pound bags on their backs down the gangplank and quickly filled waiting carts. When the decks and hold were empty, Captain Wright allowed the passengers to board. Henry and Robb took a choice spot under the front overhang out of the weather and settled down with the eighty or so other men. It was a quicker trip heading downstream with the river current rather than against it. They reached Hope by suppertime in a light, warm drizzle.

The trip downstream was a quiet one. The men on deck didn't play cards and they mostly talked about what might have been. Robb watched the scenery flow by and listened to the conversations, confirming his suspicions that most of them had found some gold, but had frittered it away in the saloons. He regretted in some ways not having gone back to see Cassie, but he'd never forget his experience with her. His group had been more than lucky to hit the right claim, a success he credited largely to George.

They reached Fort Langley and patiently waited for the *Eliza Anderson* to dock. Robb now felt the rising anticipation of getting home. Henry was restless too.

"How long will it take you to sail from Seattle to San Francisco?" Robb asked.

"Probably best part of a week, depending on the weather. I can't wait to get home."

"Me too. I'd like to thank you for all your help and advice. I'd be just like these guys if I hadn't met you and Bill. You've been more like family," Robb said.

Henry smiled and looked him right in the eyes. "You've grown up a lot, young fella, and that ain't a bad thing. You just need to get a sense of humour and get rid of some of those peculiar British ideas you've got. I can trust you, and there aren't many I can say that about."

Robb grinned. He valued Henry's judgment and he was proud someone thought him worthy, but he didn't think he'd be getting rid of any British ideals any time soon, especially now that he was going back into his father's household. They sat in the lineup silently for the rest of the evening under the tarp as the drizzle continued. Once again, the boat was full of miners returning home.

Twenty-four hours later found the *Eliza* chugging into Seattle. As soon as the gangplank was lowered, Henry grabbed Robb's shoulders in a bear hug. They shook hands, and then he turned and was gone. Robb watched his receding figure and felt a lump rising in his throat. He had to walk away, as his eyes started to moisten. *Next stop, Victoria.*

Chapter 26

There were few passengers on the Seattle to Victoria run. Robb stood looking over the rail as *Eliza* came into the dock. He noticed the palisade had been removed from the fort and the newly renovated Hudson's Bay store stood out with the new lumber, a fresh coat of paint and bigger windows. There were new houses where there had been gaps before. Tent town was empty. *Mum will be at home.*

Disembarking, he walked down Wharf Street towards the bank, pulling down the brim of his hat to obscure his face, his rifle slung across his shoulder, carrying his backpack. None of the locals on the sidewalk recognized him, and husbands pulled wives out of his way with obvious distaste. He entered the bank, the pristine, columned institution with its marble counters, and joined the customers in line. Within moments he was approached by the portly senior official, Longworth, in his black suit and starched white shirt.

"May I help you, sir?" he asked, eyeballing Robb's clothing and ragged beard with total distaste.

"Yes, I need to see the manager to make a bank deposit," Robb said quietly.

"I see. Do you have an account here?"

"Yes, I do."

"What is your name?"

"I will reveal that information when I see him. Is it still Brockton?" asked Robb.

"Yes, it is," said Longworth, trying to place the voice. "You'd better come with me." He led Robb to an alcove with a small desk and a hard, wooden chair. Robb sat down and waited, searching through his backpack for the carefully wrapped bank draft. There wasn't a customer or a clerk who didn't give him the once-over, and heads were soon bent together behind the counter with conversations in whispered tones. Robb took a perverse pleasure in the scene he'd created. *They really are a pompous lot. Perhaps some of Henry's attitudes had rubbed off after all.*

Longworth emerged from the office with the manager, Brockton, behind him.

"I understand you wish to see me about making a bank deposit," Brockton said.

"Yes, sir, I do," replied Robb, extending his hand to shake Brockton's. Brockton shook it, noting the dirt under the nails, and winced at the strong, callused grip. Robb suppressed a smile as Brockton almost wiped his hand on his trousers but didn't.

Brockton led him into the office and Longworth was about to follow him when Robb closed the door in his face with a firm, "This is a private conversation, Mr. Longworth."

Brockton sat in his swivel chair, definitely nervous, running a finger inside his tight collar as Robb rested the rifle against the wall and sat down, producing the bank draft. He could hear hushed conversations on the other side of the thick oak door as Brockton read it.

"Mr. Brockton, I'm Robb McDonald and that is a legitimate bank draft for four hundred dollars from the bank in Williams Lake for deposit."

A few silent moments went by, and then a look of comprehension and surprise came over Brockton's face. "Good gracious, Robb. I didn't recognize you. My apologies, I ..."

"You have to understand," said Robb. "There are thieves and murderers of every kind out there, and this was the best disguise I could come up with to get home safely with my money. I'd have been murdered for the boots I was wearing, let alone money. I will need a receipt for that. I also want a bath, a shave, and clean clothes before I go home to my parents. Where would you suggest?"

"The Lancaster saloon could take care of the bath; Brown's barbershop will be open until five o'clock and you have the choice of the new Hudson's Bay store or Granville's Emporium."

"I'd run too much risk of meeting my father if I went to the Bay. Thank you," said Robb.

"I'll be right back with your receipt," said Mr. Brockton, smiling as he hurried out the door and almost bumping into Mr. Longworth, who had been eavesdropping at the keyhole.

Robb smiled and nodded as Longworth regained his imperial posture and straightened his suit.

Mr. Brockton was back shortly and handed Robb the receipt, which confirmed he now had the princely sum of four hundred and three dollars in his account. *That's probably more than most of the staff have in their accounts*, he thought.

Tipping his hat to Brockton, he took his rifle and backpack, heading for the saloon where they were more than happy to accommodate his request for a bath. He was pleased to see that the tub room had a bolt on the door. *Cassie wouldn't have got in here.* He scrubbed himself down thoroughly, leaving the water a dingy brown. His hands still looked grimy despite the scrubbing. He changed into his spare clothes and threw out the old ones. He carefully removed his bear-claw pendant and put it in his backpack. Smelling a little fresher, he headed to Brown's barbershop.

Will, the barber, didn't recognize him either until he spoke. "Will, I want you to cut my hair just above my collar, not too short, and get rid of this beard or my mother won't let me back in the house," Robb said. He wasn't joking.

"Robb McDonald, well, don't you look rough! I'd never have known you," replied Will, swaddling Robb's shoulders and neck in towels. The wild stranger stared back at Robb in the mirror. With the snip, snip of Will's scissors, Robb's wavy black locks tumbled to the floor.

Will made the parting, then the final comb out. "Well, that's a good start," he said. "Now for the shrubbery here."

Robb laid back against the head rest of the barber chair and raised his chin. He could hear Will working the straight-edged razor on the leather strop to hone the edge. He felt vaguely uneasy about exposing his neck like that, but this was Victoria, not Spuzzum.

Will mixed up some soap and hot water in a mug and after inspecting Robb's chin, liberally lathered it with the brush. Robb felt Will apply the blade in short, smooth strokes down his cheeks and along the jawline.

"Do you want me to leave a moustache?"

"No, I don't think so," replied Robb. He knew they were fashionable, but he'd never bothered with one; it would just be a repository for crumbs or gravy.

It seemed to take forever but was likely not more than a couple of minutes as Will finished one side and started on the other. "There you go, lad, you look like a real human being."

Robb rubbed his hand over his bare jaw, and it felt strange. He stared at the mirror. The stranger was gone and Robb McDonald, with a tanned face and a pale chin, looked back at him. There was a mass of fallen black hair around the base of the chair.

"How much do I owe you?"

"A dollar," said Will, starting to sweep up the pile.

Robb handed over the dollar and a small tip, marvelling at the low price. *They'd be charging five to ten dollars for that up north.* "Thanks, Will. It feels good."

Feeling somewhat more civilized, he opened the doors to Granville's Emporium and was amazed at the variety of goods. It was like Cullen's store in Williams Lake but on a much grander scale. There were shelves of bottles and jars of everything imaginable, bins of penny candies, vegetables, bolts of dress material and thread, coal oil lamps, shoes, tools, nails, screws, hinges, horse harness, dog collars, combs, brushes and more. Men's clothing was at the back. Women's clothing took up a whole other section closer to the front. Robb wondered if any of Jane's skirts were on the rack.

"May I help you?" asked one of the clerks.

"I need a new shirt, trousers and a suit," said Robb.

He was escorted to the back of the store, which boasted a change room and a full-length mirror. He tried on his usual-sized shirt and found it didn't fit, as his arms had muscled up considerably. The trousers, on the other hand, were too big around the waist and hips. Robb was in the process of trying on a smaller pair when he heard a familiar, yet strident female voice. *It's Emma!* He listened intently to the conversation, meaning to go out to see her, but the tone was so imperial, he hesitated.

"How can I possibly wear my new gown to the social if you don't have the proper ribbon to go with it? she asked in a determined whine.

"Could you not use one of these other coloured ribbons? The colour is quite similar," asked the manager politely.

"Absolutely not, that's completely unacceptable," Emma declared and slammed the door as she left, sending the little bell on the door into a tinkling frenzy.

Robb looked in time to catch sight of her indignant figure marching down the street. He was shocked by her behaviour. He overheard the manager speaking to the clerk.

"That woman is the bane of my existence. She's as demanding as her mother. Even her maid is rude. There's always a litany of complaints, never a thank you. If her father wasn't so well off, I'd throw her out of this store," he said, not realizing Robb had been listening.

That's not the Emma I know. What on earth was going on?

The clerk took all his measurements and marked the alterations with chalk on the pale-gray suit material with a fine pinstripe. "It should be ready in two days time, Mr. …"

"McDonald, Robb McDonald. I'll stop in Wednesday afternoon, if that's convenient," he said, paying the whopping sum of five dollars for the shirt and trousers, still shaking his head over the profit the northern store owners were making on the miners.

* * *

He noticed many new shops, including Lester & Gibbs Mercantile. The store at the corner of Michigan and Menzies looked to be prospering. He remembered that in 1858 a large group of black people, some freed slaves from the United States but pro-British, were given permission by Sir James Douglas to stay in Canada, causing much controversy. Peter Lester and Mifflin Gibbs owned the store. Many other blacks had followed, settling in Victoria and Salt Spring Island. Robb could see a steady flow of customers going in. He made a mental note to get another pair of work boots, as his old ones had worn out. The owners were well known for the excellence of their handmade footwear.

Neither the street nor his parents' house had changed. With his rifle in one hand and his backpack in the other, he took the steps two at a time and opened the front door.

Jane saw him first, squealed and dropped a plate. His mother spun around and stood there for a split second before launching herself at him with her arms wide open. He dropped his rifle on the table and the backpack fell to the floor as he was buried alive in their welcome. His mum was crying so hard he could feel his shirt getting wet.

Before he knew it, he was sitting at the table sipping tea from a dainty china cup and eating home-made biscuits. It still felt strange. Not ten minutes had passed when the door opened and Emily came in carrying a basket of tomatoes and squash. Flinging it on the table, she pounced on Robb. He barely had time to stand up. Disentangling himself from his younger sibling, he held her at arm's length. "Good Lord, you're growing up too. You're not a child anymore. I can see I'm going to be spending my time fending off suitors," he said.

She blushed. "Don't be silly, Robb, I'm only fourteen."

"You look a whole lot older than fourteen, my girl," he said.

He offered to help in the kitchen, but his mother booted him out. "This is women's work."

"For the last six months I've been doing for myself, cooking powder biscuits and meat in my gold pan."

They looked at him as if the idea was inconceivable.

As the girls prepared the table for supper and the arrival of their father, Robb went up to his old room. It was exactly as he had left it. He checked his supply of pants and shirts. Only a couple were going to fit him. The old suit looked distinctly dull and drab. He was glad he had ordered a new one. He was also glad he'd found socks without holes and his dress boots still fit him.

He heard his father come in and with some trepidation headed downstairs to meet him. He wasn't sure what kind of reception he was going to get.

Chapter 27

William McDonald opened the door and was immediately engulfed by the three women of his household, all talking at once, their faces wreathed in smiles. He gathered from their excited outburst that his wandering youngest son had returned home.

He removed his jacket and hung it on the hook, unsure of what to expect, and tried to maintain his composure. Hearing the footsteps on the staircase, he turned and watched Robb descend the stairs. The young man looked like the old Robb, yet somehow he was different. There was a watchfulness and a wary confidence that was a bit perplexing. A boy had left home, but a man had returned.

The room was silent; the women watched as the two men put their arms around each other and stood for a few moments, not speaking. William was quite aware that he was not usually an emotional man. His wife on occasion had accused him of being "cold" but here was his son safely home. He tried to control the tremble, and Robb's arms were tight around him.

"Father, I'm glad to be back," Robb said very quietly.

William had never been one to overtly express himself. He loved the lad dearly but showing it wasn't his way. All he managed was, "Thank God you're home." Then the two men parted, held each other at arms' length and took a good look at each other. Robb saw that his father had aged considerably. His hair looked grayer than Robb remembered and the wrinkles on his face were now deep creases. He also saw that his father was in turmoil. *Have I disappointed him?*

Supper was spent catching up on the news in Victoria. Robb just sat there listening, enjoying the food and watching his family. Jane was blossoming into womanhood, not a raving beauty but a handsome woman with clear skin, glossy long dark-brown hair tumbling in waves to her shoulders and a lovely smile. *No wonder Billy Robertson is enchanted.* Emily was changing too. The little girl had gone, but there were moments when the child still came through. She had a happy, playful personality.

"Well, Robb, now that you're back, what are you planning?" his father asked.

"I will be going back north at the end of March. There's at least one more season to work the claim, but after that, I'm not sure. I own one-fifth of it. Henry sold out and has gone back to San Francisco. I met a man named Peter Dunlevey. He's a real canny businessman and he's planning on opening up some general stores. I could run one of those. On the other hand, my partner Bill and I could run a ranch, raising beef to supply the miners. Land is cheap up there. There are great opportunities, but at the moment it's a wild and dangerous place to be."

"So you're not going to stay in Victoria?" his mother asked.

"Mum, there's far more opportunity to make money up there," said Robb.

The family went quiet at that statement.

"Has Edna had the baby yet?" he asked to break the silence.

"No, she's due any day now. You got back just in time to be an uncle again," said Jane. "Matt probably won't leave her alone right now. We go over during the day when he's at work."

"Are Matt and James working at the store with you, Father?" Robb asked.

His father nodded. "Yes, they are. Victoria's grown. We've had probably fifty new houses built, lots of new folks from the east, mostly the prairies but some from Upper Canada. The store is even busier, even with the Granville as competition. We seem to be out of the fur trading business. Haven't seen any Songhees since you left. The permit office is closed 'til spring."

"There's gold up near Quesnel so I expect you'll still have miners coming in the spring," said Robb. "The Williams Lake area is very active. I don't see an end to the gold rush anytime soon. The Royal Engineers have the road widened up to Cache Creek and settlers are coming in but it's very rough right now. I've heard Sir James intends to extend the road right up to Quesnel and possibly up to Prince George."

The women cleared the dishes while Robb and his father sat in the parlour. Robb showed him the Henry rifle.

William took the rifle and thoroughly examined it as Robb explained how it worked.

"So, there's no point in me ordering muskets anymore for the Bay, just powder and balls for the existing stock. How much did that set you back?"

"Cullen wanted thirty-five dollars but I got it for twenty-five," said Robb.

His father chuckled and handed it back to Robb.

"It saved my life once when I was attacked by a grizzly," said Robb. "If I hadn't had a repeating rifle, that bear would have killed me. There was no time to reload."

His father just looked at him, shaking his head and wondering why the lad would expose himself to such danger. "Was it worth the risks financially?"

"Yes, despite the rough conditions, I've done okay. You have to watch your back all the time and be prepared to defend yourself. Murder is commonplace. I was very careful not to spend money in the saloons either." His father seemed to accept his answers.

Dishes finished, the women came in and sat down.

"So Jane, have you and Billy set a date for the wedding?" Robb asked.

"No, not yet. If you're planning on going back north by the end of March, maybe we should get married before you go. I'd really like you to be there. We've got our eye on a building lot about fifteen minutes from here, but Billy has to raise the money for it."

Later, Robb was in bed wide awake. He felt like a stranger to his family, and his experiences were so far removed from their world that he felt out of place. *If it's difficult for them to comprehend, how am I going to deal with Emma?* He desperately wanted to talk to her but couldn't just go to her house with her being engaged to Jackson. That would have been considered a severe breach of etiquette. He knew he would see her at the social Saturday and at church on Sunday. In the meantime, he had to keep busy and make some money.

Chapter 28

Right after breakfast Robb went out to the woodshed and split and stacked half a cord of wood. It was overcast and the air hung damp and heavy. His mum called him in for tea about ten o'clock. Jane and Emily had gone over to Matt's to stay with Edna. He decided to take a walk to the Bay store to say hello to his brothers. He met people on the street he hadn't seen for a while and chatted with them.

The new Hudson Bay store was a definite improvement over the old one. Like the Granville, it was big and well stocked with all the usual items. He could see his father, Matt and James serving customers. The ship in the harbour had been unloading supplies, and he could see Billy Robertson in the back room moving bags of flour, sugar and beans from the wagon to the storage area. *That would have been me if I had stayed.*

Robb slipped into the storage room to speak to Billy

"You're back! Jane's been talking about you coming home for the last month. Good to see you," said Billy with a big grin on his face.

"You too. Jane was telling me you're interested in a building lot on the outskirts of town. Where is it?"

"If you take the road to Finlayson Point, there are six lots right along the east side of the road. The survey stakes are already in," he replied.

"Who owns the land now?"

"Mr. Freeland."

"How much is he asking for them? What's the lot size?" asked Robb with a new thought flying around in his head. If he bought the lot and sold it to Billy over time, he would have a legitimate excuse to see Freeland and prove things were different now.

"Fifty dollars each. They are fifty feet by one hundred and fifty feet. The water supply in the area is good, so I don't anticipate any problem putting in a well. I just have to save the money to buy a lot before they get grabbed up or the price goes higher."

"Let me look into it. Okay? I'd better let you get back to work or Father will be after me. See you Friday night," said Robb with a hopeful spring in his step.

He caught Matt in between customers. They shook hands over the counter.

"Robb, I'm glad to see you back. I'll come over when I can. Edna's due any time. The midwife was in to see her before I left this morning; Edna had been having a few cramps."

Another customer came to the counter, so Robb excused himself and said a quick hello to James. His brothers hadn't changed one bit. His father acknowledged him with a raised eyebrow.

"Father, I won't hold up your business, so I'll talk to you later."

Robb walked down the road at a brisk pace, looking at the new homes that had gone up. A couple were frame construction but most of them were log cabins. There was a work crew busy on one opposite Lot 2, so he stopped to talk with them.

"Hello, I'm Robb McDonald. I'm interested in buying a lot around here. What's the water supply like?" he asked.

"Pleased to meet you; I'm Howard Brown. We put the well down about twenty feet and now the water's only six feet from the top. It's good water too, no salt," the man replied. "This will be a two-storey house. I need more room with four children."

"I see you've got a cellar under the house. How deep was the soil?" asked Robb.

"We got down about six feet. Saved all the stones. My dad's a stone mason, so he put really good foundation walls in for me. We'll be able to store a lot of vegetables down there."

Robb watched Howard squaring up a wooden beam with his adze, then walked across the road to look at the lots. The surveyor's stakes were obvious on all six of them. The lots were densely wooded with pine, some hillier or rockier than others. He walked the first one, which was relatively flat, but the back portion had a rocky hill. The second one was flatter, with a tiny stream in the back corner. The rest of them were pretty level but the last one was boggy. *There will be drainage problems with that one,* he thought. He stood there trying to imagine the lots with the trees cut down, a log cabin perched in the middle and a large vegetable garden out back. He decided #2 and #3 were his best options, if Jane and Billy were agreeable. Jane could have one and Emily the other. The thought also crossed his mind that it might be a good idea if he bought #4 as well, just in case he needed it himself. *It would be a good investment; he could always sell it later if he didn't need it. Land prices were rising quickly in Victoria.*

He walked back home with a spring in his step, meeting a couple of guys he'd been to school with. They seemed so young, just boys. He somehow felt older. Then he saw Ivy Marshall rapidly approaching. All the flowers and ribbons on her bonnet were bobbing up and down as she strode along the sidewalk heading directly for him, no doubt on a fact-finding mission. Robb was polite and smiled as he deliberately evaded her questions, telling her as little as possible. He could see her frustration building as she listened with pursed lips and a slight frown on her face as her interrogation failed to elicit answers.

"I only arrived back yesterday afternoon, Mrs. Marshall, so I really haven't had time to decide what I'm doing." With a quick goodbye, he turned and headed home, thankful to leave Ivy behind.

It was chaos again, and Robb quickly learned that Edna had safely delivered a baby boy just after noon. Matt had gone straight home after work to see his new son. The thought of his new nephew raised a new emotion in him. What would it be like to have a child of his own? He had to get a wife first. The constant noise level of everyone chattering was something Robb would have to get used to.

James and his wife Helen came over after supper and Robb enjoyed seeing his brother again. James's children were nearly finished school. James's oldest boy, Jeremy, told Robb he wanted to join the Royal Engineers.

"Jeremy, I've seen them working up on the Cariboo Road, and it's really hard work. They survey the road and the lots beside it and use dynamite to blow up the rock, adjusting the supporting crib work to level the road out and back fill it with dirt. It's a tough job, and they are very good at it. They are supposed to build a bridge over the Fraser near Hell's Gate but I'm darned if I know how they are going to manage that. They act like a police force up there too, settling problems with the miners and the Indians."

He wanted to discuss the building lot with Jane, so he took her aside. "Jane, I saw Billy at the store this afternoon and he told me about the building lot, so I went out and had a look at it. I want to run an idea by you. Billy hasn't got enough money right now to buy it. I'm concerned that the prices will go up shortly and it won't be affordable. What would you and Billy think if I bought the lot for you so you could get started on the house and you paid me back at a dollar a month? That way you'd own it in just over four years."

"Robb, have you got enough money to do that?" she asked.

"Yes, I do, and I was thinking now might be a good time to buy the one beside it, just in case Emily might have a need for it later."

Jane threw her arms around his neck and gave him a hug. "I'll run over to the store in the morning and ask him. I'm sure he'll agree with that idea. So, you did find gold up there. Are you rich?"

"No, I'm not rich, but by the summer I should have enough to start my own place. I have to go back north at the end of March, but I could start cutting down trees and getting your site prepared. I talked to Howard across the road. His father's a stone mason so maybe we could use him to get the foundation done. Does Mr. Freeland have an office in town, or do I have to go to his house?"

"He's got a small office beside the lawyer's office."

"Don't say anything to Mum and Father yet. I want to make sure I complete the deal before I do anything else," said Robb.

There was the ebb and flow of conversations. His mother came out of the kitchen and served a platter of fresh, warm cookies. Eager hands snatched them from the plate before they had a chance to cool. By the time the evening was over and James had gone home, Robb was more than ready to head up to his room, close the door and savour the quiet as the household settled in for the night. He thought about Emma, perplexed by her behaviour in the store, and wondered what had happened to the sweet girl he used to know.

The next morning, he decided to finish chopping the rest of the wood then go to Granville's for his suit-fitting. If he'd heard from Billy by then, he'd go over to Mr. Freeland's office.

His mum was in a fluster getting ready to take a load of baking over to Matt and Edna's. She hurried out the door with a bag brimming with loaves of bread.

"When can I see my nephew?" he asked.

"I think she'll bring him to church on Sunday," she said as she hurried down the walkway.

Chopping wood was a mindless business, but he felt it was important to keep in shape. He couldn't afford to get soft if he had to go back to panning in the spring. It had taken him weeks of carrying a sixty-pound backpack and hiking all day to harden his mind and his body. By the time he had finished chopping and stacking the rest of the cord it was nearly lunchtime. He saw Jane coming down the street toward him.

"Well, what did Billy say?"

"Yes, yes, yes. That will work for us. If you can buy it now, we will pay you the dollar a month until it's paid off," she said.

"Good, that's settled then. I'll get changed and grab a quick bite to eat before I go to Granville's to get fitted for my new suit. I'll stop at the land registry office to see what paperwork I have to do then go to Freeland's office," said Robb.

Jane put a pot of water on to heat and he quickly went upstairs to grab a clean shirt and some trousers.

She was pouring the warm water into the basin when he pulled off his shirt and started to scrub down.

He heard her gasp and when he turned her face had gone ashen. He thought for a moment she was going to faint, so he grabbed one of the dining room chairs and sat her down.

"What's wrong?" he said, kneeling before her, holding her arms.

"Your back ... the scars!" she said, her eyes as big as saucers.

"My back? Oh, that. I had a run-in with a grizzly bear. George and I killed it. Long Baptiste, our guide, took me back to the Indian village and his wife stitched me up. She put all kinds of herbs and stuff on it. It healed well. Hurt like hell at the time. You sit there for a bit. I didn't know it looked so bad," Robb said.

Robb finished cleaning himself up and shaved. By then the colour had come back in Jane's cheeks. She put her arms around him and sobbed like a baby.

"I'm okay, Jane. I really am."

"You haven't mentioned how dangerous things were up north."

"I didn't see any point in worrying you. You couldn't do anything about it," he said, putting on his clean shirt. "Long Baptiste made me a pendant with the bear's claw. I'll show it to you sometime."

"I think you've got a permanent souvenir right now," said Jane. "For heaven's sake, don't show your back to Mum or Emily. You'll give them nightmares."

He hadn't expected that reaction to his injuries. *If his sensible sister was like that, how on earth would the royal Miss Emma Freeland react?*

Chapter 29

Robb looked at himself in the mirror. His new suit fitted him superbly, emphasizing the width of his shoulders and tapering to his slender waist. The clerk made small adjustments to the shoulder seams. Robb was pleased with the light-gray colour, the pinstripe making him look a little taller.

"I'll have these alterations completed by tomorrow," said the clerk.

"That's fine, Ben. I won't need it 'til Saturday. We'll all be going to the social," Robb replied.

Robb's next stop was the land registry office. He explained to the official that he was going to purchase a building lot and wanted to know what paperwork was required to complete the transaction.

"Do I have to put marker posts at the corners, or just leave the surveyor's stakes in place?" he asked. The clerk told him to leave the stakes in place. Armed with that information, he set out for Freeland's office and found it down the side alley, with the lawyer's office fronting Wharf street.

Taking a deep breath to calm himself, he opened the door, setting the small bell ringing. No one was in the office. The desk before him was piled high with maps and papers. A detailed map of Victoria was on the wall, showing all the lots in the town. Curiosity had him looking for his father's house when he heard footsteps coming down the hall. Mr. Freeland walked in.

There was a look of surprise on Freeland's face. "Robb, you're back. What can I do for you?" he said, extending his hand, which Robb shook. "Have a seat."

"You've got some lots available on the Finlayson Point Road, I believe."

"Yes, there are six of them, and they have been surveyed."

"How much are you asking for them?"

"Fifty dollars right now. Are you interested?"

"As you probably know, my sister Jane is going to marry Billy Robertson in the spring, and they want to build a house there. They can't afford the lot yet, but I can. I took a look at the lots yesterday. Since real estate is being grabbed up rather quickly these days, I want to buy lots two, three and four today. I think it will be a good investment."

"You're buying three lots today?" said Freeland, clarifying what he thought he'd heard.

"Yes, I can go to the bank right now and get cash, or a bank draft, if you prefer," said Robb, as if it was an everyday occurrence to spend money like that. He had the satisfaction of seeing the stupefied look on Freeland's face.

"I take it your venture up north was profitable."

"You could say that," replied Robb as casually as he could.

"You go and get the draft and I'll start the paperwork," said Freeland, pulling a sheet of parchment paper from the desk drawer and checking the writing point on his quill pen.

"Alright, I'll go now. I will need a site survey from you and a bill of sale as well. Thank you, I'll be right back." Leaving Freeland looking dumbfounded, Robb headed out the door.

This time, Robb had no trouble getting right in to see Mr. Brockton. *Amazing the difference a shave, clean clothes and money can make.*

"What can I do for you today, Robb?"

"I am purchasing three building lots from Mr. Freeland and will need a one hundred and fifty dollar bank draft to complete the transaction," he said.

Brockton's eyebrows went up. "You're not wasting any time..."

"I've got time over the winter to help Billy Robertson get started on the house. Him and Jane will be getting married in either March or April. I think land is going to get really expensive as this gold rush continues, so it's wise, I think, to invest now."

"Quite so, quite so." Brockton disappeared, reappearing a short time later with the bank draft. Robb left revelling in the feeling of power that the money gave him. He couldn't believe the difference it made in how people treated him.

He returned to Freeland's office and handed the draft over to him.

"Have a seat, Robb. I'm just finishing the site survey here," he said, carefully penning in the dimensions of each lot on the map and showing the relationship to the other lots and the surveyed roadway. Robb noticed that the quill pen was completely steady in his hand. The writing was fine, the letters consistent and well formed, and every line was straight. Robb was impressed. His own writing had never been neat, and sometimes he'd left a blob of ink that had to be blotted.

Laying the pen down, Freeland looked the document over and nodded. Also on the desk was a bill of sale, which Freeland handed him to read. Robb read the document slowly. All the details seemed correct. "Would you have an envelope I can put these in? I don't want them damaged in any way. This is my very first land purchase, so it's special to me." They signed all the documents.

A tiny crinkle of a smile broke Freeland's serious countenance. "I know what you mean, Robb. I can clearly remember my first land purchase. I felt the same way. Will you be going to the social on Saturday?" he asked.

"I think so. It will give me a chance to see everyone again. My dancing hasn't improved any."

The two men laughed and shook hands, and Robb departed for the land registry office hoping all the paperwork was legal and correct.

NUGGETS

* * *

Friday, Robb went to Granville's to pick up his suit and Emily tagged along, using the excuse that she needed to buy some thread to repair her dress. She was telling him all about his new nephew who was "so cute" when Ivy Marshall met them on the street. She looked so upset she was almost unable to speak. It took her a few minutes to calm herself.

"What's the matter, Mrs. Marshall?" asked Emily. Robb stayed silent, not really wanting to get involved.

"I just can't believe the rudeness of that woman. She had the gall to tell me to mind my own business, that what she did and who she did it with was no concern of mine, and that I should stop bothering quality folk and get back to my own kind! Right there in Granville's in front of everybody."

"Who are you talking about?" said Emily.

"Emma Freeland, who else? The stupid little ninny is so puffed up with her own importance. Just because she's engaged to Captain Jackson doesn't give her the right to be so rude. It's not as if she's royalty. Her mother and father are common stock, just like the rest of us. Yes, he's made money on his land, but he was raised in the slums of Toronto before he became a surveyor. Her mother can't even read or write. The nerve of the girl! She's useless; can't bake a pie or sew a dress, has her maid do it for her, and she treats the girl and the rest of us like dirt." Ivy stormed off, still muttering to herself.

They both watched as Ivy disappeared down the street. Emily looked up at Robb. "Sounds like you might be the lucky one, Robb. I wonder if she behaves like that when Captain Jackson's around."

Robb was quiet. This was the second time Emma had upset someone with her bad behaviour. In all his seventeen— no, eighteen years (he'd forgotten his birthday in August) he had never seen Ivy that upset. He found it hard to believe that Emma had changed so much in the six months he'd been away. He decided that he would talk with her on Saturday, but at that particular moment he was certainly not impressed.

He picked up his suit, wondering if Saturday was going to be the one and only time he'd ever wear it. Emily bought her thread and seemed happy just to walk along beside him, chattering like a blue jay.

During the evening meal, Emily told everyone about Ivy. Robb wished she hadn't but kept quiet. What surprised him was everyone's reaction.

All his father said, with a growl, was, "Typical."

His mother just shook her head. "Ever since she's been engaged, she's been getting worse. She's got such grand airs. Now she's got the maid, she doesn't do anything except shop."

"I feel sorry for that girl, having to wait on her hand and foot," said Jane watching for Robb's reaction.

"Has she always been that way?" Robb asked quietly.

"Aye, right from the time they came here when she was twelve. Spoiled rotten," said his father.

Robb lay in bed that night thinking about the experiences he'd had, the people he'd met and the money in his bank account and knew in the long run he was further ahead than if he'd stayed in Victoria. He would never have been able to save enough to build a house as a hired clerk, much the same as Billy was now. It was becoming very clear that Emma would never fit in up north. A brief image of Ann flitted through his mind. But there was still a part of him that desperately wanted Emma.

He spent Friday out on Lot #2 figuring out which trees to take down. He'd leave the perimeter ones and concentrate on taking out the centre ones. Both Jane and Billy had sat at the dining room table the night before drawing a picture of the way they wanted the house set up. It would be a very simple cabin with a kitchen, parlour and two bedrooms, roughly twenty by twenty-four feet. There was room to set the house back a bit so there wouldn't be constant dust from the road. *They have enough space to extend it later if they need to.*

He crossed the road and spoke to Howard, who was atop his ladder hammering a crossbeam in place, a couple of six-inch spikes poking out of his mouth.

"You said your father was a stone mason. I wondered if he would be interested in helping us with the foundation on Lot Two."

"Will you be wanting a cellar, or just a foundation?" Howard asked, after he'd removed the nails so he could talk.

"Just the foundation, I think," replied Robb. "I'm going to mark out roughly where the house is going to go and get the trees cut down. I need to get the well guy in to dowse for the right spot for the well. Then we can decide where the cesspit will go."

"I'll be seeing Dad on Saturday, so I'll tell him and he can get in touch with you," said Howard, putting the nails back between his lips.

By the end of the day Robb had cut down two smaller trees and trimmed off the branches, creating a huge pile of pine brush. It felt good to swing the axe, feel it bite into the trunk, sending woodchips flying. He would have continued but it started to rain again, so he trudged back home, satisfied he'd got that much done. It had also occupied his time, keeping his mind off Emma. Once he had the trees down, Billy could get his brothers to help with the building.

During the meal, William asked Robb what he had done with his day. Robb told him about the tree-cutting and the foundation then started questioning his father about operations at the Bay.

"Father, where does the Bay get all of its supplies from?"

"Originally, supplies were sent out from England, but it took so long for the ships to get here that it wasn't workable even for the traders, let alone their families. We were supposed to send the otter pelts there too, but Japan's a lot closer. With the gold rush, we've been buying most of our supplies from Seattle or San Francisco for foodstuffs and tools. American drovers have been bringing herds of those Spanish cattle up the Colorado from California for a long time now. Until there's a railway through the Rockies, there's no practical way of us getting what we need from the East. Sir James told me it would be a condition for us to join the Province of Canada to have a railway from coast to coast. Upper Canada's got wheat and I'm sure the prairies will grow wheat, but we can't get it without a railway."

Previously, Robb had the impression that the general stores were gouging the miners, but now he considered the extra shipping costs by boat or mule train just to bring in the flour and beans. He realized it probably cost a lot more to stock supplies. He'd never thought about it that way before. He lay in bed that night wondering what skills he'd need to run his own store. Would it simply be easier to run a store for Dunlevey and save his money to build a house?

Robb knew a man who dowsed for water and asked him to come to Lot #2. Robb watched Ken carefully as the man mumbled something under his breath that Robb couldn't hear then walked the property. The rods in his hands acted like pointers, swinging in changing directions with Ken following. Eventually the rods crossed, and Ken stopped. He brought out a pendulum and it spun in circles or back and forth. Robb couldn't make any sense out of it

"Robb, put a stake in right here. I've got water coming to this spot from two directions at about twenty feet down," said Ken.

"Ken, how do you do that and how do you know? If I build up north, I'm going to need to dowse for my own well."

"I ask for clean, potable water, with a year-round supply." He put the rods in Robb's hands. "These ones are willow, but I've seen people use just about anything. Hold them very lightly about a foot apart, parallel to each other."

At first nothing happened, but then as Robb took a step forward the rods started to move on their own. He was so surprised, he dropped them. Ken laughed, picked them up and handed them to Robb again. "It's not witchcraft, but I don't know how it works."

Robb continued to walk as the rods led him all over the garden, and then slowly they started to swing inward.

"Slow down now; wait and see where they cross."

Robb took another step and was mesmerized as the rods crossed. It was right over where Ken had put in the stake. It gave him shivers.

"I ask the pendulum for the depth. A circle is yes, a back and forth is no. Give me the depth of the water in feet. Five feet?" The pendulum swung back and forth. "Ten feet?" The same. "Fifteen feet?" The same. "Twenty feet?" Slowly the direction changed, and the pendulum began to circle.

He looked at Robb's incredulous face. "It also takes some practice. Dig down an extra four or five feet to make sure you're deep enough. You'll want your cesspit on the other side of the property to the well and preferably downhill, so it doesn't contaminate your water supply. Anything will do for a pendulum, even a nail or a stone on a piece of string."

Robb shook his head at the mysterious process. It seemed like hocus pocus, but it worked. He paid Ken, who tipped his hat and left. He looked at the property and could envision the cabin with the well on the higher north end and the cesspit on the south.

Two weeks later the trees had been cleared and the stumps pulled out with borrowed horses. Billy dug the well at the spot marked by Ken's stake, with the help of his brothers. It was brutal work, as the land was rocky. They saved all the stones so Mr. Brown Senior could line the well. Billy dug a hole four feet wide. Eventually it was deep enough that he needed a ladder to get to the bottom, where he filled a bucket with mud and stones that his brothers hauled up with a homemade winch. Finally even the ladder wasn't long enough and he went down from the winch in a rope sling. He hit water at twenty-five feet and emerged in triumph, mud from his hair to his boots, happily confirming Ken's dowsing.

Chapter 30

Robb braced himself for the moment he walked into the hall with the rest of his family. He knew he looked good in his new suit. News that he was home and had become a land owner had gone around town. He could see heads nodding in his direction. The social was in full swing with the sounds of talking, laughter and background music. It seemed like he'd never left. As he expected, his mother joined the women at the tables on one side, his sisters fanned out to meet their friends and his father headed to the bar. Robb went with him to join James and the other men. There were a few faces he didn't recognize.

He ordered a beer and stayed with William, who introduced him to a slightly balding, middle-aged man impeccably dressed in a very expensive suit and starched shirt.

"Robb, this is John Crawford. He owns the new hotel on Douglas Street. John, this is my son Robb. He's just returned from the goldfields."

Robb was aware of his roughened hands on the man's smooth, manicured ones as they shook hands.

"I'm pleased to meet you, Mr. Crawford," said Robb. "You've got quite the undertaking. How many rooms will it have? When do you expect to have it completed?" He'd seen the framework of the building on his walks through town. It had been a beehive of activity, with a large work crew finishing the roof. The first floor had the exterior walls bricked. The second floor was still open to the elements.

"There will be twenty rooms. I've bought the lot next door, so if I need to expand later, there'll be room. I'm hoping to open in the spring. I'm glad the roof is finally on and we can concentrate on the interior. I'm waiting for a shipment of wallpaper from England for the dining room. Have no idea how long that will take. The plasterers will have to come from San Francisco to do the walls and ceilings, but I'm a long way from being ready for that. The first load of windows came in from 'Frisco a couple of days ago, so that's a start. The rain has held us up quite a bit," the man said.

"I take it this will be high-end building catering to higher-class people," said Robb.

"Absolutely," Crawford replied,

"I would suggest you have good security. This gold rush is not going to end any time soon. Every summer you are going to have hundreds of miners in tent town You will need to keep your customers safe," Robb said, thinking of wandering drunks

Crawford looked at him thoughtfully. "William said you'd been to the goldfields. I take it you speak from experience. How was it?"

"Very rough and dirty but so far I've survived it," said Robb. "I can see it could be a profitable place to have a business in supplying the miners, but it's very dangerous up there, generally speaking." He had no knowledge of the hotel business other than Mrs. Hall's house and the saloon. The thought crossed his mind that this was another avenue he could explore for work.

As he moved about the room conversing with various acquaintances, he cast occasional glances around to find Emma. There she was in a bright-pink satin dress full of frills and flounces. He couldn't see room for any more ribbon, regardless of the colour she had been so concerned about. She looked beautiful, but she was talking to a young man who wasn't Jackson. She was fluttering her eyelashes at the man, obviously flirting.

Robb shook his head. He didn't know if she was doing it on purpose to make Robb jealous or annoy him. Right now what he felt was annoyance. He turned and continued his conversation with other businessmen in the room. William and James were still at the bar. James's wife Helen had gone to chat with his mother. James introduced him to John Wood, the man who had replaced Sir James Douglas as head of the Hudson Bay post. Robb had an extensive conversation with the man.

"Are there going to be any new posts built up north?" Robb asked.

"Not that I'm aware of. I've heard that Quesnel is doing a brisk trade right now with more miners heading north. The problem is that it is quite seasonal. At least they still have pelts coming in during the winter. What did you see up there?" Wood questioned.

"I don't think the gold rush is over by any means. There are a lot of men heading up there. Some gold's been found east of Quesnel. By the time the miners get through with a creek, there are no trees and no fur-bearing animals anywhere to be found. Pelts are going to be a scarce commodity."

"Where's your claim?"

"It's up near Williams Lake," said Robb, not wanting to be too specific. "Getting supplies up there will be a lot easier once the Cariboo Road's completed. It's up as far as Cache Creek right now.

Running a general store would be good business but a risky one. You need to own a gun and be prepared to use it. Not a good place for families yet, but settlers are starting to come in. The Natives are moving out as the land is surveyed and ranchers are coming in. Tough country. I'll go back this season, but that's it. After that I'll be looking for work."

"You could apply at Fort Yale. One of the managers will be retiring soon."

Robb brightened and said, "Thank you, I just might do that. Have you heard how Sir James is doing over in New Westminster?"

"He's still involved with finalizing the boundary with the Americans and trying to set things up to join the Province of Canada. Negotiations are slow. Can't see much happening for years yet. He's not far off retirement himself, so I don't know how much he's going to get done," Wood said as he moved away to talk to another party of gentlemen. Robb decided the courier job wasn't what he wanted. Being alone on the trail to who-knew-where to deliver messages didn't appeal to him, knowing the back country the way he did now—even with his improved riding skills. Far too easy to run into trouble alone. He wondered how the circuit-riding ministers ever managed. They were probably safe enough, carrying only bibles and minimal funds.

William had been watching his son conversing with different people. It surprised him that Robb seemed quite comfortable talking to just about anyone, and he was even more surprised that he hadn't gone over to talk to Emma. He fervently hoped Robb had finally gotten over the woman.

Robb returned to the bar and ordered another beer just as Henry Freeland came over. Over his shoulder, Robb spied Emma flirting with another man across the room. *Damn her!*

"Hello, Robb. I see you've started on Lot Two," Freeland said, slapping Robb on the back in a hearty, familiar manner.

"I've made a start but the weather's not cooperating," said Robb, somewhat amused at the camaraderie in contrast to their conversation the previous spring. He opted out of further discussion when the band struck up a waltz and Emily ran over to him.

"Come on, Robb, dance with me, please, please," she said, knowing full well her brother hated to dance.

He looked down at her happy, expectant face and sighed. "Alright, but watch your feet. You know I don't do this well," he said, his right hand on her tiny waist, his left hand leading her in the correct waltz position.

"I know," she said with an impish grin, "but I just won a bet with Amy that I could get you on the dance floor."

Robb knew the basic steps but was not a dancer. Emily had improved since he'd been away and he could feel minor corrections from her as they circled the floor, tiny pressures from her hand on his shoulder if he was leading too close to another couple. He was so engrossed in keeping the tempo and not stepping on her feet that he didn't realize he was in a cluster of dancing couples, including Emma and her partner. The pink satin caught his attention and he found himself beside Emma momentarily. She glanced at him with a coy smile. His concentration broken, he almost stumbled but managed to keep a straight face and ignore her.

He was soon besieged with Emily's friends all wanting their turn on the dance floor. It was when he saw Jane with a huge grin on her face that he finally realized it was a conspiracy concocted by his sisters to keep him occupied. When the band took a break, he bowed out to head to the bar for another beer. He went over to the Robertson's table to talk to Jane and Billy about the house but was intercepted by a determined Emma.

"Robb McDonald, are you avoiding me?" she said, looking directly up at him with those gorgeous blue eyes, her lush lips in a pout.

He was silent for a moment then said, "Yes."

She looked surprised. "Why?"

"Emma, you're engaged. It's not acceptable for you to behave like that, nor is it acceptable for me to interact with you," he said, knowing he had to be very careful how he phrased it.

With a crackle of flounced satin, she spun on her heel, her face bright red, and disappeared down the hall, her back rigid and her blonde ringlets bouncing.

Robb stood there holding his beer, watching her leave. *I've burned my bridges this time.*

Jane came up to him. "What did you say to her?"

"I told her I couldn't dally with an engaged woman. Apparently, she didn't like it," he said and took a sip of his beer, leading Jane back to her table. He tried to be nonchalant, but he didn't feel good about it all. Perversely, he felt a sense of relief. He expected his woman to be attentive to him, not flirt with every man in the place. Had he become more acceptable because he had money? If so, that was a pitfall of wealth he hadn't expected. *Was she just a common gold digger?*

Jane burst out laughing. "Thank God you've finally come to your senses. It's about time someone put that bitch in her place."

"Jane! I won't have her called that, even if she's behaved badly. You'd be bringing yourself down to her level of pettiness," said Robb. "Let's change the subject and talk about your house." They sat at the table with Billy's family, sorting out the details. Robb explained that Billy could put the well in now, telling them all about Ken's dowsing and his attempt to do the same.

While they were talking, an older man came over to join them and introduced himself as George Brown, Howard's father.

Robb shook his hand and introduced him to the Robertsons. "Mr. Brown is a stone mason and has just put in the cellar in his son's new house across the road from Lot Two. You can explain to him what you want for the foundation," said Robb, noticing the Freeland family leaving, their daughter with them.

* * *

Sunday morning dawned overcast with occasional breaks in the clouds. When they got to the church, Matt and Edna were already sitting in their pew amid the gaggle of children, cradling their newest child in a white blanket of pure, fine wool. James and his brood were in the pew behind. Robb immediately went over to see the new baby. He was very fond of all his nieces and nephews. He looked down at the child. He put his arms out and Edna cautiously handed the baby to him. The child was featherweight; the tiny face, with a thick mop of black hair framed by the bonnet, looked up at him with wide brown eyes, quite content. The little fingers that gripped his were unbelievably pink and tiny. It amazed him. "Have you picked a name yet?"

"Yes, he'll be Michael William," said Matt with pride. Robb wanted children of his own in the future, but he needed to find a good woman to be his wife. He carefully passed the baby over to his mother, or "Nana" as the children called her, and watched the expression on her face. The love and tenderness were priceless. It reminded him of the Indian women in Long Baptiste's camp.

Everyone got settled in the pew as more parishioners filed in, and finally the minister came in and began the service. Robb cast a quick glance at the Freeland's pew but the family never turned their heads towards him. They seemed pretty tight-lipped, not talking to anyone.

After the service, Matt and Edna stayed to discuss the baptism with Reverend Cridge. Robb was waiting outside when he was jostled. It was Henry Freeland, looking like thunder, his face contorted and red.

"I want to talk to you right now," he said, grabbing Robb by the elbow and shoving him aside.

"What did you say to my daughter to upset her so last night?" he demanded, poking his finger into Robb's chest.

It took all Robb had not to punch the man. "Mr. Freeland, I have accepted the fact that Emma is engaged to Captain Jackson, and I intend to honour that. It's the reason I left Victoria in the spring. She's the one who approached me last night and started to flirt. I told her it was inappropriate and did my best to ignore her. I told her I wasn't interested. What else could I have done? I hope Jackson never hears of this or he could cancel the engagement. This isn't easy for me either, giving up the woman I wanted. I am quite aware I don't have the social standing required."

Freeland stood there with his mouth open then shut it, obviously considering what Robb had said, his thick eyebrows knotted in concentration. Some of the tension in his shoulders subsided. There was silence that extended to a minute as the two men stood toe-to-toe. Robb never broke eye contact.

Finally, Freeland nodded. "I understand, Robb. I need to talk with my wife and daughter. You are going back north in the spring, aren't you?" he said with emphasis on the last two words. Acknowledging Robb's nod as affirmative, he turned and walked away, deep in thought.

I think I just dodged a bullet, Robb thought as Freeland walked off. *If I hadn't handled that right, he'd have created hell in devious ways against me and my family. He's got the reputation of retaliating; all he has to do is talk to his cronies and maybe Billy or my brothers wouldn't get a promotion. That bit at the end was definitely a threat and I can't endanger any one.* His tension eased and he let out a sigh of relief as he joined his parents and siblings on the path home.

William had watched the encounter very carefully. It surprised him that Robb had held his temper. Although he couldn't hear the conversation between the two men, their expressions had given much away. He saw the fierce rigidity of Freeland's anger and Robb's measured response. Freeland had listened, the anger slowly ebbing to some level of comprehension. Robb's explanation must have been carefully couched, almost pleading for understanding, and it seemed to have worked. His son was proving to be a formidable man. He wondered what had happened up north to create that change, never comprehending his own influence on Robb.

* * *

The next day, Robb went into the Bay post and arranged an appointment with John Wood.

"Good morning, Robb, have a seat. What can I do for you?" Wood asked.

"Mr. Wood, I've thought about our discussion Saturday at the social and I would like to get some experience in the management side of running a Bay post. Is there any possibility I could work with my father and yourself while I'm here this winter? I'd be happy even getting a couple of days a week. I know it's your slow season. I worked three years with my father, grading pelts and filling orders. I worked with the Songhees quite a bit, though I understand they've been decimated by the measles outbreak. If I want to be a contender for a job at Yale or Quesnel, I need to know a lot more about ordering supplies, legal matters, accounting, wages and management of employees, that sort of thing."

Wood sat there contemplating his request. "I think we can accommodate that request. You realize I can only offer you a dollar a day at this point."

"Yes, sir. What sort of wages does a manager make?"

"Generally, two dollars a day depending on years of experience."

"Good. When would you like me to start?"

"Is tomorrow soon enough for you?" Woods asked with a smile on his face. "I see you are a man who likes to stay busy."

"When I'm not working for you, I can help my future brother-in-law build his house. I'll be cutting trees for the next few weeks." The pair shook hands and Robb went home to change into his working clothes. It looked like the rain would hold off for a while.

So it was that Robb spent the winter working in the store, learning everything he could and humbly taking home his ten dollars-a-month income. As little as it was, it meant he didn't have to dip into his bank account. It amazed him now that people could live on a dollar a day and support their families. His respect for his frugal father grew accordingly. His requirements were very few and he settled back into town life, buying flour and other food stuffs for his room and board. Being at the Bay also gave him the opportunity to meet a lot of the locals again and feel part of the community.

He spent hours with his father, studiously going over the huge ledgers of figures, and forced himself to improve his writing so the numbers and entries were legible. He became familiar with all the suppliers and how to place orders and make payments. He tallied the monthly totals and investigated any discrepancies. He made deposits at the bank. He read the Day's directives for hiring and firing employees as well as the formidable list of protocols and behaviours required of employees. Robb couldn't believe how patient his father was in teaching him. He had never before had the opportunity to spend that much time with him.

Occasionally Robb worked with John Wood, especially if he was entertaining visiting dignitaries or other Bay managers, such as the ones from Langley and Yale. Learning to speak with important people was a social necessity and sometimes a delicate political balancing act. It was an art that took time to develop. It took him a while to understand the power that important, rich people had and how they could use it to influence others in business and politics. Freeland had been an example for him. *I'm grateful to meet these people too. Whether I work for the Bay up north, work for Dunlevey or have my own store, I will need these contacts and skills. I also need to understand how businesses work in specific areas. The requirements up north are quite different from here. There's the weather, few roads, difficulty getting supplies in, no police force and a lot of dangerous miners on the road.*

The Bay had agreed to let James switch positions with his father and William was going to work at the licencing office since he was having difficulty lifting the full bags of flour. James was engaged in much the same preparation as Robb, and it gave Robb an opportunity to work closely with the brother eight years his senior. His oldest brother, Henry, who was working in Alberta, was totally unknown to him. He had never met him and only knew of him from the letters that arrived monthly for his father.

He saw Emma on the street and at the socials. Her father must have spoken to her as she never looked his way and ignored him at the dances. He was immensely grateful for that. It somehow made his loss more bearable. From gossip he'd heard she was still rude to people at Granville's and snubbed his sisters altogether. Yet there was a residual longing in him for her that hadn't quite gone away. There were plenty of young girls, mostly friends of Emily, who pursued him, but he found them mere children. There was a void there he couldn't fill.

Christmas came and went in a flurry of dinners, presents and church activities that gave him an opportunity to play with the children and become part of his family in a way he never had before. There was no longer that feeling of being a stranger.

By the end of January, the roof was on Jane and Billy's house. The log structure stood small and sturdy on its stone foundation in the middle of the lot, awaiting the arrival of the carpenter to make and install the windows. Across the road, Howard's house was finished and hummed with four active, young children. Howard gave Robb and Billy many practical suggestions. He was a good neighbour. By then, Mr. Brown Senior had finished lining the well with rocks and capped the top with planks. The hand pump was installed with due ceremony as Billy started to pump the handle, producing a flow of clear water. The following week they dug the hole for the cesspit and covered it with planks and dirt. It occurred to Rob that a cesspit was a good idea in the town when you had neighbours, but out in the country an outhouse would work just as well. Now it was a matter for Billy and Jane to build cupboards, get furniture and put in the fireplace and chimney.

The wedding date had been set for March 27. Mary, Jane and Emily were busy sewing curtains and their dresses. Robb figured his new suit was good for the occasion and his dress boots were in excellent condition. He penned a letter to George, bringing him up to date on his time at home, and established that he would be leaving Victoria immediately after the wedding, probably arriving back in Williams Lake mid-April if the ice was out on the northern routes. He posted the letter at the Bay.

On one particularly sunny day when there was little wind and the horizon was clear, Robb decided to take a day off and go out in his canoe, destination View Royal. Several hours of paddling brought him into the trading post. He'd forgotten how much he enjoyed being out on the water, and he noticed the progress some of the settlers had made on their shoreline properties since the previous spring. He also noted that there were only a few Esquimalt canoes at the dock. Jim and Harold had a couple of customers but were pleased to see him. Robb could see that the pelts on the counter were in good condition.

"We heard you'd gone off to the goldfields. Are you back working at the Bay?" asked Jim.

"No, I'm just here until the beginning of April, then I'm heading back north."

"It's quiet here," said Harold. "The measles just about wiped out the Songhees. Only a few were left so they moved across the bay and joined the Esquimalt. Long Feather and his sister survived. We don't see them much. We're still getting a fair number of pelts but it's not as busy as it used to be. There's more business now in food staples and farming tools."

Robb chatted for another hour over a cup of tea then started the paddle back to Victoria. He felt a sadness at the loss of the Native people. He couldn't imagine a disease wiping out a whole tribe, although in history class at school, he'd heard about the plagues in Europe. The Songhees had been so strong and vigorous, and so well adapted to the land, that it didn't seem possible. Images of Whalecatcher in the big canoe flitted through his mind. He thought about Long Baptiste and his family and wondered what would happen to them once the settlers moved in and displaced them.

He got back late to find the girls all excited. Apparently, Captain Jackson had arrived that morning for a brief visit. At that point, Robb didn't much care. His mum had saved him some stew and reheated it. After all that paddling, he was both tired and hungry. Sleep came easily.

* * *

Thanks to Ivy's grapevine, news spread that Captain Jackson would be residing in New Westminster on property his father owned. Emma's wedding was being planned for some time in September in Victoria. Ivy's comment had been, "Good riddance."

Robb was relieved. With Emma living across the strait, it would decrease the tensions in his family, whether he was there or not. Henry Freeland would no longer be a threat if Robb wanted to return to Victoria. He wondered how much time Jackson would be away during the spring and summer working on the Cariboo Wagon Road. Robb couldn't imagine Jackson tolerating Emma's bad behaviour. *I'll bet she's going to have some difficulty adjusting to life away from her parents under Jackson's thumb. He'd be foolish to let her get away with any nonsense, and he'd need to curb her spending. In many ways, I should be grateful to the man.*

By the beginning of March, Billy was living in the cabin. He had dutifully paid Robb his dollar on the first of the month. Robb was impressed with the place. Although it was small, it was bright and airy. All the logs had been well chinked, and it held the heat of the fire. Mr. Brown had built the fireplace with a beautiful wooden mantel. Robb had thought long and hard about a wedding gift, wondering if brass candlesticks would do, but he finally decided that the very best thing would be to give them the lot, forgiving the debt. He went down to the land registry office and transferred the deed into Billy's name, effective March 27.

Billy's brothers had helped him with the carpentry work for the long plank table and chairs, as well as the beds and dressers. The big front window faced the road, letting in a lot of light. Billy had positioned the dry sink in front of it so anyone standing at the counter could see the road traffic. The indoor toilet was a definite advantage, provided they could contain the smells. The handmade curtains and embroidered tablecloth gave the cabin a real homey look. His mum had hooked a rug that lay on the wooden floor just in front of the fireplace.

Robb took his work boots in to Lester & Gibbs Mercantile to see if they could be repaired. Peter Lester looked them over and nodded. "These have seen hard use, but I can repair them and put in new insoles."

"Good. My backpack needs to have the straps re-stitched and my leather jacket needs to be properly repaired. Would you be able to do that too?"

Lester's smooth, dark hands ran over the leather. "I'll have to replace this strap. How did you tear your jacket?" he asked, holding up the leather jacket with the one-and-a-half-foot tear down the back.

"I had an encounter with a grizzly."

The man just looked at him and shook his head. "Yes, I can re-stitch it properly. Are you going back there?"

"Yes. I will need everything by the end of the month. I'm just going to look around for the other things I need." Robb picked out another pair of trousers, two new shirts, socks, more gloves, a couple more toothbrushes, ammunition for the Henry, a new knife, rope and another tarp. The prices were right and the quality good. He rolled everything up in his tarp and headed back home.

The sight of him getting all his gear together had his mum in a tizzy. "I just hate the idea of you going back north," she said, giving him a hug.

"I know you do, Mum. Maybe I'll find a nice girl up there." He thought about Ann and wondered if she liked him enough to marry him ... or maybe it was just too soon after Emma to even consider the idea. Part of him wondered why O'Connor hadn't made a move, considering he lived in the same house. That idea irked him.

"That would be nice, Robb, if you could find a good woman and settle down," she said with a teary smile.

While they were sitting near the fire after supper that night, his father casually mentioned that Robb should probably make a will now that he owned property and had a bank account.

"Father, do I really need to do that? I'm only eighteen."

"What would happen to your property if you got killed up north? Who gets your money and the two building lots?" came the gruff reply.

"Guess I've never thought about it. You're right. I'll see Wilbur this week." He mulled over his options and decided to leave everything to his father, with the stipulation that Lot #3 would go to Emily when she married, and Lot #4 plus the bank account would be divvied up equally between his brothers and father.

The only other things he needed to do were renew his miner's licence and take a hundred dollars out of his bank account for the trip back. Robb was the first one in line when the office opened. Now miners were coming in on every ferry, their tents starting to fill the square that had been empty all winter. Once again, the church women were setting up the booth to feed them.

Chapter 31

March 27 dawned slightly overcast but dry with a light breeze; a good day for a wedding. After a quick breakfast, Robb shaved, reminding himself it would be the last time he'd be shaving for the foreseeable future. His mum had pressed his shirt. He finally got the cravat tie knotted properly, finding the collar scratchy on his neck. He looked at himself in the long mirror and was pleased with the results. By the end of the week, he'd be sleeping on the deck of the *Enterprise* looking like a pauper again. He took himself off to Matt's house to escape the chaos of his mum and sisters getting into their wedding finery, only to find it equally chaotic as Edna tried to dress the children.

Finally, it was time. They walked to the church, joining the rest of the family. Robb was in charge of holding his nephew's hand and stopping him from jumping in mud puddles. The child was deceptively cute and innocent in his little blue suit, his hair still damp and flat from his mum brushing it, but in reality, the boy reminded Robb of himself, always up to no good and full of mischief. James and Helen were already in the church plus most of their neighbours, including Ivy (of course) and the Robertsons. Robb noted that the Freelands were noticeably absent, which was a relief.

Billy was at the front looking solemn and a bit overwhelmed until Jane walked in, and then Robb watched his eyes light up. The looks that passed between the couple clearly showed the feelings they shared. His sister looked beautiful as she walked down the aisle beside her father with her dark-brown hair pulled back to a chignon at the back of her neck and a headband of white flowers. She had obviously copied the pattern for her long dress from pictures of Queen Victoria in the newspaper, with the high neckline sloping down the shoulders to large, full-length sleeves and a fitted bodice. Jane was a skilled seamstress and had changed the pattern of the skirt from the hooplike Victoria style to a slimmer, more flowing one. He knew she'd agonized over the material, with satin far too costly, and had selected a polished cotton in a grayed tone of blue trimmed with lace around the collar and cuffs. She'd put hours into sewing that dress and he was impressed. It was classic yet practical and would serve well for other occasions.

Emily was behind her in a pale peach-coloured version of the same design, her hair swept up either side with clips holding the ringlets behind her ears. Robb started to choke up. His little sisters were growing up so fast. *Dear lord, I'm going to miss them.* He looked up to see his father standing proudly watching them with a smile on his face.

Reverend Cridge performed the ceremony. Billy slipped a plain gold ring on Jane's finger, and a murmur of approval hummed through the crowd. Unlike the Sunday service, the ceremony was blissfully short then everyone gathered afterwards in the church hall for refreshments. The couple were well known in the community and were presented with many small gifts. Robb handed his envelope containing the deed to Lot #2 to Billy, but Billy was so busy he just tucked it in his pocket.

Robb made the rounds and said goodbye to John Wood and the others who had been so helpful to him over the winter. He knew he had gained considerable knowledge on the business end of things that could only benefit him later in his own ventures.

As darkness started to fall, Billy and Jane headed off for their first night as Mr. and Mrs. Robertson in their little log house. John Wood had offered his carriage, now loaded with presents, and drove the pair home with good wishes flooding in from all sides. It had been the perfect evening.

Sunday, they all met at church, this time with Billy and Jane sitting in his family pew but grinning from ear to ear. Jane came over and kissed Robb on the cheek. "We don't know how to thank you. We weren't expecting you to give us the lot. We were so happy just to get the house built. I really don't know what to say," she said, clasping his hands.

"Just be happy and have a good life," Robb said, looking down at her shining face. Looking at Billy, Robb said, "I'll be leaving on Tuesday to go back north. You make sure you take good care of her, do you hear me?"

Monday, William just sat in front of the fireplace in deep concentration. He was so used to working that he was having difficulty getting used to retirement. To get out of the house and the constant chatter of the women, every morning after breakfast he would go for his morning walk, meet other old men in town and they'd sit and talk for hours.

Robb found the house strangely quiet without Jane. Both Emily and his mum seemed to be at loose ends now that all the excitement of the wedding was over. Emily headed over to Matt's house to help Edna with the children.

Robb spent the morning sorting his clothes and checking his pack. He tucked his money in a waterproof pouch and stashed it at the bottom of the bag. He found his pendant and strung it around his neck, the bear's claw looking menacing. His good suit now hung in the closet along with his good shirts. He polished his dress boots before putting them away. Peter Lester had done an excellent job of repairing both his work boots and his jacket. Both were now serviceable and would last the season. The stitching was incredibly fine.

He didn't shave that morning and could feel the dark stubble on his chin. He put on his miner clothes; at least they were clean and not smelly yet. The boots felt good. The extra insoles would make them a lot more comfortable. He picked up the Henry and a box of ammo and headed to the old fort to get some target practice. He hadn't fired the gun since he'd been back. He'd picked up a carrying strap for it too, so he could sling it across his back and leave his hands free. He hadn't lost his touch and hit the bullseye on several occasions.

When Robb got back home, his mum had prepared a bag of flour, a bag of beans, tea, a fresh loaf of bread and sliced roast beef for him to take. *I don't have to steal it this time.* A dozen fresh loaves of bread were sitting on the counter. She had obviously been baking all day for the miner's tent where she was due the following morning.

"Thanks, Mum," he said quietly, giving her a long hug. Emily joined them and he held them for a long time.

When his father returned home, Robb handed him an envelope. "Father, I'd like you to keep this in a safe place. Wilbur made out my will just in case something happens to me up there."

William looked at him and gravely accepted it.

After supper, Robb went up to his room and lay on the bed, dozing off occasionally. He awoke around four and went downstairs. To his surprise, his father was still dressed and was waiting for him. Robb gathered up all his gear, strapped on his knife, tied the tarp in place, and the pair of them walked out of the house towards the dock. As Robb had expected, there was a short lineup of maybe fifty miners waiting to go aboard. Robb took his place; there was no fighting or shoving this time.

William stood beside his son and just watched. He looked at the waiting men, seeing the scruffy, the toothless and the dishevelled. Other than the fact that Robb was clean-shaven, he didn't stand out from the rest of the crowd. William realized that anonymity was Robb's protection; his way to not stand out, not appear affluent. He knew there were things that Robb hadn't told him, how desperate and violent these men could be. He was genuinely afraid of his son not returning.

Promptly at five o'clock, the *Eliza* came to life as the lights came on and smoke started to belch out of the funnel. As soon as the gangplank dropped, the men moved forward, giving Captain Hustler their five-dollar fare. Prices had gone up. Robb and his father had a long and silent hug, then Robb boarded. At seven o'clock, *Eliza* pulled away, and Robb waved for the last time to the small receding figure standing on the deserted dock. It was so different from when he'd left the last time, and perhaps this time was harder.

Chapter 32

The trip to Fort Langley was uneventful. Robb sat under the deck overhang and watched the scenery and his fellow passengers. The islands they passed in the San Juan strait were likely going to be ceded to the Americans. He saw the same eager desperation on the faces of the miners and wondered how many of them would actually find gold. He mentally filed the faces in his memory. He might meet some of them again. Most of them were 49'ers, but the younger ones were escaping the possibility of civil war south of the border. There was no doubt in his mind that more gold would be found east of Quesnel and the flood of foreigners would continue.

A few slices of roast beef between two thick slices of his mum's bread provided him a substantial lunch. Looking at the snow-capped mountains brought back memories of walking the trail. At least this time he wouldn't be walking from Yale to Williams Lake. The stagecoach should be running, shortening travel time from eight weeks to roughly two.

He looked forward to seeing George, Melvin, James and Bill again, but he wasn't looking forward to the backbreaking work of panning and living rough.

The *Eliza* docked at Fort Langley just as the sun was setting. The *Enterprise* was already in dock. Robb joined the *Enterprise* lineup, where a lot of men were waiting; more than had been on the *Eliza*. He figured from their accents that a significant number had walked up through the northern states. He put up his tarp against the persistent rain and sat down to finish off another sandwich. He didn't bother to light a fire that night but lay down on the hard, lumpy ground and used his pack as a pillow. Even fully dressed and wrapped in his blanket, he couldn't keep the dampness out, although it seemed a bit warmer than on the coast. He cursed himself for getting soft over the winter.

It was barely daylight when Captain Wright permitted boarding. The deck was not completely full, so Robb was able to secure a good spot. The current was so fierce that the *Enterprise* had to fight her way north, the engines barely making progress. Robb had to assume there had been heavy snows up in the mountains that were now melting into the spring flood. He was thankful when they docked safely in Fort Yale.

He immediately checked in at the stagecoach office and found out he'd have a two-day wait before the stage came in. He bought his ticket. "Is there somewhere cheap where I can stay?" he asked.

"Sure, there's a boarding house at the end of the block," the old-timer said.

He found the place with no problem. An older, rather scruffy couple ran it. Robb spent the next two nights there. It wasn't anywhere near as clean as Mrs. Hall's and the cooking wasn't as good, but the price was right. He hoped he wouldn't be taking any unwanted bugs with him. He used up the last of the bread and beef. He'd be back to powder biscuits soon enough.

Thankfully, the stage came from the north into Barnard's Express depot on schedule. Robb immediately recognized Garnet, Wayne, Ben and Howard, who still looked lethal. He tipped his hat to them as he boarded. They acknowledged him with the briefest of nods. There was no sign of Mr. Brown or Mr. Smith, but the other passenger looked of much the same cut. Robb propped his rifle on the seat and since no other passengers boarded, he placed his pack on the seat opposite him. He didn't recognize the two drivers. More cases and trunks were loaded in the back and on the roof of the coach and were tied down. The tired and muddy team were led away to a good feed of oats and replaced with four fresh horses.

Robb was now impatient to get back to Williams Lake. The road was deeply rutted and muddy, with fairly heavy traffic of walking miners and supply wagons loaded with bags and barrels likely serving the road houses. A year ago, it would have been him out there hefting a sixty-pound pack. There were even a few settlers with their covered ox carts and a myriad of young faces staring out the back watching them as the yoked oxen plodded slowly along, the husband and wife walking beside them. Robb had to admire their courage to take such risks in the wilderness. At least it had stopped raining.

It was heavy going through the mud. They stopped briefly in Boston Bar to change teams. Robb noted that all the creeks and rivers were in full spate. The steep grade at Jackass Mountain was still a formidable obstacle. The few open areas on the hillsides were dull brown, but there was hint of green on the bunch grass. Gaps in the snow above the treeline showed gullies where avalanches had cleared the slopes. In the distance, he could hear the thunder of Hell's Gate. It was a most uncomfortable ride, bouncing and lurching in the ruts. Their final stop that night was in Lytton. Robb was more than ready to get something to eat and stretch his legs. His fellow passenger remained silent, which suited Robb just fine.

The miles and days seemed to crawl by. There was still snow on the ground at Cache Creek, but it was melting fast. The Royal Engineers were busy at work with pickaxes and shovels. Robb recognized Captain Jackson, even at a distance. The man was imposing in his scarlet jacket astride the shining bay horse, directing the toiling labourers. He no longer felt any enmity towards the man. In fact, he almost felt beholden to him. *Emma isn't my problem anymore.*

He was glad he'd brought gloves along to keep his hands warm. In the mornings there was low- hanging mist along the river and he could see his breath, even in the coach. The road deteriorated after that, but it didn't stop the steady stream of miners who resolutely shouldered their packs and kept moving, and the coach horses slogged their way through the mire.

Each day moved them up the line of road houses. He knew he was home when they passed 150 Mile House and the turnoff to Horsefly. Then there was the sign for Williams Lake. They entered town, passed the government building, the hanging tree, the stores, saloons, the blacksmith and the bank. His eyes searched the street for familiar faces or any changes, but nothing seemed to have changed. The main street was just mud. Snow was still lingering in undisturbed places, and some miners were inhabiting tent town. Cullen's store and the saloon looked busy enough.

The coach pulled up outside the bank and Robb stiffly got out, slipped on his backpack and slung his rifle over his shoulder. He gave a wave to the guards and driver and headed for Mrs. Hall's.

He had no idea if George, Melvin and James were still there or if they'd already left for Green Valley. He also had no idea how he was going to react to seeing Ann. He felt about the same here as he had going up the steps to his parents' house. He had no idea what to expect.

It was Mrs. Hall who answered the door when he knocked, and her face broke into a broad smile. "Welcome back, Robb. We wondered when you'd get here. Come in," she said, ushering him into the warmth of the little house.

"Do you have room for one more?" he said.

She nodded and closed the door behind him.

He could smell the evening meal, and Ann poked her head around the kitchen door. "Good to see you, Robb. The others are out back stacking wood."

He dropped his gear in the parlour and went out the back door. James was chopping wood and George and Melvin were stacking it. "I'm glad to see you guys working. I was afraid you'd been sitting around all winter getting fat on Mrs. Hall's cooking."

They all stopped work and came over with much hand-shaking and back-slapping. They went inside and sat around talking about the winter and what they had done.

"Well, George, what have you been up to?" asked Robb as they tackled their supper. Mrs. Hall and Ann passed plates of vegetables and venison around.

"I spent a great deal of time in the gold commissioner's office looking at maps. This area really hasn't been surveyed at all. Very little is known about the geology, so I think once we've done with Green Valley, I'm going to do some mapping north of here and find out what we're dealing with. There have been a few reports of copper at McLeese Lake. What about you? How was Victoria?"

"I had a good trip home. Henry got off in Seattle. I haven't heard from him since. Even with the stagecoach, his leg was still bothering him. The stage only took ten days to get from here to Yale. It was a bit slower coming north because of the mud. The stage is the only practical way to do the trip right now, and even that is rough.

The engineers are just above Cache Creek surveying the road and widening it for travel. It's going to take them years. My family is fine. My father has semi-retired and my older brother, James, has taken his place at the Bay. I spent the winter learning the business end of things with them. My sister got married a couple of weeks ago. I helped them get a small log cabin built on the edge of town. Spent my days cutting down trees."

"And ... come on, tell us. What about Emma?" said James.

Mrs. Hall and Ann were serving up the meal and could probably overhear everything. "Well, it didn't turn out like I expected," Robb said. "When I finally got around to seeing her, it wasn't the same. She's engaged and has become this high-society woman with a maid. It just wasn't going to work. She'd be useless out here. I'm hoping to finish up in Green Valley by the end of June and join Dunlevey at Soda Creek. He's planning on opening a general store up there and I think I'd be qualified to run it."

"Well, aren't you full of surprises!" said Melvin. "Like I said last fall, this is my last run then I'm going back home. I've been away a long time and I want to see my wife and kids."

"It looks like we are all in agreement to finish up by June then," said George. "If it's still producing gold, we should sell it with a five way split and get out. I wonder what kind of a winter Bill had."

"You haven't seen him at all then?" Robb asked.

"No, he hasn't been in town. Guess we'll find out when we get there," said George.

Throughout the meal, Robb watched Ann. In many ways, she reminded him of Jane. She went about her chores with a quiet efficiency. She wasn't beautiful like Emma, but her features were pleasing. Their eyes met more than once, and she was watching him as much as he was watching her. She had a shapely figure beneath the conservative dress, which aroused possibilities. She had a ready smile and a quick wit.

"Where's O'Connor?" Robb asked.

"Oh, he got married just before Christmas and he moved in with his family. You can have his room upstairs, Robb," said Mrs. Hall.

Robb felt a glow of relief. After supper, when the others had gone upstairs, he found Mrs. Hall in the kitchen alone. Ann, apparently was out. "Mrs. Hall, could I talk to you privately?"

"What is it, Robb?"

"Mrs. Hall, I would like to court Ann, but I'll need your permission. Is she interested in me all? I do clean up pretty well."

There was a moment of silence as Mrs. Hall stood there with her head bowed. Finally, she raised her head and laughed. There was a big smile on her face. "I think she would be receptive to that, Robb. I would have no objections with you courting her, but you'll have to talk to her directly about that. She's a strong-willed woman and knows what she wants. She's turned down several offers over the years."

Robb grinned and gave her a hug. "Thank you, you don't know how much that means to me."

He heard the back door open and Ann stepped into the room, looking at the pair of them.

"You two look like you're up to no good," she said.

"You're probably right," said Mrs. Hall. "Robb here wants to have a talk with you, so you'd best go in the parlour."

Ann and Robb sat down at the table, and for a few moments nothing was said.

"Ann, I've asked permission from your mum to court you, but I guess that's up to you," said Robb, more nervous now than he had been standing in front of Sir James.

"Tell me why you've picked me when you were so keen on your lady in Victoria. Am I second best because she's chosen someone else?"

"I was never in the running as far as her father was concerned. People in Victoria are very conscious of their social standing, and my father, my brothers and myself all worked for the Bay. Emma attended the same school and church as I did. She's very pretty and I guess I was just a lovesick kid, even when we were in class. I came north to strike it rich. I thought if I had money, I'd have a better chance."

"Did it work?" Ann asked.

"No," he said. "The interesting thing I found was that after working up here and seeing how hard women like yourself and your mum work, and the challenges you face to raise a family or survive in this wild country, I realized just how shallow she was. At times she's downright rude to ordinary people. She's engaged to a well-to-do officer in the Royal Engineers, yet she constantly flirts with any man she talks to. I couldn't go along with that, and I ended it. She can't cook, sew or do anything practical. There is no comparison to women like my mother or my sister Jane. Jane made her own wedding gown and it was beautiful. Emma doesn't bother to help out in community events anymore either. Everybody else I know helps out at the church food booth selling meals to the miners. All the proceeds are going to build a new church. I knew I had made a big mistake, and now it's time for me to get on with my life."

"I am interested in you," said Ann, gently resting her hand on his. "I'm not about to rush things. We need to get to know each other. You're talking about working in Soda Creek. You have to know that my mother will be with me even if I am married. We can't really leave this house either. My father went north to look for gold two years ago and we've never heard from him since. That was a big blow to us. We depended on him. Mum opened the house up as a boarding house so we could earn a living. It hasn't been easy. Mum went to a lawyer and Dad can't be declared dead for seven years. We can't sell the house until that time even if we wanted to. Where else would we go, anyway?"

Robb looked into her face and saw the love, but also the uncertainty.

"The other thing I have to tell you is that I'm not perfect. I have a large, ugly scar on my back from that encounter with the grizzly last year. I wouldn't want to scare you. It scared Jane so much, I thought she'd faint. Also, I can't dance worth a damn, as much as my sisters try to teach me."

Ann laughed. "Since when are any men perfect?"

Robb was stunned for a moment then laughed. "I guess I'll have to get used to your sense of humour. You're going to be a challenge. We'll probably be heading out in the morning, so I'd better get some sleep." They sat for a few moments looking at each other. He wanted this woman and would care for her and provide for her. He looked into her face and saw honesty with no pretense. He gave her hand a squeeze then headed upstairs. He would have loved to give her a big hug but knew it would be considered inappropriate. With a light heart, he went to his room amid the thundering snores of his partners.

The following morning after a hearty breakfast, all of them collected their picks, shovels, tents and axes from the shed. Robb took the time to speak to both women and said, "I'll be back, but I can't tell you when." Ann squeezed his hand gently. His eyes lingered on her as they walked down the street. He didn't need to stop at the bank and he still had seventy dollars left, so they all headed to Cullen's to write letters home and top up on dried meat and food supplies.

> Dear Father,
>
> Arrived safely in Williams Lake. It was a wild and bumpy coach ride from Yale but it beats walking. There's still some

snow at the higher elevations and all the creeks and rivers are in spring flood. Still pretty cool up here, but at least it's dry. We have all decided to quit panning at the end of June and go our own ways.

Plenty of miners walking the trails, heading north. I may have a new lady in my life. Ann is Mrs. Hall's daughter and they run the local boarding house in Williams Lake where the fellows stayed over the winter. I think you will like them. Mum will be pleased to know that both of them are hard-working, practical women. Both have agreed to let me court her. I won't be jumping into anything too quick, but I like what I see, and she likes me too. We'll see what happens when I'm not mining anymore.

Love, Robb

Chapter 33

The Horsefly road was still muddy. Robb could see the ruts from the wagon and plenty of boot tracks. Snow lingered on the high ground. There was no sign of Long Baptiste when they passed the path to his camp. The pack seemed extra heavy again and Robb was very tired when they camped for the night. Sitting on a log around the fire, he could tell all of them were wanting to get it over with; just three more months of panning. He listened to the noises in the woods and paid attention to his surroundings. As a precaution, he took his rifle out of the scabbard, leaving it by his side as he lay down for the night.

The next day they slogged through the muck into Green Valley. George scanned the whole area.

The ice had broken on the creek and Chris and some of the others were working. "Something's different about the falls," he said. "It's lower than when we left. Either there's been a washout or someone's loosened some of the rocks and they've tumbled down."

The hillsides were bare of trees, but the little cabin the one crew had built was still standing. Robb waved to Chris and noticed a figure working the rocker box on their claim. It was Bill.

It was like a family reunion. All of them looked healthy and ready for another season. George inspected the falls, which had worn down to a six-foot-high flow at the rim. The area behind had eroded at least another four feet from the constant churning of water. There were several very large boulders sitting just below the falls. They set up the tents then James inspected the boundary markers, which hadn't been tampered with. The rest of them gathered firewood from the neighbouring deadfalls.

"Tomorrow we need to work with one team above the falls and the other on either side of the lots directly below. With the water level dropping, gold may have washed down into the basin. That could be to our advantage, although the rate of flow may not be as good as last year. Right now we've got spring melt," said George.

Robb looked at the creek. There was still ice clinging to the marsh grasses. There was only a hint of green on the maples and birch. Soon he had a fire going and biscuits frying in the gold pans.

"I'm glad I chose to live in Horsefly," said Bill. "It was a long, cold winter but I was in town and got fed well. We had a couple of big storms in January. I bet we had over two feet of snow here right through 'til the beginning of March. Being shut up in a cabin with a couple of guys and nowhere to go would drive me insane. I know. I've done that before."

"Did you see anything of Long Baptiste over the winter?" asked Robb.

"Yeah, I told him I was interested in Helen Raven Wing. He said he would talk to the tribe about it. Don't think they're too crazy about one of their women marrying a white man. I haven't heard back from him yet."

"Bill, we've talked about finishing up here in June and then going our separate ways. How do you feel about that?" said George.

"That would be fine by me. I want to buy land to raise cattle and horses. I won't be going back to the States. I don't want to end up in the war."

That night Robb lay in the tent thinking once more about Ann's father. He thought the man had either walked out on the women or was dead. He hadn't asked any questions and didn't even know the man's name. Ann had commented "where else would they go" if they sold the house. He didn't even know where they had come from in the first place. Those were questions he needed to ask, and maybe Pinchbeck would know some of it.

The days that followed showed a progressive warming, and finally all the ice was gone and they were able to get a good look at the section above the falls. The dislodging of the two large boulders had allowed a lot more water through, and they eagerly scoured the banks with pickaxes. The first two days they filled a flour bag with not only gold dust but small nuggets. "This is better than I anticipated," said George, stuffing the bag in their old hiding place. James and Melvin were working the bottom section below the falls and had gathered at least ten ounces.

They took turns manning the rocker box and shovelling. The returns were dwindling now, down to less than ten ounces a day. They finished with the lots above the falls and concentrated on the lower ones. There was a growing stash of gold in the log.

They discussed whether it would be better to make two runs into Williams Lake— one near the end of May and the other in June—or wait till the end when they closed down operations.

"Either way, we'd be exposing ourselves to thieves," said James.

"The daily take is going down. Are we going to sell the claim or just leave it?" asked Melvin.

"We could sell it to Chris at a low price. It would probably still produce more than their claim," replied George.

Michael Kelly showed up with supplies about a week later. The miners bought everything he'd brought. George took him aside after the trading was completed and presented Kelly with a proposition.

"Michael, we'll be finished here by the end of June. I think we're going to need some mule power to get our gold out of here. I'm expecting trouble and could use the backup. If you could get us out to the Horsefly road with the mules then have your wagon there to take all of us into Williams Lake, we'd be a lot safer. Would you consider it? We're willing to pay you and your drivers.

Kelly was thoughtful for a few minutes. "On my last delivery in June, we'll do that. It'll cost you a hundred dollars."

"Agreed," said George, shaking his hand.

Robb wanted to see Ann sooner rather than later. He was puzzled by his response to her. The feeling he had was not the same as it had been for Emma. When he thought of Emma now, it no longer aroused him. When he thought of Ann, there was a warm affection, but was it love? He sat looking at the fire and thought it a good analogy. Emma was a fiery coal, but Ann was an ember, not as hot but lasting much longer. He had no doubt in his mind that he wanted her. His body reminded him of that frequently, but he wasn't clear on her feelings for him. He admired the strength and tenacity of both Ann and her mother. They were hard-working and adaptable, and really decent people.

* * *

It was the third week in June when Michael Kelly and his son Everett made their deliveries. It took no time at all for George, Melvin, Bill, Robb and James to break camp. The night before, they had stuffed their backpacks with the gold-filled flour bags and there were still ten bags left over, which Robb put in a burlap sack. The whole valley knew they were leaving. Although the daily take had dwindled considerably, they had discussed it and decided the claim wasn't worth selling.

"If you guys want to work it, be my guest. We're done," George told the other miners. There was a mad dash as a group immediately took off to stake sections of the Green Valley claim.

As the mules were divested of the food supplies, Bill and James took the mules and loaded the saddlebags. They had sold off the tools and rocker boxes earlier. Only George had kept his tools, as he still intended to prospect at McLeese Lake. With Michael leading and Everett at the rear, the procession departed, the group looking somewhat uncomfortable on their four-legged tickets to safety.

Robb stayed at the back keeping an ever-watchful eye on the forest and rocks. He was taking his last look at Green Valley, his home for the past year, when he glimpsed two furtive forms disappearing between the trees on the high edge of the ridge. There had been a flash of blonde hair. The only person in the valley with blonde hair was Chris, and Robb couldn't believe Chris would ambush them. He nudged Everett.

"Did you see them?"

"Where?" Everett said, spinning his horse around to get a look.

"We've got company," Robb replied, pointing to the ridge. "I saw two of them up near the ridge." Everett whistled to his father, who spurred his horse on. The rest of the group jogged and bounced alongside the narrow trail, not used to riding. Robb was thankful for the few days' experience he'd had riding with the stagecoach in the fall. For over an hour they made steady progress, but the mules were tiring under their heavy loads. Michael kept up a relentless pace. They had to outdistance whoever was chasing them on foot. At one open expanse of grass Everett must have seen something, so he whistled again, indicating he was going to scout up the hill.

"Keep moving, everyone," yelled Michael. "George, keep your eyes open. They may have posted someone ahead. The Horsefly road isn't far, and the wagon will be waiting for you. Get the hell out of here. I'm going back for Everett." He galloped back down the trail to join his son. Not five minutes later shots rang out. There was a steady barrage then an eerie silence only interrupted by squawking crows.

Within fifteen minutes they came to the Horsefly road, and sure enough, Patrick had the wagon waiting. Quickly dismounting, they flung their gear into the back of the wagon and started unloading the mules.

"Where's Michael?" Patrick asked.

"Everett went after someone up on the ridge and we heard gunshots. Michael's gone after him," said James.

Patrick tied the mules to a tree and clambered back on the wagon seat. Everyone else climbed on board. He was just about to pull away when they heard horses coming. Patrick reined the team back as Michael and Everett emerged onto the trail. There was blood on Everett's sleeve.

"I'm alright," said Everett, "He took a shot at me, but it's just a flesh wound. I got him, though."

"Did he have blonde hair?" Robb asked.

"I didn't get a real good look at him, but it could have been Chris. He won't be going anywhere. My bullet hit him in the chest. He went down into the gully. I wasn't expecting him to be the problem. There are a couple of other guys in camp I figured would give us grief. Dad got the other guy."

George said, "Let me look at that arm, Everett," as he ripped an old shirt apart and quickly bound Everett's arm. "I'll let Pinchbeck know what's happened. Don't want any of the good guys getting strung up." He handed Michael the cash. "Thanks, you saved our lives back there." They shook hands and parted company. Robb watched Everett and Michael leading the string of mules down the wagon road.

Patrick clucked to the team and they were off at a brisk trot. The whole transfer had taken less than ten minutes. With all the artillery on board, they had an uneventful ride. On reaching the Cariboo Road, they had a brief halt to water the horses and grab a quick bite to eat. The main road was full of northbound miners, wagons going in both directions and two riders driving a small herd of thin cattle who looked like they needed to stop and graze.

"I just can't believe Chris would ambush us. Damn, I liked that kid. Just goes to show you that you can't trust anyone when gold's involved. He's the last person I would have expected," said Melvin.

"Did you notice the new log cabin on the south side? That's on Long Baptiste's territory," said Bill. "When I'm finished with the banking, I'm gonna head back to him and see what the tribe's decided about Helen. If I bought a thousand acres, I could buy cattle like those, fatten them up and re-sell them. They get pretty damn thin on the trail. Long Baptiste may have to move further north permanently when more settlers come in. He could rebuild his camp on my place."

It was late afternoon when they arrived in Williams Lake, and Patrick deposited them right outside the bank. The team had been driven hard and stood there, their once-shiny hides dark with sweat and their heads hanging down, sides still heaving. Robb slipped Patrick an extra twenty dollars and joined the others as they entered the bank.

Mr. Briggs took one look at them and waved them into his office.

"This is our final deposit, Mr. Briggs. We're finished in the gold business."

It took over an hour for Mr. Briggs to process their gold. Robb was quite content to just sit on something that didn't move, bounce, bray or kick. He felt drained. This chapter of his life was over, and he was too tired to think beyond that. He was also tired of always having to watch his back and expecting the worst of people.

George decided to go down to Pinchbeck's office. "I'll leave you guys to sort this out. Robb, take care of my tools and my rifle," he said, slipping out the door.

Finally, Mr. Briggs brought back their deposit slips. Robb looked at his total: Fourteen thousand, nine hundred and forty dollars! He sat for a moment. The amount was unbelievable. *I don't need to work for anybody else ever again if I don't want to.*

"Gentlemen, the bank is closed now, so I'll let you out. It has been a pleasure doing business with you," he said.

"James and I will be here in the morning for bank drafts. We're heading back to the States as soon as the stage comes in," said Melvin. The men slowly walked down the street to Mrs. Hall's, only to find she didn't have any vacancies. They had better luck at the saloon. They all sat at a table sipping on their whiskey, watching the poker games and the saloon girls plying their trade. Business was brisk. Bill and Robb went out to the canteen next door and picked up beef sandwiches for all of them.

George stuck his head in the door and saw them. James waved him over. "We got you a room upstairs. Here, tuck into some grub," said James, passing the sandwiches around. They shuffled the chairs around to make room for George. Robb went over to the bar and got a bottle of whiskey.

"I told Pinchbeck what happened," George said. "I wanted to make everything really clear. I don't want to get on the wrong side of Begby. He's sending O'Connor out to look into it. He can talk to Michael and Everett and the guys in the valley," George said.

Robb handed him his deposit slip. One eyebrow went up and there was a tiny smile on George's face.

"I left your tools up in your room," Robb said, fending off the advances of a buxom young woman.

"Not tonight," he said when she whispered in his ear that she was available.

They sat around for what was probably their last night together. The noise level and rowdiness was rising. "I don't know about you, but I'm dead tired. I think I'll head upstairs. At the moment I have no idea where I'm going or what I'll be doing. A lot depends on what happens with Ann. If you're ever back in the area, drop into Mrs. Hall's or leave me a letter at the post office. There's going to be a fight here anytime now," he said looking at the card players over in the corner. "George, Bill, keep in touch." He shook hands with James and Melvin, wished them well and headed up the stairs to his room.

Chapter 34

Robb awoke the next morning wondering for a moment where he was. It had been hard to get to sleep with all the laughter, shouting and noise of breaking glass downstairs. The mattress was hard and lumpy, but it still beat sleeping on the ground. He looked at himself in the mirror and decided it was time to shed the miner. He quickly dressed and went over to Cullen's. He bought a razor, a new toothbrush, regular shirts and pants plus a dressier pair of boots. There was a letter from Jane.

> Dear Robb,
>
> Everything is going well. Billy and I are settling into our new house. We're extremely lucky and you are largely responsible for that. I've set up the spare room as my sewing area and am supplying the Granville with skirts and dresses.
>
> Emily is helping me when she can but often is at Matt's house helping with the children. Mum and Emily are still

working at the church food booth and baking loaves of bread most days.

Ivy tells us that Emma will be married here in Victoria but will be moving to New Westminster immediately after the ceremony. Captain Jackson's parents will be coming here for the wedding and will be staying in Mr. Crawford's new hotel, which just opened. It is opulent, to say the least. They are charging five dollars a night for a room. They have their own dining room and a chef as well as a salon for the men and a separate parlour for the lady guests. The maids have their own uniforms, black with white aprons, and the male staff must wear formal suits. The valets wear black jackets with the hotel logo on the shoulder. Very grand! Keep in touch. Love, Jane.

Robb quickly penned a letter to his father.

> Dear Father,
>
> I'm no longer a miner. We finished with the claim a couple of days ago. We were nearly ambushed by some miners in the valley on the way out.
>
> Fortunately, we had made arrangements with some locals to get us out

with their mules. We got into Williams Lake late yesterday.

It's going to take me a while to figure out what to do next. A lot depends on

Ann. If things get serious with her then I'm thinking it's too risky to take women further north or even stay here. There's more gold being found east of Quesnel. The miners definitely can't be trusted. Two of my buddies are heading back to the States. Bill will be ranching somewhere locally, as he is interested in a Native woman we know. George will be prospecting north of here. Give Mum a hug for me. Let Jane know I got her letter. Today I will be shaving off my beard and getting my hair cut. Back to being me.

Love, Robb.

Robb thought about getting a bath and a shave but hesitated. In Victoria, he had discovered that having money altered people. He wanted Ann to accept him as he was. He hiked up the street to the boarding house and knocked on the door. Mrs. Hall answered and waved him in.

"Come in Robb. James and Melvin were just here. They've gone to the bank; should be right back. The stage doesn't leave for a couple of days. I've got room for all of you tonight. The miners here last night checked out early."

Robb took his rifle and pack upstairs and dumped them on his bed. On the way down he met Ann at the bottom of the stairs. "Good to see you," he said with a silly smile on his face.

"You too. Did you want some tea?" she asked, giving him a thorough inspection. "Why haven't you shaved like the others?"

"Because I wanted you to want me for who I am, not for my looks or my money," retorted Robb, trying to look serious. Both Ann and Mrs. Hall burst out laughing and went into the kitchen. Ann returned a few minutes later with a mug of tea and a plate of cookies and sat down across from him.

"I hope you weren't serious about that," said Ann.

"In what way?"

"Do you seriously think I'd pick my husband just because he might have money?" she said.

Robb watched her. "It did cross my mind. A lot of women would, you know. Not that I know a lot of women, but Emma would have. You and I haven't seen each other in over six months. My feelings for you haven't changed. I still want to marry you, but we do need to get to know each other. Right now, I have a lot of options about what I want to do next, but most of it depends on what you decide."

"Well, I'm not that kind of a woman. But what I'm going to decide right now is that you need to have a bath and a shave so I can get a good idea of what I'm going to be stuck with for the next fifty years," she said, trying hard to look stern but failing. Both of them broke up with laughter.

"Aye, captain," said Robb, saluting and heading out the door. He returned about an hour later in clean clothes, the hairy stranger banished forever (he hoped). George, Melvin and James were in the parlour, also looking quite human.

Ann came in and looked at him critically from top to bottom, her hands on her hips, suddenly blushing. "Quite frankly, I didn't expect you to clean up so well."

"So, do I pass inspection, ma'am?" he said, tugging his forelock in mock subservience.

"Yes," she said and spun around back into the kitchen. Robb could hear Mrs. Hall teasing her.

George was laughing so hard there were tears running down his face. "Robb McDonald, you have no idea how to court a woman, do you?"

"If a lady asks me a question, I give her an honest answer. What more could she want? What's wrong with that?"

"I don't think diplomacy is quite your forte. Stick to minding the store. I think you're going to have your hands full with her."

"I wouldn't mind having my hands full of her ... literally, that is. But let's change the subject. Did any of you see Bill this morning?" Robb asked.

"He headed back to Horsefly real early. He left before we even got up. He'll catch up with Long Baptiste somewhere along the way," said Melvin. "The tribe would be on their annual trek for that gathering they go to."

"I'll be heading up to McLeese Lake in the morning," said George.

"So, it's a two-day wait for the stage for you two. It's a bumpy ride but you'll be in Yale within the week. The guards are definitely nothing to mess with. You'll be safe with them," said Robb.

After supper, Mrs. Hall puttered in the kitchen, and the men sat on the porch, leaving Ann and Robb in the parlour.

"Ann, I think it's time we did some serious talking. I've got a lot of questions I need to ask you and I'm sure you've got some for me," he said, looking directly into her eyes.

"Where do we start?" she said, suddenly seeming rather awkward and unsure.

"Well, for starters, where are you and your mum from?" he asked, resting his hand on hers across the table.

"My dad was from Ireland and my mum was born in Chicago. They met when he was heading out west. I was born there. He worked as a carpenter, making furniture and that sort of thing. He decided to move to Oregon when I was about six. We came up here years ago, before the gold rush started. Two years ago, he wanted to go north so he left with two other men, and we've never heard from him since. We reported him missing to Sheriff Pinchbeck, but he couldn't find any trace of them. It's left Mum and me in a real bind. Mum started running this as a boarding house because the bank still has the mortgage on the house. As you have noticed, it's not exactly a safe place to live with all the miners around. We've been very lucky to have good neighbours, and most of the time Ryan O'Connor stayed here too, until he got married."

Robb spent the next hour telling her all about his family and life in Victoria, his job at the Bay and involvement with the Songhees and why he'd come north as a miner. "My next question to you is, if I am going to be courting you, will I be able to live here, or do I have to get someplace else to live in town?"

"Mum, can you come in here?" called Ann.

Mrs. Hall came in and sat down beside her.

"Robb's just asked if it's proper for him to stay here or if he needs another place to live while we're courting," said Ann.

"It wouldn't be considered proper at all for you to live in the same house as her during the courting period, Robb," said Mrs. Hall.

"Is there any place in particular you would recommend?"

"Mrs. Anston down the street runs a good house and her cooking's good too."

"I'll go down and visit her in the morning. In the meantime, I'm going to give you some things to think about. My work qualifications would allow me to manage a Hudson Bay post, a general store or even a small hotel. Peter Dunlevey, one of George's acquaintances, is building a new general store up at Soda Creek and likely will be involved with building a ferry to take the miners from Soda Creek to Quesnel. I've discussed the possibility of running his store with him.

"Being so far north poses a problem. I want to keep in touch with my family. Also, I have grave concerns about taking you two women into a place like Soda Creek, which would be even more dangerous than this town. If you wanted to, we could live in Victoria. Or we could live in Yale. It rains more down there but it's milder than here, with much less snow. It's a bigger place with more businesses and it's only a two-day boat ride from my folks. We wouldn't have to worry about supplies getting through in the wintertime. I'm leaning toward that option.

"In my family, the man of the house runs the household and doesn't expect his wife to work. My sister Jane sews skirts and dresses at home and wholesales them to Granville's store. Please give the matter some thought. By the way, I'm Presbyterian, if that makes any difference. What church do you go to?"

"There's just the one here. It's Methodist," said Mrs. Hall. "The circuit minister comes through twice a month."

"Next time he's here, I'll come to church with you." With that, Robb gave Ann's hand a squeeze and went out on the porch to sit with the guys, leaving the women looking overwhelmed with all the information. Ann was speechless, for once.

Chapter 35

Robb dressed in his casual clothes but left his pendant on. Somehow it was part of him. It felt strange not to be carrying his rifle, but he did have his knife attached to his belt under his coat. He visited Mrs. Anston and introduced himself. "Up until two days ago, I was one of those scruffy-looking miners. I've done with that and I'll be courting Ann Hall. Mrs. Hall suggested this would be a good place to stay since you're a good cook. I don't have any idea how long I'd be a regular lodger."

"My husband, Roy, is out at the moment. He should be back by lunchtime. Can you come back this afternoon and talk to us?"

"Certainly. I want to have a good look around town and see if there's any work available."

Next, he walked over to Sheriff Pinchbeck's office, and sure enough, he was in.

"Good morning, Sheriff Pinchbeck. I'm Robb McDonald, one of George's group. Do you have a few minutes? I'd like to talk to you about something."

Pinchbeck waved him to a chair. "What's on your mind?"

"I'm courting Ann Hall and I want to find out what happened to her father."

"Well, that's a mystery. His name was Edward, but we called him Ted. He got gold fever and headed north with Jim Barber and Vern Haggerty. Both of them were good men. I've never had reason to think they'd harm him. Their families haven't heard from them either.

"Ted was sure he was gonna strike it rich and never have to work again. The women came to me at the beginning of September to report that they hadn't heard from him. No letters, nothing. So, I rode up to Soda Creek and checked the saloon and general store. Some fellers from here had seen them at the store buying food. I asked our circuit minister who does the McLeese Lake area to check around, but the next time he was here he said they hadn't been seen in the store or saloon that anyone could remember. As far as I know, nobody's seen hide nor hair of them. If I see anyone coming back from Quesnel, I do still ask, but nothing," he said.

"So it boils down to one of two things," said Robb. "Either all three of them have deliberately gone north with no intention of returning, or something happened to them and they're dead."

"Likely," said Pinchbeck, "Could have been a landslide. That happens often enough. It's left the women in a difficult situation. The pair of them have done remarkably well with the boarding house. We've had problems a couple of times, but nothing much, really. It worked out well to have Ryan boarding there. I keep an eye on them as much as I can."

"What sort of man was Edward Hall?"

"Didn't tend to stick to one thing for very long. He was a good carpenter and could turn his hand to a lot of things. Bit of a dreamer, and none too practical sometimes. Decent sort of man, though. I can't see him just walking out on them."

"So he could have been killed and just dumped in the bush, and no one would be any the wiser."

"That's true," said Pinchbeck.

"I don't think there'd be much point in me trying to find him," said Robb, pondering the situation. "If I'm going to be around this town, I need to get some work, even if it's just odd jobs. I'm used to working seven days a week."

"You could try at the stables. I don't think Cullen needs anyone right now. I might call on you myself if Ryan's not back from Horsefly by Saturday," said Pinchbeck.

"I don't know a thing about the law, but if you want to teach me, I'd be willing," said Robb and thanked him for his time.

Cullen's store was full of miners, so Robb walked around the store checking prices. The Henry had been useful in the back country, but Robb didn't want to be hefting it around all the time. He waited until Gilbert was free and asked him if he had any handguns for sale.

"No, I don't. The cartridges haven't proven to be that reliable yet. I've heard Smith and Wesson have a couple of new ones out, but they haven't reached here yet. Your buddy Bill has a four-shot twenty-two Sharpes," said Gilbert. "I hear you're staying around here for a while."

"News travels fast. If you get any of those Sharpes in, I'd be interested. Bill used it on a rattler, and it's dead accurate close up. Do you carry wedding rings?"

Gilbert laughed. "Wait here and I'll bring out what I have." He disappeared down the hall, returning with a small, hand-carved box about a foot long. He carefully unlocked it, revealing rows of shiny, plain gold rings of different sizes. "Take a piece of string and wrap it around her finger so we can get the right size, or better still, bring her in."

Robb decided he'd better not get the ring until she agreed to marry him. He left Gilbert serving a long lineup of shaggy, dirty men.

I was one of them. Now life's different. He ate a sandwich at the canteen, feeling quite out of place in his clean clothes among the throng of ruffians. Then he went over to Mrs. Anston's boarding house. When he knocked on the door, it was Roy Anston who answered. He was a big, burly man with a luxuriant moustache waxed at the tips and braces that held up his trousers over a substantial expanse of belly.

"I'm Robb McDonald. I spoke to your wife earlier about lodging here for a while," he said, offering his hand, which Roy cranked heartily.

"Come in," bellowed Roy, "have a seat. My wife tells me you're courting Ann Hall. I wish you luck with that. She's a hard-working woman – both of them are. She's turned down a couple of fellers. The last one didn't want her mother around. She refused him right quick. Knows her mind, she does."

"If she accepts me, I'll be needing somewhere to stay until we get married. Mrs. Hall suggested here. What do you think?"

"We've got rules …"

"Let me guess, no cussing, no drinking, no smoking in the house, no women and pay on time?" said Robb.

"You've got that right!" Roy chortled.

"Could I see the room?"

"Follow me, your room's downstairs. We have four rooms upstairs, same as Mrs. Hall's," said Roy and lumbered down the hallway, past the parlour and kitchen to a room at the back. It was roughly eight by ten feet, very plain with a bed, a dresser, a chair and hooks on the wall to take clothes. A small window overlooked the back yard. A patterned porcelain washbasin and bowl sat on the dresser along with a coal-oil lamp. There was a mirror on the wall. The bed looked comfortable, and the sheets and blankets seemed clean. Robb could see washing out on the clothesline in the back garden.

"Do you have a weekly rate?" he asked.

"We charge five dollars a week, and that includes breakfast and dinner."

"Could I move in tomorrow?"

"Yes, that would be alright," said Roy.

They shook hands and Robb went back to Mrs. Hall's.

Evening brought rowdiness and noise from tent city. It was more than background noise to him, so he remained vigilant. Out on the porch after supper, Robb talked to George. "I spent some time today with Pinchbeck and tried to find out what happened to Mr. Hall. He left here with two local men, Jim Barber and Vern Haggerty. None of them have been heard from since. You're heading north around McLeese Lake. If you ever hear anything about them in your travels, would you let me know? I think it would bring closure for Ann and Mrs. Hall and settle the estate. You're always welcome if you come back here. The success we've had is largely attributable to you. Bill was right; having a geologist was a great idea. At least we knew what we were looking for."

Back inside, he spoke to Mrs. Hall. "I'll be moving down to the Anston's in the morning. They've agreed to take me on a weekly basis. Do you think Ann will take me?" he added quietly when Ann went outside to dump the basin of dish water.

"You've given us a lot to think about, Robb. It's a bit overwhelming, but I'm sure she'll give you an answer soon. It's not a simple decision to make," said Mrs. Hall, suddenly serious.

The fact that she hadn't given him an answer made Robb nervous. He went out the back door to where Ann was bringing in the washing and folding it into a basket.

"You're very quiet tonight," he said.

She looked up at him with those big, luminous eyes. "It's a big decision, Robb."

He leaned over and very gently kissed her on the cheek, holding back the desire to grab hold of her and give her a kiss on the lips.

"I admire restraint in a man," she said, turning away from him as she hauled the basket into the house, leaving a frustrated Robb on the porch.

There are times I think she's toying with me, but there's something going on. I just don't know what it is. Emma used to tease me. Lord, she teased every man. Ann's different. I see that odd look in her eyes and wonder what it means. What I feel is something deep, not just my body wanting her. On that note, he went up to his room.

* * *

The following morning Melvin and James boarded the stage. Robb spoke to Garnet and Howard. "Take good care of these two characters. They're good buddies of mine."

Garnet nodded and sat on his horse, the rifle across the saddle, ever watchful. Another passenger in a suit and bowler hat climbed on board.

Robb figured he was another bank detective. The driver chirped to the horses then the stage was gone, leaving him alone on the sidewalk. George came walking along dressed for the road, carrying his backpack, tent and tarp as well as his rifle. They shook hands and George kept going, joining the string of miners on the road to Quesnel. Robb watched his figure slowly diminish until it was just a speck through the trees. *My friends have gone. I really am alone.*

He went back to Mrs. Hall's to collect his gear for the move to the Anston's. "Is it alright if I come over in the evenings after dinner? I'd like to spend some time with you. Would your mum mind?" he asked.

Ann rested her hand lightly on his shoulder and smiled. "I'm sure that won't be a problem, and we can talk a bit more," she said. "There's so much for Mum and I to think about."

At Anston's, Robb dropped his possessions on his bed, paid his board for the week and spent the rest of the morning looking for work. There were stalls to be mucked out at the stable and tack to be cleaned, so he got hired for a couple of days' work. A dollar a day was better than nothing. Going back to Anston's for supper, he washed up and changed his clothes, leaving his boots on the back doorstep as he was smelling distinctly horsey. He quickly rinsed out his work clothes and hung them out to dry. Mrs. Anston put a good meal on the table; some corned beef, boiled potatoes and cabbage. Two of her grandchildren were there as well as two miners who were spinning tales.

"We've been hearing that there's gold's east of Quesnel near Keithley creek. Have you been out there?" the fellow asked.

"We were near Horsefly," said Robb. "Finding the gold's one problem but trying to get it to the bank's another. We really had to be careful coming and going, even if you're just coming into town for supplies. There are thieves waiting in the bushes to ambush you. You can't trust anyone, not even your own group sometimes. Be careful. On the other hand, you could just go to the saloon; you won't have any gold left anyway." He was thinking of the young fellows back in Grassy Canyon—Chris in particular.

As Robb ate his pie, he thought about how he still couldn't believe Chris had ambushed them. He thought he'd become a fairly good judge of character, but Chris had fooled him completely. He wondered if Ryan would bring the bodies back for burial or bury them out there in the woods.

"That was a good meal. Thank you. I'm going over to Mrs. Hall's," he said.

"Be back before ten o'clock. We lock the doors at night," said Roy.

"Will do," said Robb as he went out the door, taking his rifle with him. There was no way of knowing who'd be prowling after dark. The curtains were drawn in all the houses, with just a glimmer of light filtering out to the road. Mrs. Hall's was no exception. There was one older man sitting on the porch smoking. They nodded at each other. Robb just opened the door without knocking, knowing they were expecting him. He was about to call out to them when he caught part of their conversation in the kitchen.

"Ann, you've got to tell him sometime. He has to know," said Mrs. Hall.

"Mum, I'm afraid to."

"That's a chance you're going to have to take. If you don't give him an answer soon, he's going to leave. You're twenty-one. You don't want to be a spinster all your life. Someday I'll be gone, and you'll be alone. Men like Robb don't come along every day."

Robb took a breath and walked into the kitchen, startling both women. "I couldn't help but hear your conversation. What is it, Ann? What are you afraid to tell me?"

She paled, her eyes like those of a trapped animal. He could see her hands clenching and unclenching and the rapid rising and falling of her chest. *My Lord, she's terrified.*

He took her by the hand and led her out to the back porch. Gripping her gently by the shoulders, but holding her at arms' length, he said very quietly, "Whatever it is, tell me now."

She began with a few stumbling words then they became a torrent. "Two years ago, I was assaulted by a man here in the house. I'm not a virgin, Robb." She stood there, the tears trickling down her face.

Robb gently raised her face with his fingers so she had to look at him, then drew her to him. She clung to him, sobbing. He held her until the weeping ended. She stepped back and wiped her face with her hanky. His head was spinning. *Does it matter if she isn't a virgin? It obviously matters to her.* He felt a raw anger towards the man who had violated her.

"Ann, who did this to you? Was it a stranger?"

"No," she said, turning away from him. "It was my father."

Robb was flabbergasted. "Your father! Your own father?"

"We never told Sheriff Pinchbeck that he'd raped me; we just reported him missing. We couldn't tell him the truth. Mum was devastated too. She looked back at times in the past when we moved around a lot. Sometimes we left places in a hurry. She had no idea he was that kind of man. I don't think we'll ever see him again, and I'm glad of that. I'm not sure what I'd do if I saw him again. I'm angry."

"Give me a few minutes, Ann, to get my head together on this," said Robb, and they sat down on the back steps. The black star-sprinkled night with the scent of pine enveloped them. Tent city was relatively quiet.

Robb gathered his courage and said, "Ann, I've only been with a woman once. The guys set me up with a saloon girl. I was just a clumsy fool. I've seen the love that two people can have for each other with my sister Jane and her husband Billy. My parents have been married forever and they still treat other with respect. Ann, can you love me and let me love you?"

"I don't know, Robb. I hope I can."

"When I put my arms around you, are you afraid of me?"

"No, it feels like a safe place," she said.

"Well, Ann Hall, I'm officially asking you to marry me. I need an answer soon. If we're heading for Yale, I need to get things settled before the snow comes. It's the middle of July now, which only leaves me six to eight weeks to get to Yale to get work and find us a place to live."

Ann straightened her shoulders with a glimmer of her old self. "Robb McDonald, I accept your proposal. I care about you very much. We'll find a way to make it right."

He raised her to her feet, put his arms around her and very gently kissed her on the lips. He felt her hesitate for a moment then allow it. Cassie's words came back to him: "slowly and gently."

A quick glimpse at the parlour clock showed it was ten minutes to ten, so Robb took his leave. "I'll be back tomorrow," he said and hurried back to Anston's before he got locked out.

Sleep did not come easy that night. *If I ever meet Edward Hall, I think I'd kill him.* The mere thought of a father doing that to his own daughter was so disgusting it made him feel ill. It would be like his father doing that to Emily or Jane. Unthinkable! The next evening, he was going to talk to both women about Yale. He had an idea for their house that might resolve the problem until the seven years were up and Edward Hall could be declared dead.

Chapter 36

Robb slogged away at the stables all day cleaning stalls. *I think I'll stick to town life. I can make more money at the Bay or my own store.* There are two general stores in Williams Lake, so they don't need a third. He thought about Bill and hoped the tribe would see fit to allow the marriage. He had no idea how George was going to manage on his own. If he found the copper he was seeking, it would be a major undertaking to tunnel a mine. Copper was in demand.

The women at the local saloon were sitting on the front porch awaiting the arrival of the next batch of miners. Robb had an idea and walked up to the older woman, who appeared to be in charge. He could see she had once been young and pretty and was still attractive in a hard sort of way. Her bosom was still firm, and her exposed ankles still shapely. She rose to meet him as he went up the steps.

"I've seen you around. Mary here can give you a good time. It's just a dollar," she said.

"Is Cassie still around?"

"No, she's moved on. Went up to Soda Creek. I'm Jenny," she said with a flick of her hair.

"I'm not here to bed one of your girls. I need to talk to you. I'm willing to pay the dollar for some advice, private-like."

They sat at a table in the saloon and he bought them drinks. "Can you keep a secret?"

"You don't want her to know you're bedding a whore?"

"No, no. It's not that at all. My girl was raped by a miner. She'd not want anyone in town to know. I think she's afraid to marry me. How can I make love to her without hurting her?" said Robb quietly, feeling very awkward discussing this with a woman. "I've only laid with a woman once and that was with Cassie in your bath house. My instincts are as strong as any man's. I want her, but how do I slow down my urges? I'm afraid I'm going to be as clumsy as a rutting bull moose."

Jenny nodded and gave a throaty laugh, pulling her shawl around her shoulders. "I remember that well. We laughed about that for a long time." She thought for a few minutes. "Walk with me outside," she said and took him out back into the yard. They talked quietly for about twenty minutes.

Robb listened intently, trying to understand how a woman's body responded to lovemaking.

"Most of the time, miners aren't looking for love, Robb. They want sex, pure and simple. We're merely an outlet. They will take us by force if they feel like it. It's a rough life. Most of us have been beaten. But where else can a gal make ten dollars a night? It's a risky business. You are going to have to slow down and let her lead you." She gave him some specific suggestions, such as the way to use his hands and how to slow down.

He felt embarrassed, but thanked her and gave her two dollars, not one. Walking down the road to the boarding house, he couldn't imagine the life these women led.

Jenny stood on the porch watching him walk away and envied the woman who would become his wife. Men like him were few and far between.

He got a warm reception from both Ann and Mrs. Hall when he arrived, which pleased him. Just talking about her experience had been so daunting for her, but there she was looking much more like her usual self. They had two customers staying over that night, so Robb took the women out to the back porch.

"Now, ladies, we have a lot of things to talk about. I was in Cullen's a couple of days ago. He has some gold wedding bands. Ann, I'd like you to go down there and try one on to get the right size then tell Gilbert to keep it for me. Next, when is your travelling minister going to be in town?"

"He should be here for Sunday's service at nine o'clock," said Mrs. Hall.

"Good. Let me know when he gets back so we can see him to discuss getting registered and he can publish the banns. Is there anything else we need to discuss?"

"It's about this house, Robb. I just can't leave it. There's still a mortgage at the bank. I'm afraid it will be vandalized or burned to the ground if it's left empty. We've worked so hard to keep it that I can't just walk away."

"I've got an idea. Your husband has to be presumed dead for seven years before you can legally claim it, right?"

"Yes, that's what the lawyer told me."

"Here's an idea for you. Why don't you rent it to Ryan and his wife, with the option to buy in five years' time? That way it doesn't sit empty and you are free to come with me to Yale. I can talk to the bank about the mortgage. My problem is that the weather is going to close in on us by the end of September, and we won't be able to get out until spring. I want to be able to visit my family, and Victoria's only a two-day boat ride from Yale. I'll be wanting you to meet them. There's not a lot of work available for me here. I'd have a much better chance in Yale," said Robb.

"Mum, we never even thought of that. I know Ryan's family is really cramped for space. There's seven children in their house to start with. I don't know how they all fit in it."

"This house would be perfect for them. With all the bedrooms here, some of his brothers and sisters could stay here too. Pinchbeck told me that Ryan's out at Grassy Valley right now. He should be back any day now," said Robb.

Robb looked at Ann. He was glad to see the joy on her face, and the twinkle of mischief in those blue eyes again. He never, ever wanted to see the despair he'd seen last night.

They talked for another hour then Robb went back to Anston's. The following morning, Robb went over to the bank to chat with Mr. Briggs.

"What can I help you with today, Robb?"

"Mr. Briggs, I'm engaged to Ann Hall. We will be married as soon as we can arrange it with the minister," he said.

"Congratulations. I'm glad to hear that. Ann deserves a good man."

"Mrs. Hall tells me you hold the mortgage on the house. Could you tell me how much it is?"

"Right now it's approximately fifty dollars," Briggs replied.

"I'm thinking of getting a job in Yale, so both of them would be coming with me. Mrs. Hall was thinking of renting the house for the five-year period, with the option for the renter to be able to buy it at the end. Would your bank be alright with that situation? The rent would cover the mortgage payment," he said.

Briggs thought for a minute. "What would happen if the renter defaulted on the payment?"

Robb thought about it. "In that case, you could notify me by mail. I could leave some money in my bank account here to cover that possibility. That way, the mortgage wouldn't be in default. I'd pay it off myself now, except I can't get title until the seven-year time period is up."

"I don't see any reason that wouldn't work for all of us," said Briggs thoughtfully, tapping his pencil on the blotter.

The two men shook hands and Robb felt good. He planned to leave five hundred dollars in the bank and take the rest to Yale. He noticed Ryan's horse tied to the hitching rail outside the sheriff's office and headed over there.

The two men were sitting around the desk when Robb walked in. "Hello, Ryan. I figured you were back when I saw your horse outside. What did you find in Grassy Valley?"

"I was just telling the sheriff here. I found the two bodies where George told us they'd be. The crows had been at them, but I could see the wounds. I buried them out there. Didn't see any sense in dragging the corpses back here."

"Did you find out who they were?"

"Yeah, I went into Grassy Valley and talked to their mates. Got their miners' licences," he said, pulling the papers out of his jacket pocket.

"Was Chris one of them?"

"No, it wasn't Chris like you guys thought. It was one of the new fellers, an Andrew Gibson, and the other guy was Tom Brownson," he said.

"Thank God for that," said Robb. "We got to know Chris quite well, so it was hard to believe he'd ambush us, but he was the only one who had blonde hair. None of us met this Gibson guy." He was overwhelmed with a sense of relief. His instincts had been right after all.

"After that, I went to Horsefly and spoke to Michael Kelly and his son, Everett. They were very open about what had happened. Gibson shot at Everett first, creasing his arm, but Everett returned fire and nailed him with a chest shot. His arm is healing well, by the way. Michael told me that when he was riding up the hill, Brownson fired at him but missed. Michael got him. That rifle of his has the range to do that."

"From a legal point of view, will there be any repercussions for the Kellys?" Robb asked.

"I shouldn't think so. I have all the statements you fellers gave me. Pretty clear cut."

"I've seen Begby in action a couple of times," said Robb. "Wouldn't want to be on the wrong side of him. Thanks for the information. By the way, Ryan, stop by Mrs. Hall's sometime. She was wanting to talk to you."

"Sure," he replied.

Robb went to the canteen and joined the lineup to buy a sandwich. There were still hundreds of miners passing through. After lunch, he helped Roy Anston stack a cord of wood that had been delivered. He thought about what needed to be done, and the minister was the next person to deal with. As soon as he had a definite date for the wedding, he'd head to Yale. He'd really have some news to give his father. His mum would be so pleased. He was sure Ann and Mrs. Hall would get along well with them. *How am I going to make love to Ann if she's afraid of me? Will any of Jenny's suggestions work?*

* * *

Robb was eating his breakfast Saturday morning when Ann knocked on the door. Mrs. Anston answered and welcomed her in.

"Robb, I came to tell you that Reverend Jamieson came back to town last night. I thought we could go and see him this morning," said Ann.

"So you two are getting married. That's wonderful," said Mrs. Anston, instantly in a fluster.

Robb saw a resemblance to Ivy Marshall and knew the whole town would know by afternoon. "Give me a minute to finish my breakfast, and we'll go down to the church," he said. He ate quickly then washed, shaved and changed into his street clothes.

Minutes later he and Ann were walking down the wooden sidewalk towards the church. He felt oddly possessive and protective of her, slowing to match her stride and keeping an eye open for the miners on the street.

Reverend Jamieson was in the rectory sitting at his cluttered desk, obviously working on the next day's sermon. He was a middle-aged man, short and wiry, in the early stages of going bald. Robb could well imagine him riding through the wilderness to tend his extended flock. He had the air of a dedicated, no-nonsense individual. He warmly welcomed them when they knocked on the door.

Robb felt nervous. "Reverend, my name is Robb McDonald. I have asked Ann to marry me. She wishes to be married here and for you to perform the ceremony."

The minister questioned both of them at length, inquiring extensively into Robb's background and beliefs, work background, his relationship with his family and if he could support Ann. Finally, he seemed satisfied that Robb would be a suitable husband.

"I was a miner for two seasons, so I have lived rough. My father has spent his life working for the Bay and all four of us boys were taught to work hard and be frugal. I found enough gold that we can get by quite nicely. I didn't indulge in the saloons, like most, so I am quite capable of taking care of her and her mother."

"You have to get registered beforehand. In a bigger place, the registrar would be a separate person, but out here I serve that role as well as the ministerial one. I can publish the banns, starting tomorrow, and they must be published three times. The earliest you could get married would be September fourteenth."

"It is our intention to move to Yale immediately after the service. I will be going ahead to make arrangements for living accommodations," said Robb. "I need to get Ann and her mother there before the weather sets in. What is your fee for the service?"

Reverend Jamieson took a large leather book from the bookcase, made room for it on the desk and proceeded to enter their names in the register. "It will cost you five dollars," he said.

Robb rummaged through his trouser pockets and produced five dollars, which he handed to him.

While he was completing the registration certificate, the minister asked, "Who will standing for you, Robb?"

"I was thinking of asking Gilbert Cullen."

"Good choice. And you, Ann?"

"My mother," she said.

Outside the church, Robb held her hand. It seemed natural. Now he understood what Billy had meant about finding the love of his life. He saw the happy smile on her face and felt a warmth inside him.

Sunday morning, the little church was packed full of worshippers. Robb recognized some of them from his walks about town; they were faces he had seen on the street, now looking much neater – the men in their suits, children freshly scrubbed in their good clothes and women in their bonnets and good but plain dresses. There wasn't the emphasis on fashion that was so prevalent in his church back in Victoria. No one was trying to outdo everyone else.

Robb could feel people's eyes on him as he stood beside Ann, and he felt proud. Although his clothes were clean, he wished he had his good suit to wear.

Reverend Jamieson led them through the service. He preached about hard work and honesty and the evils of greed. Everyone joined in the hymns. Since they were familiar to him, Robb added his slightly off-key tenor to the other voices. When the banns were announced, there was a slow buzz of conversation.

Robb caught up with Gilbert Cullen and his wife before they left the church.

"Gilbert, Ann and I were wondering if you would be able to stand with me at the wedding," said Robb. "I don't know many people in town."

"It would be my pleasure," said Gilbert, shaking his hand. "I'll get someone to mind the store that day."

Robb watched as Ann and Mrs. Hall were engulfed by the women of the congregation in a round of congratulations. He saw her shy smile blossom into full-blown laughter at some of the comments she was receiving, and he found twenty pairs of feminine eyes thoroughly scrutinizing him.

Ryan came over and introduced his shy, young wife, Caroline. "Hey, Robb, Mrs. Hall's going to rent her house to me," he said, all excited. "The rent's a good deal and she's leaving most of the furniture. Caroline's two brothers are going to come with us, lots more room there."

"Glad to hear it, Ryan. You can pay your rent each month to Mr. Briggs. I'm heading for Yale as soon as the stage comes in. I'd appreciate it if you would keep an eye on my two, will you? I have to find a place for us to live and some work," said Robb, keeping a wary eye on the miners passing by the church's white picket fence.

Ann joined him, slipping her arm through his, and Mrs. Hall gave him a hug.

"Mrs. Hall, can I call you by your first name? Mrs. Hall sounds so formal," said Robb.

"You can call me Althea then."

"Althea, that's different."

She took his other arm when he offered it and the three of them headed back to the boarding house.

Two days later, Robb said goodbye and boarded the stage, carrying his pack and his rifle. The bank draft was carefully folded in his back pocket.

Travel on the stage was no longer a novelty and he spent his time contemplating his options. The seven days passed quickly and uneventfully. The Royal Engineers had reached 70 Mile House. The gully they were working on looked particularly precarious. He didn't envy them their job; the recent rains had made the hillsides treacherous. Once again, he glimpsed Jackson's red jacket and felt somehow that he owed that man a great deal. If Jackson hadn't become betrothed to Emma, he would never have found Ann.

They arrived in Yale late afternoon. The raging Fraser, the narrow roadway and the plunging hills never failed to impress him. He had clear memories of walking that road when it had been a lot narrower. Even one year of heavy traffic had made a difference. The gold rush of 1858 at Hill's Bar had almost overnight created a new town, and now Yale was a major supply depot for the whole interior. There was a sternwheeler at the dock, the *Henrietta* not the *Enterprise*. *River traffic must be much busier, requiring more boats*, he thought.

This time Robb followed the detective into the bank. He asked for the manager and was given a seat. While he was waiting, he watched two of the guards remove crates and trunks from the stage, that were obviously

335

heavy from all the grunting and groaning as they hauled them to the vault. The remaining two guards were on high alert at the doorway with their rifles ready, scanning the street for potential dangers.

With the crates safely under lock and key, the guards left, leading their horses down to the Barnard's Express stables at the corner of Albert and Front streets, just ahead of the now-empty stage. The detective was closeted with the manager for about fifteen minutes then it was Robb's turn.

"I'm Robb McDonald. I've been mining up near Williams Lake and I'll be moving here with my wife and mother-in-law near the end of September. Mr. Donaldson, I'd like to open an account," he said, eyeing the nameplate and carefully placing the bank draft on the desk.

Mr. Donaldson checked the slip and did a double take on the amount. "Welcome to Yale, Mr. McDonald. Looks like you've been one of the lucky ones. Very few survive to enjoy the fruits of their labour."

"I also need your advice. I'm going to need a job and accommodation for my family. I have experience working for the Bay but I'm not sure if they have any vacancies, and I wouldn't mind running my own business. Who would be the best person to talk to?"

"There is a small hotel, just behind us on Douglas Street, where higher-class people stay, which would be suitable for your womenfolk. The mayor is probably your best bet for business matters. His office is on Block Eighteen on Douglas."

"I appreciate your time," Robb said. He could almost see Mr. Donaldson rubbing his hands together at the prospect of more business.

It's time I sent Father a letter to keep him up to date. He headed into the post office and put quill to paper. The Branch and Bennet's saloons on Front Street were doing a brisk business with miners who had probably arrived on the *Henrietta* that day. *I don't think they stand a chance coming north this late in the season.* He needed to find a house away from the docks and felt the responsibility that now rested on his shoulders to provide a safe place for Ann and Althea.

> Dear Father,
>
> I have a lot to tell you. I will be getting married on September 14 to Ann Hall. The one and only church in Williams Lake is Methodist. Reverend Jamieson published the banns last Sunday. Williams Lake is just too dangerous with all the miners around, and I don't like the idea of us being isolated over the winter. Here in Yale, you're only a boat ride away if we want to visit. Much easier to keep in touch. I arrived here this afternoon and will try to find a house and a job. I'll be checking in with the Bay tomorrow, and if that doesn't work out, will be scouting for other business opportunities. You can send any mail care of the post office here

instead of Williams Lake. Once I've got things settled, I will make arrangements with you to ship all my stuff, including my good suit. Give my love to Mum, Matt, James and the girls. Love, Robb

He arranged for a mail box with the postal clerk and went up the street to find the hotel. It was a small, wooden, two-storey structure, freshly painted. The lobby was smartly decorated and brightly lit with coal oil lamps and wall sconces. The woodwork was gleaming. The rooms leading off the lobby had walnut woodwork and frosted glass panes in the doors. Posted in the front window was a sign listing the code of conduct and the cost of the room: three dollars per night. *That'll keep most miners away,* thought Robb. He could hear voices of other guests from the parlour.

The clerk at the reception desk was an immaculately dressed individual with slicked down, short-black hair and a moustache, in a well-tailored suit. He eyed the rifle and Robb's travelling clothes with disdain tinged with alarm.

"I'd like a room for two or possibly three nights," said Robb, laying down his three dollars. That had the man's attention. "Do you have bathing facilities here?"

The man's interest was piqued. "Each level has a bathing room at the end of the hall, sir. I do have a vacancy on the second floor, room number eight," he said.

Robb signed the register and took the room key. "Do you serve meals?"

"Yes, breakfast is at eight, lunch at noon and dinner at six o'clock."

"Will I be able to have dinner tonight?"

"Yes, I'll tell the cook to expect you."

Robb went up to his room, which was really quite luxurious. The walls and ceiling were plastered, and the tall windows had brocade curtains. There was a dark walnut bed with a real mattress and the linens were pristine. Freshening up and changing into his street clothes, he left his rifle and pack in the room, and headed down to the dining room.

He was shown to his seat by the clerk, where there was a full place setting of silver prepared for him. Robb acknowledged the two couples already seated and sat down, thankful he'd been drilled in etiquette back in Victoria. He initiated a conversation with the older gentleman nearest to him and introduced himself.

The one couple were visitors from New Westminster, but the older man, a Mr. Collins and his wife, lived in Yale. Robb explained that he was looking for a job and a house. He asked the other couple how Sir James was doing, as he had worked with him in Victoria. He was told that the Douglas family were settling in well. By then, they seemed much more at ease with him.

The arrival of the meal stopped conversation. The serving staff brought in a tureen of pea soup with freshly baked bread. Robb found it delicious. The next course was a whole leg of ham, carved to perfection, with scalloped potatoes and carrots. Dessert consisted of fruit-filled pastries. He couldn't help but compare this meal with the beans, jerky and fire-cooked flat bread in camp. After the meal, the men retired to the drawing room while the ladies disappeared into the parlour.

Robb politely refused the tobacco offered. "Mr. Collins, I need somewhere decent to live for my wife and mother-in-law, preferably away from the saloons. Are there any houses available for sale or rent?"

"I can't think of any right now, except for a couple, but they're on Front Street, so not desirable for families. I can certainly understand you wanting to keep the women folk safe. On Douglas Street or even up on Mary Street there are lots for sale. Johnny Ward is building a house on lot number eleven. It will be a storey and a half. There are several good carpenters in town; Seth Armstrong's one of them. You might look just north of China town on block seven too. What are you going to do for work?"

"I worked at the Bay in Victoria for over three years, so I thought I'd go there first."

"If that doesn't work for you, try Oppenheimer's Store. He could always use someone," Smith replied.

"Thank you for the information," said Robb, excusing himself and leaving the two men to puff on their cigars.

* * *

It was raining the following morning. Robb dodged from doorway to doorway until he reached the Bay store. The store was full of miners. *Hard to tell if they're buying supplies or trying to stay dry,* he thought. He asked to speak to the manager. An older man, probably as old as his father came over to the counter.

"My name is Pearce. How may I be of assistance?"

"I'm Robb McDonald. You may know my father, William McDonald."

"So you're William's youngest boy. Not hard to see the resemblance. Come into my office," he said, ushering him behind the counter and down the hall.

"So, I hear William and your brother James have changed positions."

"That's true. He was finding the lifting difficult, so the licence office will be much easier. Mr. Pearce, I'm looking for work. I've been up at Williams Lake and will be moving here with my wife and mother-in-law at the end of September. Do you have any positions available? I've worked all the jobs and spent the winter learning the management ones with James."

"I'm sorry, Robb. I don't have any vacancies. We've already reorganized, and my replacement is ready to take over."

"Thanks, anyway," said Robb with a sinking feeling. "Are you retiring here?"

"No, my wife and I will be moving to New Westminster. No miners there," he said. "Try Oppenheimer's. They might have something, and there's always the fort. They have their own provisioners. It's just the other side of the reserve lands."

They shook hands, and Robb went back out into the rain, crossing Albert Street. Oppenheimer's was located in the middle of the block. The store reminded him very much of the Granville in Victoria, catering more to Yale's residents than the miners.

The manager was a Mr. Thomson, a fifty-something man with rolled-up shirt sleeves and braces. Robb explained his mission and the man called him into the office. "What sort of work experience do you have?" he asked.

Robb gave him his work history.

"I can't offer you a management position, Robb, but we do have a couple of positions open in the store serving the customers. One of our staff is leaving at the end of the month. John's going back to the States. It pays a dollar a day. Would you be interested in that?

"We get married on September fourteenth and it takes a week to get here by stage. The beginning of October for sure. I'm prepared to work for a dollar a day," said Robb, keeping his fingers crossed.

There was a brief pause then Mr. Thomson shook his hand. "Welcome aboard."

"My next problem is finding somewhere for myself, my wife and mother-in-law to live on a temporary basis until I can build a house. Any suggestions?" asked Robb.

"Come with me," said Thomson, leading him out of the office and up a back staircase to the second floor. Half of the area was storage for dry goods. A partition wall divided the room, and Thomson opened the door. Inside was an area about twenty-by-thirty feet with windows facing the street and waterfront. There was a bed, a table, a chair and an armoire. In the corner was a pot-bellied woodstove. A man's clothing was thrown across the unmade bed and a dirty plate and cutlery were still sitting on the table.

"Once John goes back to the States, this room will be empty. You can use it for your family, if you wish. We have found it advantageous to always have someone on the premises. It tends to keep thieves from breaking into the shop after hours."

Robb looked around, mentally dividing the room into three smaller rooms— two small bedrooms and a living room cum kitchen area. "Is there an outhouse and well out back?" he asked.

"All of us share it," said Thomson.

"This will work for us, at least on a temporary basis, until the house is built," said Robb. He went out of the store and surveyed the backyard area. It was full of packing crates and debris, but the outhouse was by the back fence and the well was close to the building. *It's not quite what I had in mind, but it will just have to do for now,* he thought.

He was elated that he'd found a job. *I really don't have to work, but I don't want to touch that money, or it'll be gone in no time. If my father can raise a family on a dollar a day, then by God, so can I.* The rain was easing off, so he quickly made his way to Barnard's Express, where they confirmed the Thursday departure. He bought his ticket and spent the rest of the afternoon wandering around Yale, checking out the stores, the building lots and Seth Armstrong's carpentry shop. Seth wasn't there. Robb discovered the church, St. John the Divine on the corner of Albert and Douglas, the gaol and Chinatown. He decided to look for the mayor's office tomorrow and see what building lots were available on Mary and Bridge Streets.

As he lay in bed that night, he felt a huge feeling of relief that as menial as the store job was, it was a brand-new start. Both Ann and Althea were common-sense women, and they would cope with new surroundings. *For once, they wouldn't be the ones cooking for strangers and doing mounds of laundry every day. A new start for them too.*

Wednesday dawned cool and gray, but dry. Robb ate a superb breakfast, paid the clerk for that night and headed out the door to try and catch Seth Armstrong before he was off to work on a house somewhere. Seth's house was a wooden storey-and-a-half home with a wide front porch and a one-storey add-on at the back that was probably a summer kitchen. Most of the homes in the area seemed to be that design. A man with wavy red hair, probably in his early thirties, was just loading his tools onto a wagon fully loaded with planed pine planks. The team waited patiently. Robb introduced himself and explained his situation.

"I'm starting work at the Oppenheimer's store the beginning of October. I need some simple but sturdy basic furniture for my family: a table, four chairs, a double bed, a single bed, a wardrobe to hold clothing and perhaps a chest of drawers. I intend to build a house in the spring. When does the frost go out of the ground here?" Robb asked.

"You'd be looking at the beginning of April for sure. There are a dozen building lots for sale at the end of the road, but more are being severed all the time. You might wanna wait until you're living here to get a better deal. The lots have been selling for thirty or forty dollars. I can certainly work on the furniture for you. I can't promise I'll have it all ready by the time you get back. I've got to finish a house I'm working on," Seth said. "I'll keep my eye open for any good quality second hand stuff too, just to get you started." They shook hands and Seth drove off down the muddy road.

Robb found the mayor's office and they spent several hours discussing business in the town. Robb told him about Bill's idea of a feeding lot for northbound cattle near Williams Lake.

The mayor liked the idea. "One thing, Robb—with the amount of snow they get up that way, you can't just turn the cattle loose over the winter and expect them to survive. This area isn't like California. They'll starve to death unless you feed them hay, and there's not much of that around. We haven't got the land cleared yet for hay or corn production, except on a very small scale, like one milk cow for a family. Salmon's a major food source here for both the Native people and us. Fish gets us through the winter more than beef. Some of the ships are bringing in barrels of brined pork. That sells well."

"There'll be a drop in the number of miners shortly, I expect," said Robb.

"A lot head back to the States for the winter. The stage doesn't run from October to April, but the steamers still get through from here to Victoria. The Fraser doesn't ice over generally."

"I'll be needing firewood to heat the upstairs room at Oppenheimer's."

"There's plenty for sale all of the time. They're cutting timber everywhere for houses. You won't have a problem getting wood."

"Is there a Methodist church in the area?" Robb asked.

"No, just St. John's at the moment."

Robb thanked him for his time and headed back to the hotel. Yale had a lot of possibilities, and he felt reasonably content that he'd made a good choice for his new family.

Chapter 37

The stage trip north seemed interminable. Robb was impatient to get back to Ann. The road was heavy with fully loaded wagons taking winter supplies to the northern towns. Many miners were heading south. The pines were a dull brown/green with their heavy loads of pine cones, punctuated with the yellowing leaves of birch. He could hear the bellowing calls of elk somewhere in the hills and the constant honking of southbound geese flying in the valleys between the mountains. Mornings were chilly the farther north they went. Riverbanks were full of Native families salmon fishing along the rivers as the mass of bright-red fish swam upstream to their spawning grounds. Sadly, it reminded him once again of the now-vanished Songhees.

There were two other male passengers on board. One was a minister going to Cache Creek and the other a relative of someone in town. Just north of 70 Mile House, traffic slowed as the Royal Engineers were still working on that difficult gully. Jackson, astride his horse, was immediately visible in his red jacket, directing traffic onto a temporary one lane path that bypassed the cribbing section the road crew were working on. There was a brief moment when their eyes met and there was recognition. Robb smiled and tipped his hat. Jackson acknowledged and watched him as the stage went through. *He'll be heading to Victoria very soon for his own wedding,* thought Robb, envisioning Emma in some satin creation bedecked in ribbons. *Good luck to him.*

Five days later the stage reached Williams Lake, and Robb headed straight for Mrs. Hall's. He ran up the steps and through the front door, propping his pack and rifle in the corner. Both women were in the kitchen. He grabbed Ann and held her tightly, burying his face in her hair. *Oh Lord, she felt and smelled good.* He glanced up to see Althea standing by the sink with a meat cleaver in her hand over the carcass of a chicken.

He pulled back and saw the twinkle in Ann's eyes.

"I'd better behave myself," said Robb. "It's not a good idea to upset your mother-in-law when she's got a cleaver in her hand."

The two women laughed. Robb was too excited to sit, and he paced around the parlour getting in their way, talking a mile a minute.

"Robb, sit down and tell us about Yale," said Althea as she handed him a cup of tea and some biscuits.

"The good news is that I've got a job as a clerk at the Oppenheimer Brothers store. The pay's not much but will keep us going. Also, they're going to let us have the room upstairs over the store until I can get a house built. It's very sparse but there's not much available. I met Seth, the local carpenter, and he's going to make us some furniture. I'm sorry, ladies, but it's just one big, bare room with a woodstove. I'll get some lumber and build partitions when we get there. We'll need to take bedding and dishes."

"Whoa!" said Ann, amused at his enthusiasm.

There were no guests that night, so Robb had supper with them and told them all about Yale. "There are still miners to deal with, but from what I could see, they confine themselves to Front Street where the saloons and the stores are. I was thinking, Althea, that it might be a good idea for you to take your sign down. You don't need to take in boarders any more. You're going to need time to get things packed up. I will set up an account with Gilbert for you at the store if you like, so you can get whatever supplies you need. Do you need to get new dresses for the wedding?" he asked, glancing at Ann and thinking of the hours Jane and Emily had spent sewing theirs.

"That would be nice, Robb. Thank you," said Althea, looking a bit overwhelmed. Then she started to weep. Ann immediately put her arms around her mother and the women stood there for a few minutes.

Robb was totally taken aback. He'd only ever seen Althea as the woman in charge, the woman who could handle anything. "Have I said or done something wrong?"

"No, no, Robb," said Althea, wiping her face and blowing her nose. "It's just been a very long time since a man, or anyone, for that matter, has been so concerned about us."

He hesitated for a moment then put his arms around them. "I take family duties very seriously. I know you've had to be self-sufficient, and it's that courage I've admired all along. Now it's my job to provide for and protect you as best I can. You've got my word on it. You'll have to get used to that, because it's important to me," he said quietly. *I'm not Ted Hall,* he thought.

Both Ann and Althea were very quiet after that. He left shortly thereafter to get a room at Anston's and listened for the sound of the bolt sliding into place on the door as he left the house.

He suddenly realized that even though he was taking over their lives, they had been independent. He'd have to make allowances for their strength of will and character.

The next few weeks were busy ones. Althea only had two small trunks, so Robb built wooden crates to take their belongings. Ann used the blankets that had been on the upstairs beds to pack away the china they weren't using, as well as the few family pictures of Althea's parents and siblings that left pale rectangles on the bare walls.

Robb picked up the ring and a new shirt for the wedding. He also wrote to Bill and George. He had no idea when those two would get back to Williams Lake; maybe some time before winter set in, maybe never.

> Dear George,
>
> Ann and I will be married on September 14. Immediately after that, the three of us will be moving to Yale. I have a

clerk's job at Oppenheimer's and rooms over the store for the time being. Hope you've found the copper deposits you were looking for. Keep me posted on that. It occurred to me that investment in a copper mine might be a good idea. Haven't heard from Bill at all. Keep in touch. You are welcome any time if you are coming south. Sincerely, Robb.

Dear Bill,

Haven't heard from you. I'm hoping you and Helen Raven Wing are together now.

Ann and I will be married on September 14 then we are heading to Yale. I spoke to the mayor down there and he thought your idea for starting a feed lot for the northbound cattle was a good one. He also said that those California cattle don't survive our winters if they are just turned loose. They have to be hay fed. Thought you needed to know that. Apparently, the British breeds are hardier than the California breeds that come up through Washington state. If you're coming to Yale, look us up. Would be glad to see you. Sincerely, Robb.

He watched as Mrs. Cullen put the envelopes in the Green Valley mail slot. He wondered if he'd ever hear from either of the men again. It seemed like another lifetime ago.

The fourteenth was getting closer. Robb stopped in at the stage office to book three tickets for Yale, only to discover that two of the four seats were already booked. "Fred, I need three seats as Ann and Mrs. Hall will be with me. We're going to have two trunks and four crates of household goods. How about I rent a horse and ride along with the guards? I rode with the guards once before and didn't have any problems."

Fred looked a bit uncertain but grudgingly agreed.

* * *

September 14. Robb bathed and shaved with care. *This is it.* Promptly at 1:30, Gilbert knocked at the door. Mr. Anston let him in. The entire Anston family were going to the church too.

"Have you got the ring?" Gilbert asked.

"Yes," said Robb, almost fumbling it.

It seemed to him that a lot of the townsfolk were heading for the church. When he got there, the church was packed. Robb and Gilbert took their places in the front pew. Robb's heart was pounding. Reverend Jamieson talked to him for a few minutes then looked towards the church door and smiled. Robb turned and there was Ryan escorting Ann and Althea. They had both bought new dresses; not frivolous, fancy clothes but simple ones. Ann looked radiant in her new honey-coloured dress, holding a posy of wild flowers, as mother and daughter walked down the aisle arm in arm.

Robb hardly heard a word of the service. He was totally overwhelmed with the woman standing before him. Under Reverend Jamieson's bemused direction, he went through the ceremony. Robb saw Ann's lips form the words "I do" and felt his whole heart go out to her as he gave his oath and slipped the plain gold band on her finger. Althea stood to the side, a teary smile on her face.

"I now pronounce you man and wife. You may kiss the bride," said Reverend Jamieson with a big grin, and a hum of voices rose from the congregation.

Robb kissed her firmly on the mouth. "I've been waiting a long time to do that," he mumbled under his breath. He looked up to a sea of smiling faces, and for the first time noticed the bearded, hard-looking character in the back row, complete with backpack. "George!"

After signing the register and receiving their certificate of marriage, they worked their way to the front door of the church with the good wishes of all their neighbours. Robb grabbed George by the shoulders. "It's so good to see you. I can't believe you came back."

"I just arrived."

Ann gave George a kiss on the cheek. "Come and get something to eat. The church women have put on a lunch for us."

"Ann, are you sure? I'm badly in need of a bath and a change of clothes."

"You're a friend," she said and led him to the table set under the trees and laden with sandwiches, pies, cakes, biscuits and a large bowl of punch. Robb stood and watched as George chatted with Gilbert, Roy and other men who knew him from the winter. It was Mrs. Cullen who called the crowd to attention and made a special presentation to Ann. "On behalf of the ladies auxiliary, we are proud to honour you on your wedding day with a quilt in the log cabin pattern you like," she said, handing over the multicoloured bundle.

Ann's mouth dropped open as she gazed at the quilt, running her hand over the minute stitching. "How did you ever find the time to do this? We've only been engaged six weeks."

"We all pitched in. There's a piece of material from each one of us in that. We did the squares, but Mrs. Rafferty put it together and did the quilting. It's something to remember us by."

Ann was speechless.

Gradually, the crowd dispersed. Althea was staying for a few days with the Cullens. Robb, quilt firmly tucked under his arm, walked Ann back to the house. He opened the door for her, and they stepped inside. Robb bolted the door, took off his jacket and looked at her. They were alone.

She placed the quilt on the table and opened it out fully. "I can't believe they did this. I'm so grateful. I recognize some of these pieces. That's a piece of material from Betsy's dress, and that one's from Caroline's little sister."

Robb stood quietly for a moment. He wanted her so badly. Now they were married, but he was still unsure how to proceed. He put his arms around her, held her tightly and kissed her deeply and passionately. She put her arms around him as he pulled out her hairpins until her tresses tumbled to her shoulders, and proceeded to kiss her cheeks and neck.

"I love you, Ann. Tell me what to do. Tell me what you want. I want you to give yourself to me." His voice was a hoarse whisper as he ran his fingers through her hair. He could feel every inch of her body against his.

She led him to the bedroom.

He undid the buttons on the back of her dress then stripped off his shirt. She slowly removed her dress, revealing her body clad in a dainty petticoat, drawers, camisole and stockings. She kept her eyes down, seemingly unable to look at him. His eyes devoured every inch of her. She looked at his smooth, heaving muscular chest and tentatively touched him.

Jenny's advice came in flashes. Desperately trying to control himself, Robb tried to slow his breathing and turned away. *Slowly and gently? Bloody hell!*

He felt her behind him, her fingers stroking the scar on his back. He'd totally forgotten it. He turned to her to see her reaction, but she didn't seem fazed or about to faint.

"Do you not want me?" she said, looking so sad.

"It's not that, Ann. I want this to be pleasurable for you. I don't want to rush you. I want you to come to me."

The look on her face changed to a rather sheepish smile as she sat down on the bed and pulled him down beside her.

"How on earth do I get you out of these things?" he said, fumbling with the ties and laces of her bodice as he planted kisses down her neck and shoulders, his hands tentatively exploring the curve of her breasts.

* * *

Robb awoke in the morning to the smell of sizzling bacon. He put his hand on the bed but found the other half empty. It took him a moment to remember where he was. Most of the bed clothes were in a heap. Then he smiled to himself. His wife was one amazing woman. He quickly gathered his clothes that had been strewn all over the floor, got dressed and went out into the kitchen. Ann was standing at the stove making breakfast and had set the table for two.

"Well, Mrs. McDonald, how's the old married woman?"

She laughed. "That sounds so strange."

He gave her a kiss but she shooed him into the parlour. "That's quite enough from you, now. Would have thought you had enough last night. Have a seat or I'll be distracted and burn your breakfast."

He sat down laughing as she put a plate heaped with slices of fried potatoes, bacon and toast in front of him. "Sit with me," he said. "I'm not one of your boarders."

She looked around the parlour. Two trunks sat there with their lids open. The four crates were nailed shut already, stacked against the front wall. The rest of the room was bare. "Upstairs is totally empty. There's just the bed linens we're using down here, a few dishes and our travelling clothes. Otherwise, we're ready."

"Was I too rough with you last night?" he said, looking at her with concern. "I'm afraid I got carried away."

She paused for a moment. "I think you're going to have to curb some of your enthusiasm when my mother will be sleeping just the other side of the wall."

"You mean I'm going to have to be quiet?"

"Yes, something like that."

"I'll try to keep that in mind," said Robb.

They walked to church for the 9:30 service to be greeted with knowing looks, smiles and not-so-subtle winks from the men. Robb was glad to see Althea and gave her a big hug.

Althea immediately went to her daughter, and he could see the two heads together. Ann seemed to be reassuring her mother.

Robb wanted to tell her that her daughter was fine, but Althea probably needed to hear it from Ann, not him. George joined them in the pew, freshly shaved, bathed and in clean clothes.

Reverend Jamieson delivered a rousing sermon on faith, hope and charity extolling his flock to help the poor and be generous in spirit. Robb was there but really wasn't paying attention. He had too much to think about.

357

After the service, they all sat on the front porch of the house, with Robb and George discussing the copper mine. "I'm going to be filing a claim tomorrow with the gold commission for a piece of property up at McLeese Lake. I've found a lot of copper, some molybdenum and probably a bit of silver, quite valuable," said George. "It's not the same as mining for gold. Copper's used for a lot of things in industry, like pennies and wire. But it means either excavating a shaft or doing an open-pit mine to extract it. There's no local place to smelter it either. It means forming a company and getting investors just to get the equipment. It will be a long-term project, probably the rest of my life. By the way, there's a lot of gold being found east of Quesnel. I'm predicting a big strike up that way soon."

"I've had enough of panning and living rough. I don't want to live that way anymore, never knowing if someone's going to ambush me, never knowing who to trust. I've got the women to think of too. Keep in touch with me, George," said Robb thoughtfully. "My priority is to build a house for us before I commit to anything else." He proceeded to tell George all about Yale.

Chapter 38

Tuesday morning bright and early Ann and Althea boarded the stage, sitting opposite the two male passengers. Robb helped load the trunks and crates. It reassured him to see Garnet and his cronies sitting on their horses, rifles at the ready. Robb mounted his rented horse, the Henry in the scabbard, and as the stage pulled out of town, he waved goodbye to George, Ryan, the Cullens and Anstons. He wasn't sure if he'd ever come back to Williams Lake.

Depending on the width of the road, sometimes he rode with Garnet and Wayne behind the coach, or up front with Ben and Howard. Sometimes he rode beside the coach, pointing out things to Ann and Althea. The scenery was incredibly beautiful in its fall colours. In calmer parts of the Fraser, ducks were gathering for their migration south. For several days it rained, and as usual the road turned into a sea of muddy ruts. Many miners were making the trek south. The road houses were accommodating to the women, seating them away from the men. Several times, Robb slept on the floor when only one bedroom was available. Ann and Althea were used to sharing. Those nights, Robb missed feeling the warmth of her body beside him.

Eventually they came to the detour section around the gully. From the scattered rocks and debris, it looked like the crew had blasted recently. They were now clearing rocks from the path and tossing them into the canyon. Jackson was on his horse, supervising the traffic. Robb stopped and introduced him.

"Captain Jackson, I'd like you to meet my wife, Ann, and mother-in-law Althea," he said. Then he turned to the women. "This officer is the man who will be marrying Emma Freeland shortly." He was fully aware that Jackson knew exactly who he was. He wanted Jackson to know he was no longer competing for the blonde in Victoria.

Jackson tipped his hat to the ladies then indicated they'd better move on so as not to delay the wagons behind them. They hadn't advanced more than a quarter of a mile when all the horses became restless. Robb started having trouble controlling his horse. The ground trembled, then there was a deafening roar as a section of the canyon wall slid down behind them, in a billowing, choking cloud of dust, boulders and trees. Robb had a momentary glimpse of men being swept over the edge into the Fraser and a horse and red-coated rider cartwheeling into space.

He heard the women scream and fought to stay astride his terrified horse. The noise was deafening. Gradually the noise stopped until only an occasional rock bounced down the slope. The two wagons behind the stage had survived it, but the road behind them had vanished. Soon figures were running from all around, peering over the edge for survivors. Robb dismounted and could hear the screams of the injured horse thrashing around on rocks below. It was Jackson's bay.

"Poor bastard, his back's broken," said Garnet, as he aimed his rifle with care and fired. Then it was quiet. The dust was still billowing down below. They were all scanning for bodies. Robb was looking for any sign of the red jacket.

"There! Over there!" someone shouted, pointing to a ledge about halfway down the cliff face. Robb craned his neck and he could see part of the red jacket and the right arm behind a stack of boulders. There was no movement.

"I'm going down," he said.

"I thought you were afraid of heights," said Garnet.

"I am, but I don't have a choice here. I know that man. Knot my rope to yours," he said, tying his end around his waist. With Wayne's rope knotted to theirs, there was about sixty feet of rope. Robb hoped it was enough.

"I'll tie it to my saddlehorn," said Garnet, testing the knots and backing his horse up to keep the line tight.

Robb heard the faint sound of Ann screaming, "No, Robb, no!" but by then he was over the edge, working his way down. The soil was loose in some places, his boots sliding. Carefully, hanging on by his fingertips, he sought firmer handholds and tiny grooves in the canyon wall big enough for his boots. He was afraid to look down. Now the roar of the Fraser obliterated any sound of the voices above. He yanked on the rope for a bit more to be let out and lowered himself one toehold at a time. Slowly the row of faces above him disappeared. He stopped about forty feet down and carefully looked to his right and left. He could see a partially buried upside-down boot sticking out of the dirt. *If that boot has a foot in it, the man's dead.*

To the left, he could see the top of the boulders. He put his weight on his right foot and kicked a notch into the dirt. He grabbed a rock to shift his weight, but it came away in his hand. It took him a few minutes to find a secure handhold, and then he shifted his weight. Gradually he positioned himself so the rocks were below him; that's where he had seen the jacket earlier, although it seemed eons ago. Robb finally felt the boulder under his foot and put his weight on it. It held. He let out his breath and looked around. Ten feet from him, behind another boulder, he could see the jacket. Crawling on his hands and knees, he edged towards it. Jackson was lying facedown, partially buried in dirt. Robb took out his knife and dug into the dust, carefully scraping it away from Jackson's face and shoulders. There was a fluttering of the eyelids.

He's alive! Robb redoubled his efforts, exposing the man's chest then hips. It seemed to take him forever to get Jackson's body out as he resorted to using his bare hands. The left arm was severely deformed, probably broken. Robb tried to turn him over, but Jackson screamed.

A shower of dirt and pebbles from above startled him. Looking up he saw two pairs of feet coming down the rock face. One of the men had a portable stretcher strapped to his back. *Thank god, I've got help coming.*

Robb cut Jackson's left sleeve, exposing the deformed arm, broken above the elbow. He found a small chunk of driftwood and bound the arm to it with strips of the sleeve then started to make a sling from the remaining strips.

Finally, the two men found their way onto the boulders. They positioned the canvas and pole stretcher beside Jackson. It took the three of them to turn him onto his back to position him on it. For a brief moment Jackson opened his eyes and looked at Robb. "We'll get you out of here," Robb said, looking at the blue eyes staring out of the swollen, bruised face. There was a flicker of recognition.

The two engineers buckled the strapping tightly around Jackson, securing him firmly to the stretcher. They untied the ropes from around their bodies and wound the lines around the stretcher. One of them took off his belt and buckled it around the two lines, centering the ropes over the middle of the stretcher.

Three jerks on the lines and slowly, slowly the stretcher and Jackson's suspended dead weight moved up the cliff face. One of the engineers motioned to Robb to start climbing. Robb tugged three times on his rope, and it tightened dragging him upwards. Going up was quicker than going down. In his mind, Robb could see Garnet backing his horse to pull him up. He prayed the lines would hold as he was exhausted. Two ropes suddenly flew past him. They must have got Jackson safely to the top and were now going to bring the engineers up. As it was, the shadows were lengthening. Finally, he was dragged over the lip of the canyon wall. Hands grabbed him and pulled him to safety. He looked up at Wayne and Ben. It was all he could do to stand. Feeling weak and shaky, he leaned against Garnet's horse. "Thank you, my friend. I'm glad that's over," he said, glancing at the knot of engineers placing the groaning Jackson onto a wagon. *God help the man; who knew what other injuries he had?*

Suddenly, Ann was there with her arms around him, totally disregarding his filthy, torn clothing. "Thank God you're alright. Why did you do it? Why did you risk your life for him?"

He put his dirty, bloodied finger over her lips. "Hush. Everything I have right now, I owe to him. You and I have a brand-new life together. If he hadn't become engaged to Emma, I would never have gone up the Fraser; I would never have been a miner; I would never have found you. Do you understand? I owe him for everything that's good in my life. Because of him, I have a future, or should I say, we have a future." With that, he kissed her and slowly they walked towards the coach where Althea was waiting.

CPSIA information can be obtained
at www.ICGtesting.com
Printed in the USA
LVHW111941300622
722490LV00002B/2

9 781525 549373